"IT'S A THRILLER"

Saturday Review

"SURVIVOR is exactly what people once had in mind when they said that they'd rather stay at home with a good book."
Los Angeles Times

"To gain an idea, however hazy, of SURVIVOR's excitement and perspicacity, one might imagine an Agatha Christie mystery crossbred with Henry James's ASPERN PAPERS."
The New York Times

"SURVIVOR is a fast-paced tale . . . impossible to put down."
Baton Rouge Advocate

"Brandel tells his story like a chain-smoker—blowing some of it right in your eyes while the rest of it drifts here and there; it's a foolproof entertainment with flair."
Kirkus Reviews

BY
MARC
BRANDEL

SURVIVOR

AVON BOOKS
A division of
The Hearst Corporation
959 Eighth Avenue
New York, New York 10019

First Avon Printing, February, 1977

AVON TRADEMARK REG. U.S. PAT. OFF. AND IN
OTHER COUNTRIES, MARCA REGISTRADA,
HECHO EN U.S.A.

Printed in the U.S.A.

To Antonia

You are myself, myself, only with a different face.

—DOSTOEVSKI

1

IT WAS AN UNEXPECTEDLY SAFE SECTION. Farther west, hostilities had intensified as darkness fell. To the north the open ground was disputed territory. I would have hesitated to walk across it by day. At night it was a tacit no-man's-land.

Five blocks south of Central Park I felt unusually safe. With one of the big openings of the year taking place at the Museum of Modern Art—contributing members by invitation only—the police had made a show of force in the area. There were pedestrians on Fifth Avenue, men and women strolling down from the Plaza or up from Fifty-second Street.

I mingled with them. Wariness, the common mood of the city, left me for the moment as I watched the taxis and limousines turn in toward the museum. I was on the lookout for a man alone, about forty years old, vain, not too sure of himself and with a poor memory for faces. Although I had given it a good deal of thought, I hadn't quite made up my mind what a man like that would be wearing. Something between the cautious dullness of a tux and the cynicism of anything really far out.

A taxi passed me, faltering as it turned. The man alone in the back didn't look perfect. The tartan cummerbund suggested a commuter to me, a mother somewhere, prudence. But he was the best so far. I hurried after the taxi as it joined the line dropping passengers at the entrance to the museum.

I had rehearsed every inflection of what I was going to say. All I needed was two minutes during which he was too confused to be sure whether he had ever met me before or not, too uncertain of his ground to assert any independence.

"Hi, there." As the man in cummerbund turned away

from his taxi, I lifted my sari to my knees and skittered toward him. "We were expecting you at Walter's."

"Oh. . . . Hi. . . . I . . ." Tartan Cummerbund looked confused, all right, but also unmistakably suspicious. He was going to be difficult, but at least he hadn't said, "Walter who?" I had spent hours choosing that name. Apart from its almost anonymous blandness, there seemed to be more Walters than anything else in the columns that spring.

"Where were you?" I did my best to sound accusing. "Walter kept calling your answering service and we had oysters oreganata to start with, everybody was asking about you, they're all inside, and you missed a marvelous Montrachet." I slipped my hand under his arm. "Come on."

"Walter who?"

I should have known from that cummerbund. He was probably the kind of meticulous prig who had researched his family tartan. Looking away to give myself time to think, I caught sight of another man alone getting out of a limousine beside me. The plum-colored jacket, the maroon bow tie looked promising. As his car drove away he remained rigidly still; he appeared to be slightly drunk. Perfect. I clasped the back of Cummerbund's neck and brushed my cheek against his.

"You're sweet to ask me, but I promised someone else." I released him.

"There you are." I put my hand on the plum-colored sleeve. "I was going in without you."

I had picked an easier one this time. The vague hazel eyes in the well-fed, well-massaged face took me in as calmly as a refund in the mail. Unexpected but not unwelcome. He patted my hand against his sleeve, fumbling in his pocket for his invitation card.

It was only a few steps into the lobby of the museum. For me they were steps back into the past as well as toward the realization of years of anticipation. I was sixteen when I first discovered Tagliatti, coming across some reproductions of his paintings in an art magazine at my English boarding school. I can remember the grained reading-room table, smell its sour varnish, feel the irk of the school uniform as I leafed through the tedium of Bond Street galleries until, as I turned a page, there they were. Two New York scenes and an adobe house with figure. I

10

stared at them, impaled by their directness. They seemed so brazenly addressed to me it was unthinkable to let anyone else see them. I tore them out at once. For weeks until the end of term I visited those reproductions daily, furtively, my life centering around them as some of the other girls' lives centered around a teacher they had a secret crush on.

I still kept them, tattered and fragile now, between the pages of an atlas in my apartment. I had taken them out, stared at them with that same shock of recognition when the *Times* announced this retrospective show of Tagliatti's work at the Museum of Modern Art. I knew at once I couldn't wait another twelve hours until the general public was admitted. I had to get in on opening night.

"Please." The man in the plum-colored jacket was standing aside for me at the door.

The lobby surprised me. I had been expecting to join an audience. It was evident from the flash of teeth, the bird cries of mutual recognition, that for most of this swirling crowd of people they themselves were the show. I glanced at my companion. Clasping his invitation in his extended hand, he was gazing around with that hesitant immobility which had attracted me to him outside. I steered him firmly toward the rope barrier that still separated me from the paintings upstairs.

If he had any desire to linger in the lobby, greet any friends he might find there, he didn't show it. He was as easy to steer as a dummy on casters. The girl at the barrier plucked the card from his hand as though removing a price tag. Instantly unhooking the rope, she handed us catalogs with what seemed to me an unusual deference. I wondered if I had accidentally picked some celebrity as my escort. I observed him in the elevator. He was older than I had thought: in his late fifties probably. His immaculate hands, the skin of his face, his white hair, all had a preserved look, as though some process of decay had been arrested at a chosen moment. I had been wrong about his being drunk. His inertia was part of his personality.

The elevator door opened. I forgot him immediately. I had to clench my legs together to keep from running from one painting to the next. I forced myself to take them as they came. There were forty-three in the show—virtually all the oil paintings Tagliatti had completed in his lifetime. Arranged chronologically, the canvases in the first room

11

had been painted in the South of France just before the war. *Quai, St. Tropez. Café Owner. Woman in Garden* "(Mrs. Eugenia West). From the Wexford Bone collection," the catalog added. *Street, Le Lavandou.*

Although I had never seen as much as a black-and-white reproduction of these early paintings, I recognized them all as unmistakable Tagliattis. He had experimented and developed later, but style is a truer index of character than a man's face; the essence of his work hadn't changed over the years. A representational painter to the extent that Chirico and Francis Bacon are, Tagliatti is usually grouped with the surrealists, although there are no dismembered camels or melting phones in his paintings. Their expression of something beyond their subject matter is in their execution, as emotion is in a voice regardless of words.

I had never been able to define what that emotion was. Protest? Affirmation? Anger? I looked into Mrs. Eugenia West's eyes, at the mouth that was two curt streaks of paint. Had Tagliatti loved her? Hated her? He had painted her with an impersonal vehemence that was hard to relate to such everyday feelings.

I had already spent ten minutes with Mrs. West. Moving on to the next canvas was like breaking out of an embrace. *Beach, Le Lavandou.* I was held again for another ten minutes. I had to raise my catalog between my eyes and the beach, the plump white-skinned woman lying there, before I could turn away this time. Who was she? It didn't say. "From the Wexford Bone collection" again. Lucky Bone, whoever he was. *Casino, Hyères.* There was an unmistakable expression of anger and contempt in the way he had grouped the figures around the roulette table. I forced myself to move on.

It wasn't easy. I kept getting hypnotized. There was one painting in particular that I was able to turn away from only because someone bumped into me. *Chair, 1946.* "From the Wexford Bone, etc." That's all it was—a wooden chair, set slightly to the left of the canvas, within the exaggerated perspective of two walls and a floor. The right-hand wall was faintly striped, suggesting bars, a cage. The floor was squared like a chessboard. What held me was the unbearable sense of isolation, of anguish that those few harsh lines and planes managed to express. That chair existed in hell. I was grateful to the elderly woman

12

who freed me from it by pushing in front of me. She said she was sorry. We smiled at each other.

An hour and a half later I was back in the South of France. The crowd in the lobby had thronged upstairs by now. Presenting their profiles to the paintings, they formed an animated chain around the walls. I added my spurious apologies to their clamor as I squeezed my way back to Mrs. West. One of the few identified portraits in the show, it fascinated me as a clue to Tagliatti's personality, his life. There was a brief biography of him in the catalog, but it was as unrevealing as a timetable. "Paul Francis Tagliatti. Born in St. Louis, December, 1917 . . . Studied at the St. Martin's School of Art, London . . . Returned to the United States, 1938 . . . One-man show, sketches and water colors, Haggard Gallery, 1945 . . . Died in Tetacata, Mexico, April, 1952." These barren facts were gilded for me by all the tales and rumors I had heard about him. To many of my generation Paul Tagliatti has become a legend, an archetype. Since there are no biographies of him yet, he is a more convenient hero than Jung or Joyce. Anyone can claim him for his own. He is supposed to have been a prodigious drinker, a head, a rebel, a bitter exile. There is a story that he spent several years in prison, persecuted by the American government. There are admirers of Hesse who claim he was a mystic, a recluse, hiding in various parts of the world under a series of assumed names. There are other, to me more appealing stories about all the women who loved and helped him.

Was Eugenia West one of them? She was sitting in a basket chair in the sunlight. She appeared to be wearing nothing but a muslin wrap-around, held at the waist by a sash, a frivolous bow. Mimosa, the wall of a house, part of a window shimmered behind her. She looked about thirty-five. There was a wanting expression in her eyes, a hunger, that made me feel Mrs. West had been easy to go to bed with but difficult afterward. Nineteen thirty-eight: crisis everywhere and sun in Provence. Paul Tagliatti was twenty. . . .

"Walter who?"

Tartan Cummerbund had crept up behind me. I decided to ignore him. Nineteen thirty-eight. May or June, from the light. I was sure Mrs. West was American. Rich? With a villa in Le Lavandou? Who was Mr. West? Was he there too that summer? Had she been in love with Paul Tagli-

13

atti? Untying that bow, dropping her wrap-around in a shuttered afternoon bedroom . . .

"I don't know anyone named Walter." He had one of those primly insistent voices. Even some of the peacock people around me were giving him their divided attention. "Do you know what I think?" He didn't expect an answer. "I don't think we've ever met before. I don't think you know me."

I gave up and smiled at him. Sooner or later he would get to the point, accuse me of having invented Walter to try to cod my way in without an invitation. It was none of his business, but it happened to be true, so I would have to be pleasant. I hate pretending to be friendly to people; it is simply sometimes necessary in my precarious way of living.

"Of course I know you." If I let my imagination work by itself, without trying to reason deliberately, I can often feel, guess a few facts about someone. "I met you with your mother." I was sure he had a mother. I was sure, too, he didn't live in New York. There was something about him that made me think of Southampton, the way other men make me think of Madison Avenue or Wall Street. "In Southampton last summer. You were wearing the same jacket." It was at least two years out of fashion with those buttons. "And we—" Did he dance? I decided to finesse it. "And we did a what's-its-name together."

"Sure." I'd been lucky. "The Dunes Club dance. I remember you now." His voice brightened with mistaken conviction. "You had on a green dress."

"That's right. With a white belt." I knew that from then on I could say almost anything. It was as though I had just told his fortune; a few meager facts had convinced him. If I said now that I'd spilled wine on his mother he would remember that too. *Beach, Le Lavandou.* I was tired of him.

"Shall I tell you something funny?" He was a great one for rhetorical questions. The plump white-skinned woman on the beach was an American too. I had identified her from a later portrait, *Lilian Alan Fletcher*, painted in Provincetown. . . .

"The funny thing is I still can't think of anyone I know named Walter." I had been dead right about him: he was a meticulous prig. The counted, the predictable have always dismayed me. When I broke away from my money-

14

cosseted mother five years ago, my declaration of independence was prompted by the urge to pursue not so much my own happiness as the unexpected. I was going to have to do something drastic about this cummerbund pest.

"I'm afraid we'll have to go now." The man in the plum-colored jacket was moving toward me. Behind him, the elderly woman who had bumped into me earlier reached out as though to detain him; I had the impression they had been talking together. I took his arm gratefully; I wasn't going to have to do anything about Cummerbund after all. It wasn't until we were crossing the lobby that I wondered why my companion had come and retrieved me. Did he think he knew me?

His driver was waiting outside. I hesitated as the door of the old-fashioned limousine was opened.

"You can drop me at the Plaza, Berman."

The oddly preserved face turned to me.

"And then Berman can drive you home if you like."

"It's all the way downtown."

"It doesn't matter."

There was no sense in refusing. The two-dollar cab fare meant too much to me and there was no other way of getting back to Macdougal Street. By this time of night hostilities would be open. The desperate looters who had been reconnoitering all day would be staked out in ambush in every street and subway station. I might be able to get as far as Forty-second Street; beyond that, no matter how I zigged and zagged, there was no route that was passable for a girl alone.

"Thank you." The padded armrest between the back seats reminded me of my mother's old Bentley. Victoria Station. Being picked up by the chauffeur on my way home from boarding school at the end of term. I leaned back with the same sense of relief.

"Did you like the paintings?" My companion was sitting as though scaffolded beside me, impervious to the acceleration of the car.

"Yes."

"I thought you did."

"I never realized he was only thirty-four when he died."

"I *thought* you liked them."

I had been in New York for two years—long enough to recognize this form of conversation. "They don't expect you to listen," Evelyn Waugh wrote about them. I still

15

couldn't help listening; I only occasionally expected to be heard.

"What's the Wexford Bone collection?" Sometimes a question would get through.

"You seemed particularly interested by the early paintings."

Only sometimes.

"I was looking at that portrait of Eugenia West." If I was going to talk to myself I might as well talk about something that interested me. "I was thinking about her. She had a villa near Le Lavandou. That's where she sat for him. In the garden before lunch. She used to go to bed with him in the afternoons. She was a rich American and she was hopelessly in love with him. She used to give him money to gamble with at the casino in Hyères."

"I *thought* you liked the early paintings best." He seemed to feel he had made his point, said everything he had to say about that. He didn't speak again until the car stopped in front of the hotel. The driver opened the door.

"Where do you live?"

He wasn't getting out. He might have been waiting only so that the driver could hear me. I didn't think so. For the first time I sensed a purpose in his immobility. It startled me, like a cat that had been there all the time, unnoticed until it purred. I remembered the way he had said, "It doesn't matter" when I told him I lived all the way downtown. He was evidently a man who was used to having his own way. For a moment I was inclined to resist him; I impulsively resist any domination; but he had been more than helpful to me.

"A hundred and seventeen Macdougal Street."

"A hundred and seventeen." His movements as he got out of the car were as deliberate as his stillness had been. "We never introduced ourselves." He was waiting again, leaning toward me.

"My name's Jane Claire."

"Jane Claire."

His masklike face withdrew a little and then returned. He was making up his mind about something.

"I'm Wexford Bone."

2

"WHAT DO YOU DO after you have been raped?"

The mimeographed question had been left in my mailbox while I was out. I thought about it as I climbed the scuffed wooden stairs to my apartment. I couldn't answer it from experience. Statistically that makes me one of the lucky ones. Women in America, according to some police estimates, are getting raped every forty seconds. But I'm also one of the lucky ones who don't believe statistics have anything to do with them. I probably inherited that from my Irish grandfather. "The life expectancy of an infantry lieutenant on the Western Front," he used to tell me, "was five days."

"You were there four years without even getting promoted."

"For God's sake, girl, I'm not talking about myself."

As a child I could understand his indignation. I still share his attitude. I don't imagine I am magically exempt from harm. I am five feet four inches tall, weigh a hundred and ten pounds, have never learned karate and don't carry a Mace gun. But one thing sure: whatever happens to me will have no connection with the predictions of any computer.

What *do* you do after you have been raped?

I turned the key slowly, as silently as I could, slammed the door back against the wall and snapped on the lights. I can make my door secure enough once I'm inside, but anyone could open it when I'm out. Fortunately, there are few places in my loft apartment where an intruder could hide. I looked in the closet and the bathroom before bolting and chaining the front door.

I knew what I would do first after I had been raped. Douche. I looked at the leaflet to see if I had the right answer.

"Do *not* douche."

17

Why not?

"It will destroy evidence."

I kicked off my sandals and folded my dress away: six yards of pale blue Indian silk; like the little black dress of more provincial times, a sari is acceptable anywhere. I sat down on the bed and went back to the leaflet.

"Call the police. Make them take you to the nearest precinct station. Insist on a physical examination within six hours." It reminded me of one of those guides for tourists, each instruction anticipating the next hassle.

"Expect detailed, intimate questioning from the police. Do not feel guilty. Being raped is not your fault. . . . This leaflet has been distributed for your protection by a voluntary, non-profit-making women's organization."

There is a notice board beside the door: my small collection of modern Americana. I pinned the leaflet next to a quotation from the Chairman of the Foreign Relations Committee: "To hell with world opinion."

I would still douche, I decided, taking off my tights. "For your protection." What protection was evidence? Was it even justice those non-profit-making women were after; there could obviously be no question of restitution; or was it revenge? Why else call the police? A desperate lot the police seem to me. Perversely frivolous. There they go, towing away cars, closing skin movies, harassing whores. Stewards enforcing the company's regulations while the ship sinks.

Like most people I know, I have no doubt the ship *is* sinking. "At this moment in history we find ourselves threatened by extermination that no one wishes, that everyone fears, that just may happen 'because' . . . ." R. D. Laing isn't the only one who can see that all over the world are the engineers, the politicians, the futurologists, the multinational executives, compulsively making sure he's right.

I'm not going to go on about ecology.

But as we increase our knowledge, all we seem to do is build a wider and greater hell on earth.

Why?

Kelly and Koestler say the answer is in ourselves, in our individual characters. Maybe it's because we're too frightened of *not* surviving. When I first came to New York I had a theory about that—about survivors. I thought there are people in every generation whose urge to

18

survive is so strong they endanger everyone else. And themselves. They are attractive and vital with their secret purpose. We love and follow them. And they are the enemy. I spent days in the public library trying to find out if there could be any truth in this theory. I followed every lead I could—anthropology, social science, the psychologists. A number of books about animal behavior taught me a great deal about the behavior of animals. All history engrossed me; I went through the newspapers, going back fifty years: the war, the depression, the Twenties. It was the day-to-day behavior of people that enthralled me. In the end I forgot all about my theory. I became interested in what we've been, what we've done for their own sake.

I still spend a good deal of time in the past. The present seems to me already too late. The answer to that "because," if there is one, lies in earlier years, before decline became fall.

In the meantime it was Friday tomorrow. I needed money for the week end. I have had several "good" jobs since coming to New York. "The really fun things," I found myself writing as a junior editor on a magazine, "are those little extras that will change your whole personality, that pair of loopy earrings you never felt were quite you." I work two days a week as a waitress now, two or three days as a temporary secretary, occasional evenings as a cashier in a movie house.

The two things I am determined to avoid, either separately or together, are marriage and a career.

My mother has spent her whole life insulated by trust funds; perhaps that's why I have no hunger for money. Her lawyers pay the rent on my apartment; space is as precious to me as land was to my father's family in Ireland; I atone for this self-indulgence in guilt and with a weekly letter to my mother. For the rest I need less than ten dollars a day.

I decided I would comb my hair back the next morning, put on a skirt and go and type somewhere.

"Wait here, Berman."

I was dressed, waiting for the employment agency to call me back about that day's job, when I heard his voice from the street. It didn't surprise me. I imagined him pausing in the hall, looking at the three battered mailboxes. "J. Claire" is penciled on a strip of adhesive tape

19

stuck to the middle box. I listened to him climbing the stairs. There is no bell. He knocked.

"Who is it?" From the first we played silly games like that with each other. There was never any trust between us.

He was wearing a gray tweed suit that morning. It made him look less indefinite, more recognizably a man who owned things. He didn't ask if he could come in. I closed the door after him without saying a word either.

He strolled possessively about the room, looked at the photograph on the wall over the bed. It was an early one, taken in 1953, before he grew his beard; I found it in a bookstore on Eighth Street and had it framed; Solzheitsyn seems to me one of the few people alive who have earned the right to be serious. Bone studied the pained, determined face. I couldn't tell whether he recognized it or not. My desire to find out broke the silence.

"My uncle Patrick."

Bone nodded. I had found out nothing. He moved on to the bookcase.

"I have to go to work in a few minutes."

"What kind of work do you do?"

"I'm a secretary." I didn't explain I was other things, other days.

"You're not American, are you?"

My mother made sure I was an American citizen from birth. I didn't feel like explaining that either. "I wasn't born here."

"I've never been to Ireland."

"Would you mind telling me why you came here, Mr. Bone?"

"Why did you pretend you knew me last night?"

"I didn't have an invitation card."

"You're very interested in Tagliatti, aren't you?"

"I like his paintings."

"How do you know so much about his life?"

"I don't."

"You told me he borrowed money from Mrs. West." He had been listening to me, all right, on the way to the Plaza.

"I was guessing."

He didn't press me; he was a master of silence; he stood there, filling space, until I went on.

"There's no point in trying to explain. You wouldn't be-

20

lieve me." I walked over to the bureau and picked up my handbag. As I passed him I could feel his anger as clearly as the waft of an air-conditioned store. It frightened me. He smiled; it was a commendably genuine smile; he could control his features like puppets.

"I'd believe you if you told me the truth."

"It's a trick, a game I play. Looking at things, trying to feel, trying to imagine something from them." It reminded me of old ladies in summer hotels, seeking revelations in the feel of a proffered wedding ring. All they sought was attention.

"You got a psychic message from Mrs. West's portrait?" He didn't believe a word of it. He probably thought I had known Mrs. West somewhere, heard about Tagliatti from her.

"I'm going to be late for work."

"I came here to offer you a job."

"I've already got one." I wanted to get him out of there before the agency rang me back and confirmed that.

"I'm looking for someone to do some research for me."

"I've had no experience."

"You read a lot." He was looking at my bookshelves again. "History, psychology, social science. That should be a help to us."

I didn't say anything; let him explain himself for a change.

Instead of explaining, he surprised me. There was a sudden unexpected liveliness in his eyes; he no longer looked blandly ominous; he looked amused and intelligent.

"Do you think our only hope lies in everybody making everything his business?"

For a moment I almost liked him: quoting Solzhenitsyn at me to let me see he had known all along it wasn't my Uncle Patrick over the bed.

"What kind of research?"

Bone picked up the catalog I had brought home with me the night before. "I'm not satisfied with this. The listing of the paintings. Especially the dates. Some of the dates. I was talking to Edna Haggard about it last night." I had the impression he was watching me to see if I reacted to her name. I tried not to, while I wondered if she was the elderly woman who had bumped into me in front of that painting, *Chair*.

21

"She gave Paul Tagliatti a one-man show in New York in 1945."

"She owned the Haggard Gallery?"

"Yes." He was looking at the catalog again. "*House, Cuernavaca,* 1939. Paul lived in Cuernavaca in '51, '52, but I don't believe he ever went there before the war. I want someone to find out things like that, put the paintings in their proper order, get the dates right."

"Did you know Tagliatti?"

"Very well." For once his hesitation didn't seem deliberate. "We were close friends for twelve years. I was with him in Mexico, in Tetacata, when he died."

"What did he die of?" It was perhaps the only genuinely spontaneous question I ever asked Bone.

"He was shot in a quarrel with a drunken Mexican." He made it sound like a death from natural causes. "He was very ill at the time anyway." He put down the catalog, closing that subject. "Have you ever heard of Kevin Fallon?"

I had. For one thing, I had read two biographies of Tyrone Fallon, his father, one painfully researched and the other absurd. Both had had a lot to say about the tragedy—as the silly book put it, The Curse of the Fallons. The elder son, Tyrone Junior, had hanged himself; the younger son, Kevin, had chosen a slower way out. Tyrone Fallon himself, the first American to win the Nobel Prize for Literature, had been found frozen to death in the snow twenty yards from his own house. It was that kind of family.

"I know who he was."

"He was a friend of mine. Years ago. It was Kevin who first introduced me to Paul Tagliatti."

"Why did you ask me about him?" For reasons I wasn't going to explain to Bone, I had a personal interest in Kevin Fallon. There was a photograph of him, a poignantly attractive young man, in one of the books about his father. I tried to find out all I could about him. A man I met at a party told me Kevin had once worked at the Rowland display studio in the Village. I knew about the Rowland studio; it had been in the loft that was now my apartment. After that I often thought about Kevin Fallon; I imagined him working here in this same space, existing here thirty years ago. I tried to re-create the whole period in my mind: the radio playing all day; the Andrews Sisters and the Battle of the Bulge; commercials masquerading as patriotism; "Lucky Strike green has gone to war." A dozen black girls painting faces on masks; the smell of paste and excelsior. Kevin, dark, young, diffident, making papier-mâché angels for Lord & Taylor's windows . . .

"How much do you earn as a secretary?"

I had almost forgotten Bone was there.

"Four dollars an hour."

"I'll pay you two hundred dollars a week and your traveling expenses."

It sounded suspiciously generous to me. "Just to catalog some paintings?"

"You'll have to trace people who knew Tagliatti. Talk to them. Find out what he was painting at that time. That's why I mentioned Kevin Fallon. You could start with Kevin."

"He's dead."

"He gets a small income from his father's copyrights." It was like Bone to put the practical details of existence first. "He lives at the Milroy Hotel on Eighth Street." He took a pigskin wallet with gold edgings from his pocket and slipped out some twenty-dollar bills. They looked as fresh as innocence as he held them out to me.

"A week's salary in advance to show you I'm serious."

I didn't take them. I knew he was serious; I didn't think he was telling me the truth. He didn't seem to be offering me a job so much as buying me off. I've had a lot of experience of that; my mother has, in her own way, been buying me off all my life; she has her reasons. Bone had none that I could see.

"Why do you think I'd be any good at this job? If I took it."

He didn't answer. The phone was ringing: the employment agency calling me back. I knew almost at once that I wasn't going to answer it. Bone seemed to know it too. He waited, still and patient, until the ringing stopped.

"After you've seen Kevin, come and have dinner with me tonight." He dropped the twenty-dollar bills onto the table.

As he walked toward the door I saw the notice board with the leaflet pinned to it behind him. "What do you do after you have been raped?"

It wasn't revenge those non-profit-making women were after. It was vindication. I suddenly understood that. It

23

was vindication I wanted from Bone now. I let him get his hand on the latch.

"I suppose you know Kevin Fallon worked here, Mr. Bone."

"Here?" He dropped his hand.

"In this building. This apartment. He worked in a display studio here thirty years ago."

"How did you know that?"

"You wouldn't believe me if I told you." I smiled at Bone; I felt vindicated.

"Kevin did work in a display studio for a while." He gave me his commendably genuine smile back. "He had an unexpected talent for making angels out of shredded paper. It was the only talent Kevin Fallon ever had." Bone opened the door.

"Berman will pick you up at seven."

3

THE WEST SIDE OF WASHINGTON SQUARE is a bad block. Chicly radical once; Eleanor Roosevelt lived there in the late Forties, stalking brisk as a giant insect across the park in the early mornings. It's a hangout for creeps now.

Although they weren't likely to use force by daylight, only approach me with the threat of it disguised as begging, I turned off down Third Street and took the long way around. My mental plan of New York is heavily marked with recommended detours.

"One was forced to travel even at noon as if one was going into battle." Horace Walpole wrote that about eighteenth-century London. There seem to me other similarities between the two cities: the helplessness felt by many people; in Walpole's London one fifth of the population were alcoholics; they were prepared to kill, if they had to, for the oblivion of gin; magistrates had them publicly hanged by the hundreds. The violence of the law deterred none but the executed. It was pride, that curious Victorian sense of purpose, that finally brought relative order to London.

The Milroy hotel was a relic of Harding's normalcy. There was no pride here. The desk clerk looked out of place aboveground. I waited while he fiddled with the switchboard, snapping switches in an irritable, purposeless way, before he sidled over to me. He brought the smell of musk and disinfectant with him.

"Mr. Kevin Fallon, please."

"Who?"

"Kevin Fallon." The "Who?" was automatic. It's one of the things I've learned to accept about New York—these pockets of resistance against any demands of the present. They aren't confined to run-down hotels.

"Number 34." He peered at the rack and shook his head. "His key's not here."

25

"He might be in his room."

"When he's in, he's usually in and out."

He left me to think that over while he went back to his switchboard. A few indirect words, scarcely a movement, Bone would have had Kevin Fallon in the lobby by now. I don't have the presence for it; no one's ever been frightened of me in my life.

"Who wants him?" The smell of musk and disinfectant again.

"Mr. Wexford Bone."

"Who?"

Most of the lobby had been boarded off and rented to a firm of real estate agents. Once spaciously residential, the Milroy was doomed. Space has too much scarcity value now to be lived in. There were no chairs on the lobby side of the partition. I waited by the door, where the air was a little fresher.

Kevin Fallon would be in his middle fifties by now. I was expecting the worst. The figure that hobbled out of the elevator still shocked me. The clerk nodded dismissingly in my direction. The toothless old vagrant in the long belted overcoat managed a few more steps toward me. I hurried to meet him. Close to, the face looked soiled with living. The bones beneath it seemed to have worn away; they no longer supported the skin. But the frightening thing was that, like some familiar object lost at the bottom of the garden for years, it was still just recognizable as itself. It was still grotesquely the face in the photograph I'd found in one of the books about his father.

"Where's old Wexford?" The words were mumbled into the coat collar.

"He's at the Plaza. He asked me to come and see you."

"I'm not going all the way to the Plaza for that son of a bitch."

I was surprised by the abrupt perky humor in the voice. Kevin Fallon looked down at his feet. "I don't understand what's wrong with these shoes. I only just got them. They hurt like hell." A brief dry sound changed the complaint to mockery.

I was glad to glance down too. It seemed a cruelty to keep looking at that face. He was wearing brand-new construction boots. The white cotton laces had been threaded through every hole and tied in a neat bow at the top.

"Would you like to go somewhere and sit down?"

"I wouldn't mind a cup of coffee." The quick, punctuating humor—it wasn't quite laughter—seemed to make a mockery of that too.

I helped him toward the door. Our progress outside was silent and irregular as I steered him through groups of incurious sightseers straggling about in the spring sunshine. I couldn't stop thinking about those boots. Had he gone into a store, chosen them, tried them on? I once spent several hours thinking about Oscar Wilde's elbow until I could picture it quite clearly: his individual skin, the form of *his* bone. I couldn't imagine Kevin Fallon buying those boots.

We found a coffee shop halfway down the block. "How are *you* today?" The woman behind the counter greeted us with averted eyes and heart-shaped menus. Each item was followed by an obituary of its ingredients. "From selected Texas herds tender-fed on . . ."

"Just coffee for me."

"That's a fifty-cent minimum for coffee."

Kevin Fallon hadn't taken his hands out of the pockets of his long tubular overcoat since he had appeared in the lobby. His menu rested on the counter, unnoticed or forgotten. He was looking at his feet again. I found it possible to believe he never ate anything.

"Two coffees," I told the waitress quickly.

Kevin Fallon's silence was different from Bone's: there was no demand in it; he wasn't going to ask me why Bone had sent me to see him; he didn't care. It was enough for him to be sitting there, to be sitting anywhere resting his feet.

"Mr. Bone——" I began.

"Old Wexford. I haven't seen him for years."

"I'm working for him——"

"He went off somewhere after the war. After the battle of the Village. Did you ever hear about that battle?"

"No." At least he was talking. I might be able to get him around to Tagliatti presently.

"Anyone—If you weren't in uniform, the G.I.'s figured you were queer. They used to beat you up in the bars. It wasn't like Viet Nam. Everybody was on the army's side. Old Wexford was 4F. He had an ulcer."

I leaned against the counter to get closer to him. It wasn't only that it was hard to follow the sequence of his words; it was hard to hear them. He never looked at me, mumbling into his coat, punctuating himself with that

27

gentle mocking sound. "We could never figure out what Bone was doing down here. He had a lot of money. He came from some place like Charleston, only smaller. He was the kind of kid who'd been taught to shoot ducks. He was always oiling his British shotgun. The son of a bitch was as fat as a whale. He used to buy us drinks."

I could reconcile that with the present-day Bone; the power to frighten had come later.

"Bone said you were friends."

"He didn't have any friends. He was a prick. All he had was money. He used it to make people hang around. Everybody else was so goddamn broke."

"He said you introduced him to Paul Tagliatti."

"Old Paul."

"How long did you know him?"

"Before the war. Old Paul. After Pearl Harbor . . ." He was obviously remembering something that still hurt him. "I guess I behaved like a shit. I did a lousy thing to him."

"How?"

"He was a hell of a painter."

We agreed about that. Then I saw that Kevin Fallon was talking about his feelings thirty years ago.

"Do you remember what he was painting when you knew him?" It was the question Bone had sent me to ask. I didn't really expect Kevin Fallon to answer it.

"There was one he did of the Sixth Avenue El."

"The El?" That startled me. There had been no painting of the El in the show at the Museum.

"It used to go past the Minetta Tavern. They tore it down and sold it to the Japanese."

"Anything else you remember?"

"Some Mexican ones."

"This one?" I had brought the catalog with me. I opened it at the *House, Cuernavaca*, dated 1939, which Bone had questioned. Kevin Fallon didn't take the catalog from me. He nodded in a way that didn't necessarily mean yes.

"Do you know when he painted it?"

"He didn't paint anything when we were in Mexico. We were both too drunk. He did a few drawings."

"When were you there with him?"

I got the answer to that indirectly, through fragments of reminiscence.

"We were hitchhiking down to Acapulco. A goddamn

28

American woman picked us up. She didn't want to take us both at first. Only Paul. She had some dogs in the back of the car. Great big bastards." Each sentence seemed less an effort of recall than a discovery. "We were going to walk along the beach from Acapulco to Panama. We were going to catch fish and live on them. We figured it would take about four years. The war would be over by the time we got to Panama. We were going to ask who won. We couldn't catch any goddamn fish. The lines kept getting snagged in the rocks. We had to go back. Old Paul went around doing drawings of the tourists. That's how we got the bus to Mexico City. My father cabled me some money there." There was no perkiness, no humor in his voice as he spoke about his father. "I didn't want to come back anyway. Anyone could see we were going to get into the war. I'd been to military school. I knew there'd be more shit in the American army than there was in the S.S. I was as scared as old Wexford was of getting drafted."

It sounded like late 1940 to me, or maybe the spring before Pearl Harbor. They might have stopped off in Cuernavaca on their way to Acapulco, but Tagliatti evidently hadn't painted anything there then.

"Did Tagliatti come back to New York with you?" I asked.

"I think he went to Provincetown with Lilian. We had an apartment on Greenwich Avenue after that. We couldn't sleep in it. The bedbugs were as big as mice. I caught one that had a pint of blood in him. We could have given him to the Red Cross. I guess I went to Sarah's."

He was staring at his coffee. He hadn't touched it.

"That was when old Wexford showed up in the Village."

"Don't you want your coffee?"

"Sure." For the first time he took his hands out of his pockets. He kept them below the counter; he was showing them only to me. They were fine hands, a delicate harmony of bones and muscle, still unexpectedly youthful. But they were no longer his. He had no more control over them than over a pair of startled birds. I wondered how long it had taken him to thread those white cotton laces into his boots.

"Shall I put sugar in it?"

He shook his head. "Sugar makes you vomit."

29

I lifted the cup for him. He sucked down some of the coffee. "Old Paul." He seemed glad to get back to his reminiscences. "A lot of people were scared of him."

"Why?"

He didn't answer. He was staring at his boots again.

"We should have made it to Panama," he told me. "It would have saved old Paul a hell of a lot of trouble. Me too. We always said we'd go back to Acapulco after the war. I don't know. I got busted. Then Paul had that show and made some money. They pulled all my teeth out in Lexington, Kentucky. The U.S. Government gave me some choppers. They hurt worse than these goddamn shoes." He was back in the present. He looked vaguely around the coffee shop. For all its heart-shaped menus and pastel colors, the place was as characterless as a paper clip. I wondered why.

"It was all right for a while." He had his hands safely trapped in his pockets again. "There were still people around. You could still sit in the circle in Washington Square. I don't see anyone I know any more."

Only the desk clerk. It wasn't difficult to imagine Kevin Fallon's life at the Milroy. The stained ceiling over the irregularly made bed. Grime seeping in like the sound of traffic. Four flaking walls. The clang of steam pipes. "When he's in, he's usually in and out."

"Did you hear that about nuns?"

I hadn't noticed the man come in. He stood just inside the door: middle-aged, brush-cut, a conformist in dress down to his polished loafers. He waved his arms, shouting into the arrested stillness of the coffee shop. "Did you hear that about nuns? They can commit murder, nuns—murder. The police can't touch them. Did you ever hear that?"

He genuinely seemed to want to know if we had. His arms stopped waving. He held them out to us, pleading for our answer.

"Didn't you ever hear that? Any one of you?" His voice dropped, quavered; he had lost his audience; sudden lunacy in cities is too common to hold attention. He left furtively; no comment followed him.

"That'll be a dollar eight." The waitress had let herself be startled for a moment; it annoyed her that she had. Kevin Fallon and I were a disparate pair, God knows; she had never liked the look of us sitting there at her counter; she was coldly determined to get rid of us now.

Outside on the sidewalk we walked a few steps without purpose. I found myself holding Kevin Fallon's arm. A black limousine was idling farther down the street. Like Bone's it reminded me of my mother's old Bentley; it pulled away before I could see if Berman was driving it.

"Do you want to go back to the hotel?" I hoped he didn't; it wasn't altogether self-interest that made me want to keep him with me; it was partly the thought of what he would be going back to.

"I don't know what I want to do."

"Does it hurt to walk?"

"I'm getting used to it."

"Would you do me a favor?"

"Sure." His head bobbed up; he smiled at me. For a moment I saw not the caved-in mouth, the grained skin, but quite clearly the face of the young man in the photograph. It was one of the most vulnerable faces I have ever seen.

"Would you spend the afternoon with me? Tell me about Paul Tagliatti. Anything you can remember. Take me to some of the places you used to go to together. Show me where he lived."

4

September—November, 1941

HE WASN'T LIVING ANYWHERE THAT WINTER. After the bedbugs drove them out of the apartment on Greenwich Avenue, Kevin moved in with his girl, Sarah, who gave violin lessons and had a job as a hat-check girl in a restaurant uptown. Paul spent some of his time at her place with Kevin, but not too much, and he never slept there. Sarah had a way of looking at him and he didn't want to get into a three-way situation with Kevin. His real home was the Old Colony bar.

There was a floating group of regulars there, mostly young men of about his own age and their occasional girls. They were glad to include him in their aimless drinking: a half dozen people spilling out of a booth, beers all over the table. Paul would sit drawing on odd bits of paper.

Strangers drifted in—older men on a bat, salesmen taking a day off. Live ones, the regulars called them. A live one would get restless after paying for three or four rounds; he wanted to go on somewhere else. Between the Old Colony and the next bar, it was usually possible to con him out of some hamburgers. That took care of the eating problem.

Paul was not particularly friendly with any of the group except Kevin. Much of their conversation consisted of scraps of old jokes: "I said kidleys, did'll I?" "Funny ha-ha, or funny peculiar?" They were only reluctantly bohemian; most of them would have preferred nine-to-five lives. The war in Europe had ended the long depression at last; there were jobs to be had; but not for them: nobody wanted to hire them; there was no future in it. Sitting around the Old Colony bar, pooling their nickels for beers and cigarettes, they were waiting to get drafted.

They were more interested in Paul than he was in them. None of them had ever been outside the United States. He had been "all over the world"—France, Italy, Spain, even Greece. He was as good as an encyclopedia when it came to settling arguments, full of exotic information: the sequence of Henry the Eighth's wives, the rites of the Roman saturnalia. Although it was understood that he had been born in St. Louis, there was something fictional to them about this detail. He no longer had an English accent; he had learned to pronounce words like "new" and "glass" in the American way; but he was still obviously, intriguingly foreign.

He didn't talk much, and never about his painting. After a summer of hard work in Provincetown, during which, he told Kevin, he had completed six paintings— "One of them's the best thing I've ever done"—he was going through an interval of quiescence: watching, absorbing. Outwardly he was concerned only with the details of survival, the necessity of finding—as the French say, "touching"—the few cents he needed every day.

He would have had no trouble finding a girl to help support him; several around the Old Colony invited him to share their apartments with them. He didn't want to expose himself to their inevitable demands. "What are you thinking about, Paul?" Angela Anson, Kevin's half sister, was living in a women's hotel uptown. Paul kept in touch with her; she had a suitcase full of his things—sketchbooks, materials, several carefully rolled paintings; but he had no inclination to resume his affair with her. The few times they saw each other she talked to him earnestly about employment opportunities, a steady job retouching photographs. Angela had joined the series of wistful girls in Paul's life who wanted to domesticate him.

For forty cents he could sleep at the Mills Hotel on Bleecker Street. A single cubicle, narrow as a closet, the plywood partitions rising six feet on either side of the bed, chicken wire from there to the ceiling; a rough sheet as the only bedclothes: steam heat was cheaper than delousing blankets. The hawking and coughing, the protesting sleep-cries of the hundred men filed away on each floor. Crowding into the shower room, jostled by varicose flesh. No drunks, no liquor, no smoking in the cubicles. In by ten and out by seven-thirty. The trouble with the Mills

Hotel, Paul told Kevin, was that it was sometimes hard as hell to get the forty cents.

When he couldn't afford the Mills, he had to find someone who would put him up for the night. There was a girl he met at the Old Colony named Priscila Franklin who got alimony from Philadelphia and had an apartment on Bedford Street. Priscila's demands didn't threaten his independence.

"You won't try anything if I let you stay?" Lurching back to her place after the bars closed; fleeing across the intersections. Not out of fear of violence; crime was gangsters and stick-ups in banks; the only menace in the streets was the knife-edged wind.

"No."

"Promise?"

"I swear." Paul meant it. A pretty girl with huge dark eyes, Priscila wasn't more than twenty-five, but something had gone wrong with her glands, or perhaps it was only the drinking and the hot dog diet: her body had the wrinkled softness of a partly deflated balloon.

It was a one-room apartment with a double bed. She told Paul he could sleep on the floor. "You won't try anything, will you?"

"No." It had been some time since he had had the money to buy new socks or underwear. He went into the bathroom to wash the ones he was wearing. Priscila's voice hunted him through the door. "Paul? Paul." He hung his wet things on the hot-water pipe, wrapping them around it like bandages. They would be as stiff as paper in the morning. "Paul?" He took a shower; his toothbrush was in his jacket pocket; with his blond hair he didn't need to shave more than twice a week. "Paul?" He fastened a towel around his waist and opened the door.

Priscila was sitting up in bed in her slip. "You can come in with me if you promise not to try anything."

He dropped the towel and got into bed. His body was pale and lean; Eugenia West, Lilian Alan Fletcher, a number of other women had found its engaging adolescence erotic. Priscila decided after all to take off her slip.

"Promise you won't try anything if I turn the light out."

It was usually about an hour before she let him get to sleep. She wasn't inventive; she pushed herself against him, complaining he was taking up too much room; she got her hands on him on the pretext of making him shift over. He

34

lay as close to the edge of the mattress as he could. She wanted to change sides. Rolling herself under him, she pretended to be caught in the sheet. Finally, she got him inside her. She struggled and whined and encouraged him by digging her nails into his back.

In the morning she was sullen and hostile. "You promised you wouldn't try anything if I let you stay."

He spent at least one night a week at Priscila's. He couldn't wash his clothes at the Mills Hotel. It was against the rules.

Kevin insisted, with his perky humor, that this was Paul's only reason for putting up with Priscila. But Paul had another, more involving interest in her. He was fascinated by the quality of isolation in those huge dark eyes; he was sifting and sharpening his ideas, making notes for a portrait of her.

Duke, the bartender at the Old Colony, was fond of Paul. He enjoyed chatting with him in Italian, complaining about "those bums," as he called his other customers. He had been born in Sicily; he was impressed by Paul's manner, a grace which he unconsciously associated with the rich, the *padrones* of his childhood. Because of this, Paul baffled him; he couldn't understand what he was doing hanging around a joint like the Old Colony. "With your looks," he would tell Paul. "Your—you know what I mean—" Fumbling for the right word, he would settle for education. "With your education, you could go anywhere in this town." He would often stand Paul a drink. More importantly for Paul, Duke would lend him the sixty cents he needed to by an evening's work as a dishwasher from an employment agency on lower Broadway. Fridays and Saturdays were the most likely days for a job. If there was nothing going, Paul always walked straight back to the Old Colony and repaid Duke at once. He had nothing to pawn except his reliability; it was necessary to redeem it.

The work, when he got it by paying the sixty cents in advance, was rushed and unpleasant: scraping the congealed food off the dishes; fitting them into a rack; pushing it through the canvas flap into the scalding steam; dragging it out the other end. From six to nine the dishes piled up, precarious and unsavory; at ten he was given a meal; another period of frantic activity when the movie

35

houses emptied around eleven. At three or four in the morning, after mopping the floor and trundling out the garbage, he got paid off. Six dollars in cash; no tax; no Social Security. His employers rarely asked his name. Outside in the chill streets, the smell of grease and boiled greens was like wax in his nostrils.

It was too late for the Mills. Any other hotel would cost at least a dollar. Those were the nights Paul began to rely on Bone.

Kevin and Paul had taken to stopping by Bone's apartment two or three afternoons a week. It was somewhere to go. There were art books and magazines to look at, a couch to sit on. There was never any liquor or beer; Bone didn't drink; buying rounds in the Old Colony, he ordered ginger ale for himself; but he always had coffee, Danish pastries, doughnuts in his alcove kitchen. Bone had a weakness for sweet things; in Vienna he would have gained ten pounds in a week. Paul and Kevin could fry up an egg if they felt like it; they helped themselves.

One afternoon Paul found a drawing of Carracci's in one of Bone's art books. He helped himself to some of Bone's typing paper; he was an excellent copyist; he would have made a superb forger; but neither of the drawings he made that afternoon was a copy. In one he deliberately left out all shading; in the other he omitted all Carracci's lines. It was an exercise for him, nothing more. He lost interest in it after an hour or so and wandered back to the Old Colony with Kevin. Bone found the drawings later when he was replacing his art books in their proper spaces on the shelves. He didn't mention them to Paul the next time he saw him.

Paul was drunk the first night he spent at Bone's apartment. Drunk, Paul was helplessly indiscriminate. He would attach himself to anyone, to any blurred face in sight, like a survivor to a sea-washed rock. Leaving the Old Colony with Bone, he bullied him into buying a pint of whiskey. He sat on the couch in Bone's apartment, drinking it and talking about Walt Whitman. Paul hated Whitman that night with a quite personal hatred; he seemed in some piercing, hallucinatory way to associate the poet with Eugenia West.

"Humiliation," he kept saying. "Every line of Whitman's revels in self-humiliation. And that's all she

36

ever cared about too. Exposing herself, being humiliated, like that fucking Whitman." Paul wanted, and felt he was increasingly unable, to make that quite clear.

When he woke up in the morning he was fully dressed on the couch. Bone, in pajamas, was tucked into his studio bed on the other side of the room. Bone's jacket was hanging neatly over the back of a chair. The two drawings Paul had made, mounted on expensive cardboard, were lying on the desk. After a night's drinking, Paul often woke at that age full of restless, apparently clearheaded energy, a sense of impatient purpose: he wanted to go out to Connecticut for the day, look at some trees, some white frame houses. He took Bone's wallet out of the pocket of the jacket and helped himself to a five-dollar bill. As he replaced the wallet he saw that Bone was awake, watching him.

Bone didn't say anything. His eyes closed. He pretended to be asleep.

Paul washed his face in cold water and left.

A circle had been completed. The drawings Bone had appropriated, the mutual knowledge of Paul's theft formed the halves of it. From then on each had an understanding of the other. Bone had a realistic estimation of Paul's talent and of his casual ruthlessness. Paul had a tacit understanding of Bone's knowledge. Neither was to be immediately affected by the existence of this circle. It was later to determine the outline of both their lives.

The next time Paul took a night's work as a dishwasher he rang Bone's doorbell at four o'clock in the morning. There was a reek of garbage and stale grease about him, but Bone could see at once that he was sober. Paul had a bath and slept on the couch. In the morning he helped himself, openly, to a clean pair of Bone's socks.

He didn't overdo it. On the whole, except for the nights he slept there, he saw less of Bone after that than before. He and Kevin found other places to go and sit and keep warm.

By the end of October, Paul was getting restless. The interval of quiescence was over. He wanted to get that suitcase back from Angela Anson, to set up a blank canvas and stare at it. He wanted to paint. He needed a place;

Lilian Alan Fletcher was still on the Cape; he wrote to her. Provincetown was like a police state in the wintertime, she replied; Kevin's father had been arrested there as a spy during the First World War; she couldn't risk having Paul back there with her now.

There was a possible studio he knew about, a loft with a couch, a table and a few chairs in it, on Fourteenth Street. It was going for five dollars a week, but the owner wanted a month's rent in advance. Paul decided to get a job. If he worked until Christmas he could buy himself two or three months in that studio.

All the stores were taking on help that November. To be a salesman in most of them you needed a dark suit, several clean white shirts, black shoes; Paul had none of those things; but there was one store, he knew, that encouraged more relaxed, informal wear among its staff. He borrowed a jacket from Kevin and had his own trousers pressed, waiting in a curtained booth, pulling them on still warm from the steam. He walked up to Abercrombie & Fitch.

The woman who interviewed Paul was immediately impressed by him, by what she thought of as his cultured accent, his clean-cut appearance. He was so young, too, even younger than he looked; his age made him exactly the kind of personnel she was looking for: a bright kid, still safe from the draft, who could be kept on after Christmas and become a useful member of the team. She wrote, "Trainee Sales, Permanent" on his card and hired him at twenty-two dollars a week.

Paul had filled in his name as David Tyrrel on the application form, and his age as nineteen. It had been an essential precaution. If he had given his real age, which was twenty-three at that time, he would have had to produce his draft classification card. He didn't have one.

Paul had never registered for the draft.

5

"I'LL HAVE SOLE TOO, PLEASE."

It was the first time I had ever eaten in the Oak Room. Bone had his own chosen table. He sat on a banquette facing the room. I sat across from him with my back to it.

"You've done very well." He was looking at the report I had given him; I had kept it short and factual.

1941
Jan.–May. In Mexico with Kevin Fallon. No paintings. Sketches of tourists in Acapulco. Sold to tourists. Other drawings and sketches.

June–Aug. In Provincetown with Lilian Alan Fletcher. Six paintings. *Lilian. Tyrone Fallon House. Dunes, with Figures.* Property of Boston Museum of Fine Arts, Lilian Alan Fletcher Bequest. *Girl on Wharf. Street, with Figures.* Now in Wexford Bone collection. Sixth painting—subject unknown. Present whereabouts unknown.

Sept.—Oct. In New York. No paintings. Several sketches, including pencil drawing "Duke," bartender at Old Colony. Two studies from Carracci, acquired by Wexford Bone.

Nov. Rented studio on Fourteenth Street. Two paintings. *Girl in Bed* (Priscila Franklin). *Man Sleeping* (Mills Hotel). Both in Wexford Bone collection.

"It's surprising he painted so much that year." Bone sipped his ginger ale. He still didn't drink. "It was an unsettled year for Paul." He scratched at his fish. "It was an unsettled year for everyone. The war. Everyone was sitting on the edge of the war." He wasn't interested in what he was saying; he was thinking about something else. "I've got that drawing of the bartender."

"I'd love to see it."

"I've got most of Paul's sketchbooks. I could have photostatic copies made of them for you."

"It'd be a great help."

"How did you know—" He folded my report and put it away in his pocket. He was getting to the point. "How did you know about those studies from Carracci?"

"Kevin remembers them."

"How did you know I had them?"

"Kevin said Paul did them in your apartment. Didn't he leave them there?"

"Yes." Back to his fish. I don't know what Bone thought then; he probably didn't believe I had accosted him by chance outside the Museum of Modern Art; he had seen me talking to the man in the tartan cummerbund a moment before I approached him; perhaps he thought I was working for them, for the Donners. Perhaps I only puzzled him.

"You must have spent a lot of time with Kevin."

"From noon until about six o'clock." Bone knew that; I had seen the black limousine again several times that afternoon; Berman *was* driving it.

"How is he?"

"All right."

"It was difficult for Kevin. Having a world-famous father." Bone was thinking about something else again. "There was nothing Kevin ever really wanted to do."

Except find a purpose, create one from need. "It's a way of life," Kevin had told me that afternoon. "When you're on horse, there's something you have to do. You wake up in the morning and you have to get it. You *have* to."

"He never had any talent, nothing he could use to compete with his father." Bone had a purpose; I could feel it across the table. He put down his knife and fork. "It was difficult for Paul too. He had too much talent. Can you imagine the responsibility of a talent like that?"

"I've been trying to."

He smiled. "His talent ruled Paul like a fate. Fate as the Greeks understood it. He knew he could never escape it." There was an unmistakable sympathy, a sincerity in Bone's voice. Again, for a moment, I almost liked him. "Paul could have had such an easy, pleasant life," he went on. "People would have given him anything he wanted. He

40

was that sort of person, so—It was more than just charm. Have you ever seen a photograph of him?"

"No."

He took an envelope from his pocket and slipped out a post-card-sized photograph. A young man was leaning back on a sofa, his legs stretched out. He was looking directly into the camera. My immediate impression was of the beauty of his face: a romantic beauty, the blond hair like an aura, the eyes hopefully innocent. Although there was nothing sentimental about it, it was a beauty that would have been better suited to an idealized illustration than a photograph. Except for the mouth. The mouth was not innocent; it was determined; the lips were decisively set in repose, renouncing the possiblity of impulsive response. I wondered how old Paul had been when it was taken. If I'd had to guess I would have said twenty or twenty-one. The clothes were no help to me in trying to date the photograph. Paul was wearing a gray pin-stripe suit with narrow lapels and no cuffs to the trousers; it had an incongruously present-day style to it. I looked at the back of the photograph; it was stamped with the photographer's name: Howard Coster, Victoria Street.

I glanced up. Bone was watching me in that same waiting way as he had when he mentioned Edna Haggard's name to me.

"You can keep it if you like."

"Thank you." I put the photograph away in my bag.

We finished our fish; I chose strawberries from the trolley. Bone had an éclair; he still liked sweet things.

"I'll have my attorneys write to you." He had reached a decision. "They'll pay your salary and send you any money you need for expenses. If there's anything you want to know, you can always get in touch with me through them." He was taking it for granted I was going on with my research. By that time I was taking it for granted too. That afternoon had given me a glimpse of a personality that interested me too much to stop. It was Paul Tagliatti's independence that fascinated me. Most of us feel alien, out of place, at times; but we resist it; it disturbs us; we have an urge, however ineffectual or suppressed, to fit in. It had obviously never occurred to Paul that he could be anything but out of place, a stranger everywhere. He seemed to have known that the only way he could be accepted was by deliberately disguising himself. And he had bothered to do that only when he had some immediate, practical reason to pass unnoticed: at the Mills Hotel; applying for a job at Abercrombie & Fitch.

"Can you tell me anything about his parents?" I asked Bone. "About his background?"

"Not very much, I'm afraid." He wiped a speck of cream off his lips. "The family were originally Italian, of course. From Milan, I think. There are blond Italians in Milan. They settled in the North of England, in Manchester, sometime around the 1880's. They were in the cotton business and quite wealthy at one time, according to Paul. His father sold his share of the business soon after the First World War and took to a wandering life in Europe. France, Italy, Switzerland, Spain, Greece. Paul used to say his father was always looking for the perfect place to do nothing. I think both Paul's parents died when he was thirteen or fourteen and after that he was brought up by an aunt in England."

"His parents must have been in the United States during the First World War."

"Yes?"

"Paul was born in St. Louis in 1917."

"Yes." Bone looked as if I had presented him with some astonishing new fact. "In St. Louis, yes."

He raised his hand for the check. The waiter brought it as though he had been living only for this signal. Bone examined the figures, appeared to be adding them up and wrote his name beneath the total in a neat, careful hand.

"I'll send you all the information I can through my attorneys. The names of people who knew Paul, places he lived. I may not be able to give you the exact dates. I only know what Paul told me, things he told me from time to time. It's up to you to try and put it all together."

"Do you want me to go on sending you reports—what I think he was working on, what happened to the paintings?"

"You've made a very good beginning." Bone nodded as he stood aside for me at the door. We walked through into the lobby.

"You'll send me those photostats of the sketchbooks?"

"Anything you need." He stepped back a little to let a man with a brief case pass between us. "I'll help you in any way I can." He moved away toward the elevators. "Berman will drive you home." He was gone.

I found Berman waiting for me by the door. The back of the limousine no longer reminded me of vacations from boarding school. It no longer reassured me. I felt Bone had been presenting himself to me, showing me only what he wanted me to see. I knew he was using me, manipulating me in his own way for some purpose of his own.

I couldn't understand what it was he was after.

6

I ALWAYS DISLIKE ENGLAND when I'm away from it. I spent too many years in boarding schools there. Among other myths which I absorbed at those schools was the idea that children whose parents spoke with identical accents, no matter which part of the country they came from, were a genetically superior group; that marriage and motherhood were a duty for the superior; black immigration was "a pity"; Ireland "a problem"; and Jesus Christ an unfortunate eccentric, but from a very good family. (God the Father, etc.)

It would be unfair to say I was taught these things. I was taught very little. They were simply there like the chill in the classrooms and the smell of furniture polish. It took a long time to get rid of them, to stop them influencing my own thoughts and attitudes. I shall be a God-fearing atheist as long as I live. It took me less time to unlearn the little I had been taught; as soon as I started reading books for myself I found that most of that was either irrelevant or untrue, and it was easy to forget it. But this whole convalescent process of recovering from my education in England left me with a counterinfection, a mild prejudice against the country and its institutions.

Then I go back there. They're still aimlessly rebuilding the airport. The porter calls me "Love." The bus conductor talks to himself; anyone who cares to is welcome to listen. London, as I lurch toward it on the upper deck of the bus, is calm and flat and shabby. There are flowers in the parks and on barrows at street corners. Except for a few areas, frequented mainly by Americans, the city turns out to be unbelievably easygoing. I begin to absorb its cheerful apathy as I once absorbed its less engaging influences. I begin to like the ridiculous place.

I found a small hotel in South Kensington. For a few days I had to keep reminding myself I could walk back to it at night, could walk anywhere any time. I had to force myself not to stop, and want to run, at the sight of two men loitering ahead of me in a quiet street. If they tried to pick me up, I had to remember I could ignore them and walk on.

The St. Martin's School of Art is in Charing Cross Road. Municipal architecture is often a reflection of the intellectual mood of the times. The niggling solemnity of the building reminded me at once of much of the English writing of the Thirties, the Left Wing Book Club and the peevishness of Oxford Socialism. The date over the door stopped me. It was 1938. Paul Tagliatti had been at the St. Martin's from 1935 to '37. After some mumbling interrogation from an elderly man in the hall, I was allowed to talk to the librarian.

She was a nice girl with solid legs. When I told her I was interested in a painter who had studied there, she invited me up to her office. The corridors on the way were busy with students: most of the men bearded; most of the girls individually dressed and attractive. A single face stood out like the moon. He didn't look different from the other students in any way I could define, but it was impossible not to know at once that he was an American; I was still wondering why when we reached the librarian's office.

I asked her about the date on the building.

"I suppose that's when the school was opened."

"But there was a St. Martin's School of Art before that. Long before that."

"Before 1938?" That seemed to astound her. She was probably about the same age as me, twenty-four or -five, but her own birth hung like a curtain between her and the past. For a moment I envied her. We were both swimming in the same sea, but she still had sight of the land, a steady fix on the present.

She took out some files. "You're right," she told me. "There was a school here as far back as 1910. Look." She had found an old prospectus.

"Maybe they rebuilt it in 1938."

She discovered they had. I thought it was just possible that one of Paul's teachers might still be alive somewhere; I asked if she could look up the old class lists. She was sorry, but she couldn't; the school had no record of any of its students before 1954. "There was a fire," the girl told me. "All the old files were destroyed."

45

She shook her head. She wasn't shaking it at me. Someone was standing in the doorway behind me. By the time I
turned around, whoever it was had gone.

There didn't seem to be any point in wasting any more
of the girl's time. I started to thank her. She seemed to
want me to stay; she asked me the name of the student I
was interested in. She had heard of Tagliatti, had seen
reproductions of his paintings. "He studied *here?*" We
talked about him for a few minutes. She asked me where I
was staying. We talked about hotels, furnished rooms,
three girls sharing.

There was a run in her tights, high up on the left thigh.
With those solid legs she might easily have chosen to wear
longer skirts. In one of those moments of sudden empathy
I could understand why she didn't. Her face was homely
and practical, the face of a friend; she wanted to show she
had more to offer than friendship. I felt that a number of
hopeless young men were sure to take appalling advantage
of that offer; they would repay her sturdy affection with
demands; she was the kind of girl who would always attract dependence.

I wandered around the school for a while before leaving. I tried to imagine what it had been like in Paul's day:
smaller, darker; the docile prewar students.

"Beautiful."

As unmistakable as the moon. The young American was
leaning against the wall, watching me with exaggerated admiration. I still couldn't figure out what it was about him
that made his nationality so obvious. There was a tame-
ness about his face that was almost innocence, but innocence is no longer a particularly American characteris-
tic, even if it once seemed so to Henry James.

"Beautiful," he repeated. I walked out into the street. At
the corner of the block I stopped and looked in a window.
Flogging Through the Ages. Venus Under the Lash. It was
a pornographic bookstore, English style. There was a shelf
of secondhand books on the sidewalk; I picked one of them
out. *A History of Spanking.* Turning the pages, I caught sight
of the copyright date. Nineteen forty-one. Night bombing;
the threat of German invasion; rationing and the blackout.
But someone had filled out all the forms; managed to obtain scarce paper from the government; had found the labor and the perseverance to publish this book. *A History*

46

of Spanking. To me there was something more lifelike about that than blood, toil, tears and sweat.

I put it back on the shelf; I waited another two or three minutes. The young American hadn't followed me. It was no use pretending I wasn't disappointed.

Beautiful! The token speech of my generation. Great! Wide! Yes! Beautiful! The words as empty as the "Where *did* you get that dress?" of my mother's friends. I'm not even pretty. My mother has assured me of that repeatedly. My mouth is too large, and my forehead bulges. My nose is straight, but insignificant, and though my teeth are small and were uncomfortably braced during most of my teens, my lips bulge too. "Like a little monkey," in my mother's words.

Trafalgar Sqaure was almost deserted; you probably have to know a lot about pigeons before they're interesting. The girl in the library—her voice, her presence—lingered so insistently in my mind she might have been sitting beside me. She made me feel like a stick; compared with her I was so hopelessly unengaged; I was like some don at an Oxford college, endlessly researching Etruscan civil law. I decided to go to the movies. Films have a hypnotic effect on me; I can sit in a cinema and think about nothing for hours. The plot of the movie means very little to me; I notice some peculiarity about one of the actors' ears. I sit waiting for him to reappear so I can have another look at his lobe or his concha. I begin to feel a sense of intimacy with him, as though we shared some secret together.

It was late when I got back to the hotel. Although the building, the elevator, the plumbing were almost comically English, none of the staff seemed to be. The French girl at the desk had mislaid my key. She found me another one. I had decided Bone could afford the extravagance of a room with a private bath. I undressed to take a shower. The door of the bathroom opened just before I reached it.

"Beautiful." The young American advanced into the bedroom and stood screwing up his eyes at me. "Did I startle you?"

"No."

He had. Like that waitress in the coffee shop, I was angrier about that than about anything else. "Get out," I told him. "Go on, get out."

"I've been sitting on your john for hours." He seemed

47

to think that gave him some squatter's right. "In the dark."
His eyes were beginning to focus. I got a bathrobe from
the closet and put it on.

"Now, go on, get out."

"Don't you want to know why I'm here?"

"No." My anger was passing. What was it about him
that made him so unmistakably American? He had an earnest look, but I've known earnest Frenchmen. Perhaps the
French manage their earnestness better, without looking
naïve about it.

"I saw you at the St. Martin's this afternoon."

"I know."

"I heard you tell that girl in the library where you were
staying."

"All right, now you've seen the place for yourself, you
can go on home." I opened the door for him.

He might look naïve, but he had the intuition to do the
one thing that could disarm me. He started to take his
clothes off. His shoes went first. They were expensive moccasins, out of place with the jeans that followed them. He
pulled off his shirt and undershirt together.

"Now you can't throw me out."

I closed the door as he hopped on one foot and then the
other, tugging off his socks. He stood up in front of me.

I liked him better naked. With his shoulder-length hair,
his beardless face, he looked physically uncommitted; he
might have been waiting for a word from me to become
whatever I wanted, male, female, neuter.

"You're not American, are you?" He sat on the edge of
the bed.

"I wasn't born there."

"Don't you hate Americans?"

"Why should I?"

"Ask the Cheyenne. Ask the Ute."

"There weren't all that many red Indians in Ireland."

"We're spoilers. We're rapists. The Indians knew that
America was a paradise—" He went on about the pristine
rivers, the forests, the buffalo. I knew what he was up to.
Having taken off his clothes, he was trying to shed his nationality too, to reduce himself to skin and hair, my inescapable kin. He would start on the white man in a moment, stripping himself of that identity too. I didn't want
to listen to it; I had read too much about Carthage, Islam,
some of the present-day African republics.

48

"How long have you been having an affair with that girl?"

He stopped, silent, in the middle of a sentence.

"Who?"

"In the library."

"What did she say about me?"

"You didn't hear me tell her where I was staying. Your girl friend shook her head at you, telling you get back downstairs, long before we started talking about hotels."

"She's not my girl friend."

I picked up his clothes and made a bundle of them. "You can get dressed in the corridor." I pushed them into his arms. "You're not very convincing about the Ute, either," I told him. "You've said it all too many times."

"I'm not having an affair with her, anyway."

"You're her dream. Passive. Dependent."

"I'm not passive, either."

"Maybe not all the time. But you're adaptable." I didn't want to go on about that. I didn't care whether he was sleeping with the girl or not. "Why did you ask her where I was staying?"

"Because you're beautiful."

I opened the door.

"Because you're interested in Tagliatti."

I'd guessed that was it. Men don't see me for a moment in a crowded hall and find out where I live and break into my room. Not young men, anyway. There was something else that still bothered me. I hadn't mentioned Tagliatti to the girl until after she'd given this friend of hers that signal, telling him not to worry, she'd find out all about me for him. She'd been expecting me. They'd both been expecting me.

"How did you know I was coming to the St. Martin's?"

"I didn't."

"Who told you?" I was still holding the door open. There was the sound of someone coming down the corridor.

"Oh, hell." He put the bundle of clothes down on the bed and hurried over and closed the door. "You're not the only person who's working for Wexford Bone."

7

His name was Walter. It suited him. He was as adaptable as putty. There seemed to be no core to him. He was whatever he sensed I wanted him to be. I couldn't help liking him.

"I was at the Art Students League," he told me. "I guess anyone who's trying to paint is unconsciously looking for some example. Someone who's done it the way they want to. That's how I felt about Tagliatti. It was only a couple of reproductions. I wanted to see the real paintings, the ones Wexford Bone had, so I wrote to Bone."

"How did you know where to find him?"

"Will you do me a favor?"

"Go on about Bone."

"Will you take that robe off?"

I handed him a towel. "You can put this around you." He dropped it on the floor.

"I like being naked with you. It's natural. I just want you to be natural too." He would be telling me he only wanted to wake up with me in a moment. "Come on." He was hovering in front of me, looking sad and gentle. "Please."

I hung my robe back in the closet.

"Beautiful."

"Don't say that again."

"You've got a great body. Like a dancer."

"I walk a lot." I caught his hand before it reached my breast; his fingers felt unexpectedly cold.

"You wrote to Bone," I reminded him.

"Not now."

"He offered you a job." I let go his hand. It dropped slowly to his side.

"Please."

The way I feel about making love with someone often depends on how he feels about himself. I don't mind a

50

man's being proud of his penis, although it seems an arbitrary thing to be proud of; but if he chooses to consider it a weapon, I can't oblige with cowed gratitude. A man's shoulders, his way of standing, his waist can be weakingly attractive; but there are few things less erotic to me than that length of hose between his legs. As Joyce suggested, it's an essentially absurd object, and I can't see its erection as either an achievement or a threat. It seems useless to me except as a connection.

"You're doing research for Bone?"

Walter was far from flaunting his erection. From the way he snatched up the towel and tried to hide it from me, it might have been something imposed on him, like a shackle, a pain and embarrassment to him.

"Yes. *All right*," he said hopelessly. "What else do you want to know?"

The trouble is that if you feel like that about men it puts you under an obligation not to use your body as a weapon either.

"You can tell me the rest in the morning," I agreed.

He was tense and bony in bed. For a moment as we met there, I found myself thinking about Eugenia West, an afternoon lassitude, the scent of mimosa from beyond the shutters. Paul Tagliatti's young, lean body . . .

Walter was touching me; his hands were still disturbingly cold; it struck me that this unfamiliar familiarity, the feel of his long hair against my face, would become irrevocably part of my memory. Long before we were connected to each other, I felt a vivid sense of immediacy. This was the present. It was great. Yes! Beautiful!

One of the lovely things about having an affair is that for a time you celebrate each other. Anything either of you does or says is of immediate interest; there is a deference between you, a welcome when you meet after parting; you grant each other an unaccustomed importance. It's a gift of gratitude for shared discovery.

We went out to breakfast together: a difficult thing to do in London; the English expect people to eat breakfast at home. We eventually found an American pancake place. The waiter was Spanish; he seemed charmingly eager to celebrate us too.

Walter and I sat side by side, birthday new to each other in our intimacy. Neither of us wanted to be the first

51

to start asking all the questions that still separated us. We talked about our childhoods. He told me his name was Walter Oliver; his father owned a paper mill; they had a big house out on the Island, Southampton.

"I've only been to Southampton once. What was it like growing up there?"

"I've *never* been to Ireland."

I tried to tell him about it. Grandfather's house on the west coast; I spent every summer there until I was twelve. The gentle kindness of the people. "Welcome home, Jane," they used to say every July.

"Don't you ever want to go back there?" Walter asked.

It's a desperate thing to be born in Ireland, and leave it. Nowhere else will ever be home. But once you've left, how can you go back? You've changed.

"My grandfather's dead now. The house has been sold. There's nothing to go back to," I told Walter.

"I know. I feel the same way about the South Shore. Walking along the deserted beaches in winter. The excitement of expecting something to happen. But I'm not a kid any more."

We had run out of common childhood experience by the time we finished our coffee. It was no use trying to keep it up. Bone might have been sitting across the table from us.

"What are you supposed to be doing exactly, Jane?" I was grateful to Walter for being the first to give in.

"Making a list of the paintings, the dates, where they are now."

"That's all?"

"I want to find out all I can about Paul Tagliatti. But that's for my own sake."

"That's all Bone told you?"

"What else is there?" I knew there was something else.

"I mean, he didn't say anything about me?"

"No."

Walter ordered more coffee for us. It was my turn to ask questions.

"How long have you been over here?"

"A month. About a month."

"How did you recognize me at the St. Martin's?"

"Bone sent me a photograph of you."

"Where did he get it?" It wasn't a question I expected

Walter to answer, only an echo of admiration for Bone's deviousness.

"It looked as if it was taken in the street."

By Berman? That day I was walking around with Kevin?

"Have you got it?" I asked Walter.

"Somewhere."

The coffee came. We went on exchanging information like compliments. Walter told me Bone had hired him to do the same job as me; catalog the paintings. I told Walter about the period I had covered in New York: 1941, the paintings Tagliatti had finished during that year.

"He did the portrait of Lilian Fletcher in June." Walter had found out more than I had about that summer in Provincetown. "She was having an affair with a young Portuguese fisherman. The local people used to get hairy about rich women like Lilian carrying on with their kids. She invited Tagliatti up to Provincetown to confuse them."

"Wasn't she having an affair with Paul?"

"He was too old for her by then."

"He was only twenty-three."

"You didn't know Lilian."

"Did you?"

"Of course not." Walter was tracing patterns on the back of my hand with the tips of his fingers. "But I know a lot about her. She never liked Tagliatti's portrait of her. She stored it away. It didn't show up until she died." The contact of his fingers was becoming less and less impersonal. "The crazy thing is, I know—I'm pretty sure, anyway—that he did a painting of that young Portuguese fisherman too. But no one's ever been able to find it."

Paul had told Kevin he had finished six paintings that summer. I had been able to name only five in my report to Bone.

"It wasn't part of the Lilian Alan Fletcher bequest?" I asked Walter.

"I've seen everything she left. Everything in that collection in the Boston Museum."

My hands have always been particularly susceptible, perhaps because they're my earliest association with desire. Helplessly in love with a boy at eleven, I found tormenting excitement in holding his hand.

"We might as well work together from now on," Walter suggested.

I agreed. The movement of his fingers stopped. We didn't discuss our agreement any further until we were in the street.

"If we work together, you'll have to tell Bone," I said.

"Why?"

"Aren't you supposed to send him reports?"

"Not about us."

"About how you're getting on. They'll be exactly the same as mine."

We were walking toward the park. "You can take all the credit for anything we find out, Jane."

"That's not fair. If you don't seem to be getting anywhere he might fire you."

"You needn't even mention me."

We found a bench and sat down. "I don't care if he does fire me." Walter took my hand again. "I don't need Bone's money anyway."

The sun was warm. Walter leaned back, stretching his legs. I wondered how old he was. Maybe twenty-five, I thought. Only a year older than me. I wondered how he had learned, what it was in his background that had made him such a persuasive liar. Almost everything he had told me was either a lie or a half-truth; I was sure of that.

But I couldn't help liking Walter.

8

WE PARTED FOR THE AFTERNOON. I went to see an art dealer in Bond Street. He had been a friend of my mother's and offered me a cup of tea. I thought he might know if there were any Tagliattis in private collections in England. He didn't think there were. "Unfortunately." He was interested, in an indirect English way, in why I wanted to know. I explained that I was looking around for a collector in New York. He could understand that.

"There's a considerable premium on Tagliattis at the moment." He might have been talking about Swiss francs.

Walter was waiting outside the restaurant in Soho where we had agreed to meet. I stopped half a block away and watched him. I've always liked doing that with someone I care about, seeing them without their knowing I'm there. They seem more complete alone, because nothing in them is a reflection of me. Walter looked older by himself. He was standing quite still, his feet apart, his clenched hands on his hips. His attitude reminded me of some civic statue. *Youth. The Future Is in Their Hands.* Although nothing he had said had indicated it, it struck me that he was in some secret way ambitious.

I walked on. As soon as we touched, we welcomed each other. He looked at me as though he were unwrapping a gift. Entering the restaurant with him I felt much prettier than I am. We hardly talked until we had ordered dinner.

We started with avocado. I asked Walter if he had found out anything about Paul's life as a student in London.

"He didn't paint anything then," Walter told me. "Nothing he kept, anyway."

"Do you know where he lived?"

"What does it matter?"

"I'd like to see the house, maybe the room he lived in."

"What for?" Walter lowered his spoon; there was a war-

55

iness in the way he did it, like someone pushing aside a book, preparing to give you all his attention.

"I've told you, I'm interested in everything about him."

"He didn't leave any paintings *there*."

When I was fourteen I spent a summer in France, near St. Jean-de-Luz. My mother was married to a Frenchman at the time and had a villa there. An English couple lived across the road. I never spoke to them, but sometimes I would see one or the other of them coming back from the village with a shopping basket. Never together. It wasn't until the end of the summer that the woman in the post office told me about them. They had a daughter of sixteen. She was said to be "grosse, grosse, *grosse*" by the few local people who had seen her. She had to be kept under constant constraint to stop her eating herself to death. The story didn't surprise me. I had known all summer there was something I didn't know. I felt the same way when Walter said that.

"He didn't leave any paintings *there*."

"What do you think Bone's after?"

"How many are there?"

"Who knows?" Walter went back to his avocado, the wariness gone. "There could be any number of them. He moved around a lot. All his life. He was always leaving his paintings with people to look after for him."

"That portrait of the young Portuguese fisherman?"

"That's one. He wouldn't give it to Lilian. He said it was one of the best things he'd ever done. He wanted to keep it. He took it back to New York with him after the summer in Provincetown."

"How do you know?"

"Lilian Fletcher's sister is still alive. Natalie Alan Donner. Lilian used to write to her. Mrs. Donner let me see the letters. There was a whole lot in them about that summer in Provincetown."

I thought that over for a while. The skins of our avocados were taken away.

"The portrait of the Portuguese fisherman might have been in the suitcase he left with Angela Anson," I suggested.

"Who?"

"She was Kevin Fallon's half sister." I told him as much as I knew about that. "I think he got all his paintings back

56

from her later that year, 1941, when he moved to Fourteenth Street."

Walter started his macaroni. He didn't eat meat. Some of the "Nature" role he had played for me the night before was genuine enough.

"I'd give anything to see that picture. Imagine it, Jane. Maybe the greatest Tagliatti of all." He was slipping into a role again. "It's crazy to think of it hidden away somewhere. Like a secret truth in a dark, locked room, waiting to be discovered." He was full of wonder, a believer in magic. He must have thought it was the side of him I liked best. He reached across the table toward me.

"That portrait couldn't be in England, anyway." I held my hands together in my lap; it was hard enough to keep him in focus without letting him stroke my fingers.

"Why not?"

"He left here in 1938, three years before he painted it."

"He came back."

"When?"

"During the war."

I waited for Walter to go on. The three-year period from the job at Abercrombie & Fitch, the studio on Fourteenth Street, until the exhibition at the Haggard Gallery was a part of Tagliatti's life I knew nothing about yet.

In the outline of Paul's movements Bone had sent me, he had simply written "1942–'45, War."

"I don't know how he got here, what he was doing, but he sent Lilian a post card from London in 1943."

"He wouldn't have brought any of his paintings with him; he'd have left them in New York."

"Not if he thought he wasn't going back there."

I thought of the group at the Old Colony, dispersed by the draft; Angela Anson wistfully trying to domesticate him. He had had little enough to go back to.

"He might have had some friends over here," Walter went on. "People he could trust to look after paintings for him."

"I suppose he might."

"Did Bone give you the address of anyone in England you ought to look up?"

Bone's outline mentioned only Eugenia West. I had already found out from a man on a newspaper, another friend of my mother's, that both Eugenia and her husband, Nigel West, were dead. I recalled the photograph of

57

Paul which Bone had given me: the incongruously present-day style of his suit, the narrow lapels, the trousers without cuffs. There was another time men had worn jackets and trousers like that: in England during the war; they were called utility suits then. I remembered the photographer's stamp on the back: Howard Coster, Victoria Street.

Walter's knee touched mine under the table; it was the lightest pressure; a subtle friction; I could feel it all the way up both thighs. My divided self. I didn't trust Walter for a moment; I wanted to trust him. I wanted to give in to him; I didn't want to help him in his treasure hunt. It was no good Walter talking about secret truths in locked rooms. He was interested only in the cash value of those lost paintings.

So was Bone.

"I don't have any leads in London except the St. Martin's School of Art," I told Walter.

He took his knee away. I insisted on paying my half of the check.

Outside, night had come with crawling taxis. A girl in a belted raincoat weaved by on a Honda. She had just taken her clothes off in one strip club; she was on her way to take them off in another; I could feel her hard young weariness as she passed. Across the street a cigar store was closing for the night. It looked as though it had been there a long time. This part of London had been bombed very little. It had changed, certainly, in the past thirty-five years, but the changes had no depth; they were only an addition. The prewar Soho Paul had known and recaptured in one painting at the Museum of Modern Art, *Café, Greek Street*, was still here, overlaid with a coating of decay and repair.

It must be possible, I thought, as an act of will, of patience and knowledge and imagination, to reconstruct what he had seen and felt here as a student, as a complete skull can be reconstructed from a few fragments of bone. I had some of the knowledge already. Before leaving New York, I had spent three days at the Museum of Modern Art memorizing Paul's paintings like verses; I could recall the emphasis of every brush stroke. I had photostatic copies of his sketchbooks, some of them going back to his days at the St. Martin's. They contained more than drawings; he had had the habit of writing things beside his sketches: impulsive thoughts and feelings, quotations from books he

58

was reading, ideas that occurred to him, reminders to himself about things he had to do, occasionally the name of someone he had just met.

All I needed was a few more facts.

Walter took my hand as we crossed the street. I would have to get away from him for a while. He wouldn't mind that. That girl in the library would be happy to welcome him back after his short absence.

9

THERE WAS A HOWARD COSTER in the phone book with an address in St. John's Wood. The woman who answered said her husband couldn't come to the phone. Could she help? She had a friendly voice with a slight Northern accent. I could guess she hadn't been to the kind of English schools I had.

I asked her if Mr. Coster was a photographer.

"Yes." She hesitated. "He's retired."

When I mentioned Paul Tagliatti, she was interested at once. "Do you know, I heard he was dead." She sounded as if she didn't believe it. I told her I was afraid it was true. She invited me over. "Come after five, when the shop's closed."

It was an antique shop. A woman in her sixties was taking in a tray of horse brasses from the sidewalk. She was tall and thin and was wearing no-nonsense woolen stockings, a straight skirt and a knitted cardigan. Her white hair was piled on top of her head in the style of the suffragettes, like a cottage loaf.

"I'm Joan Coster."

We shook hands. I helped her carry in a pierced fiddleback bench.

"I'm afraid it's been restored." She showed me the leg that had been replaced. "Can you imagine, they didn't even bother to use walnut." She was sharing an outrageous secret with me. Within a few minutes we might have known each other for years.

She locked the door and placed a "Closed" sign in the window. We sat in the kitchen upstairs. "Howard's resting in the front room," she explained. "He'll be in for his tea presently." The tea came out of a mahogany canister lined with zinc. She showed me the beveled joints. "Think of the

60

workmanship." And then, regretfully, amused at herself, "I know I ought to sell it."

Objects, things, usually bore me. Exclaiming over them is my mother's favorite substitute for conversation, her way of avoiding more demanding subjects. Joan Coster managed to personalize everything she touched; the canister seemed to be sharing the room with us, like a cat. She wasn't avoiding getting to the point of my visit.

"I was thinking about Paul after you called." She brought him into the conversation as casually as she offered me the sugar bowl. "He was an extraordinary boy."

"Did you know him well?"

"We saw a lot of him at one time, in the Thirties. We knew so many people in those days, but Paul's always the one who stands out most clearly in my memory. There was something, I don't know, so vivid about him. I keep expecting him to walk into the shop one day." She passed me the milk. "Knowing someone's dead never really changes them, does it?"

"When was the last time you saw him?"

"During the war."

"What was he doing over here then?"

"He was living somewhere down in the East End, I think." She didn't ask why I was interested. I was from a long way off, New York; the reasons for my questions presumably belonged back there; they didn't concern her. "He didn't seem to be in the army or anything of that kind. At least, he wasn't in uniform. I've got a photograph of him somewhere that Howard took at that time. I'll try and find it for you if you like."

I thanked her and told her I already had a copy of it.

"How long was he here?" I asked.

"Two or three months. Most of the summer."

"Where did he go after that, do you know?"

She shook her head. "That was the last time we saw him."

Paul had simply turned up at Howard Coster's studio in Victoria Street one day in the middle of the war. For the next few months he had dropped in two or three times a week, and then he had simply stopped coming. It was typical of him that he had explained so little about what he was doing, the practical circumstances of his existence. It wasn't, I think, that he was particularly secretive; it didn't occur to him that such things were interesting.

61

I waited a moment before asking the next question.

"When he was here then, did he show you any paintings he had done? Did he have any of his paintings with him?"

She glanced away from me toward the door. "He did bring some paintings into the studio one evening. He had them all rolled up in a cardboard tube with oilcloth around it." There was the sound of someone moving in the next room.

"Do you remember them? Do you remember what they were?"

"I didn't see them." She seemed to be preparing herself for something. "We had a cottage in Sussex we used to go to for week ends, to get away from the bombing. It must have been a Friday evening. I was in a fuss, packing up, afraid of missing the train. Paul was in the studio, showing his paintings to Howard. They were hours over it. I just kept wishing Paul would hurry up and leave. It seems awful now." She didn't mean it seemed awful because they were original Tagliattis, as sound as Swiss francs, but because she would never see him again.

"Perhaps Mr. Coster would remember those paintings. If he—"

She wasn't listening to me. Neither was he. He came straight to the table and stood waiting while she poured him a cup of tea. He was a short, strongly built man; over seventy, I suppose, but still full of sturdy energy. He was dressed in a way that was fashionable among English painters forty years ago: wide corduroy trousers, a flannel shirt, woolen tie, a loose tweed jacket. Bristles of white hair covered his head; it was a remarkable head, a geometric rendering of bone structure, all planes and caverns; a jutting nose and chin, the frontal bones armoring the eyes so effectively they almost hid them.

"This is Howard." Joan Coster introduced us only with this simple statement of his identity. He didn't appear to notice me. He was holding a large book, resting it on the table. It was open at a photograph of Michelangelo's *Pietà*. He turned the page; I caught a glimpse of Adam.

"We were talking about Paul Tagliatti." She spoke the words slowly and clearly as though she had rehearsed them.

Howard Coster moved his marvelous head slightly; he might have meant it as a nod. She put milk and sugar in his tea and placed the cup beside the book.

"I was remembering the evening Paul came to the studio in Victoria Street during the war. He came to show us some of his paintings and I was in such a bother I couldn't look at them."

Howard Coster's attention was still on the book; he turned another page.

"Paul's dead." She spoke with the same deliberate clarity: a conscientious friend delivering a message. "He died in Mexico."

"He was such a dear chap." Howard Coster looked at me for the first time. I didn't surprise him; I might have been sitting there in his kitchen every afternoon for years, as familiar as his wife.

"I can't help feeling that about him. He was such a dear fellow."

I still thought for a moment longer he was talking about Paul. He wasn't. The book was open at Michelangelo's *Christus*. He was staring at it with deep tenderness; I saw the glistening of tears in his remote eyes; he touched the anguished mouth with his fingers. He was talking about Jesus.

"Such a dear chap." He picked up the book and his tea and left. Joan Coster closed the kitchen door after him.

"He had another stroke about two months ago." Her voice was as cheerfully matter-of-fact as when she had been showing me the tea canister. "I don't think he knows who people are any longer." She started to clear away the cups. "Sometimes I don't think he knows who I am. But it doesn't matter, really, because he doesn't think about it."

I pretended I had to leave. She told me not to be silly; she wanted me to stay; she enjoyed having someone to talk to. We settled back at the table. She got out a basket and started to darn a pair of her woolen stockings.

She didn't mention her husband's condition again. She talked about the days before the war, the studio in Victoria Street, Paul.

10

1935–1937

PAUL WAS SEVENTEEN when he first came to London and began studying at the St. Martin's. Both his parents were dead. For the past three years he had been living with an aunt in Brighton, going to school there. After he settled in London he rarely went back to see her; they agreed he couldn't afford the fare; there was very little left of his father's money; his aunt sent him three pounds a week to live on.

He knew no one in London. He lived in a series of furnished rooms—Chalk Farm, Earls Court, Notting Hill—moving every few weeks. They were all the same once he had closed the door on himself: cells without bars.

His isolation was increased by his appearance. Seeing him for the first time many men felt it was a pity he wasn't a girl; if he had been they could have found him beautiful. Inevitably, because of this, he attracted men who preferred boys; they were always trying to pick him up; he reacted to their advances with startling, savage anger. He took to carrying a book with him everywhere he went; absorbed in reading on buses or the Underground, he was less likely to be accosted. In the streets he kept moving with pointed intentness, afraid to stop for a moment and invite approach.

He thought sometimes of disfiguring himself. One evening he did take a razor blade and deliberately cut his cheek, trying to change the dimple that enhanced his prettiness into a scar. The silent efficiency of the blade made him feel sick; the cut healed in a few days without leaving a mark.

He might have been happier if he had been homosexual, but his femininity was only in his face. He was feverishly attracted by women; the thought of their bodies tormented

64

him. He masturbated frequently, carrying on what H. G. Wells once described as a one-sided affair with his mattress.

There was little in the popular culture of those days to incite his eroticism: no strip shows, no nudes in magazines or movies, no pornography available except to the rich. Paul didn't begin life classes until his second year; he had never seen a naked woman; he longed to, as a religious might long for revelation.

The girl students in his own year at the St. Martin's did not attract him. In their uniform calf-length skirts and sensible sweaters, they were not the stuff of his fantasies and desires; they were persons, known to him by their surnames. Beade, Pavitt, Johnson; barely imaginably sexual. One or two of them, admittedly, were rumored to be "loose"; some of the male students claimed to have kissed them; but these were the least prepossessing of all, lank-haired with bad skins. Paul was never stirred to think of intimacy with any of them.

This was true of most of the girls he saw around London. Outside of the few areas where the wealthy met each other, there were few pretty or provocative girls to be seen. The typists and shop assistants on the buses and the Underground were of the same breed as the first-year art students. Resentful, lumpishly dressed, they appear in Paul's sketchbooks as a subspecies of females, suggesting boiled food, washing up, rather than love-making. Their resentment was understandable; the young were an unpopular minority. The Victorian idea of them as an ungrateful tribe who had not yet earned their right to a place in the nation was still widely ingrained. It was a virtue to bully them; having no sense of themselves as a group, they did not think of protesting. Instead, they did their best to suppress the evidence of their youth; they anticipated middle age.

There was one group of working girls who had escaped this grim leveling. In appearance they were almost indistinguishable from the rich; they wore fur stoles and well-cut suits, or, in bad weather, smart belted raincoats; they moved with a subtle friction of silk as their knees brushed against each other. The evening streets were resplendent with them: London's army of prostitutes.

Soho, their main parade ground, was only a few minutes' walk from the St. Martin's. Paul hurried there the moment his classes ended; they were just appearing on duty at that hour, staking out the few yards of sidewalk they would patrol during the long night watch.

He soon knew most of them by sight. For hours every evening he would range the streets, looking for his favorites; it reassured him to find them there. He gave them names in his mind, Sandra and Lily, and the one who attracted him most of all, a tall French-looking girl at the bottom of Dean Street, Madelon. They were truth to him, the essence of experience. Above all, they were vividly available.

Madelon might be available, but Paul had no idea how much she charged. If it was over a pound, he could never manage it. The money from his aunt arrived every Friday; after paying for his room and breakfast he had two pounds left; on Saturdays and Sundays he splurged on movies; by Tuesdays he was always down to a few shillings, walking to the St. Martin's and back, subsisting on a meat pie a day from a coffee stall. To spend a whole pound one Friday would mean a dismal weekend, lying reading in bed through the cold hours; there was no heat in his room except a coin-in-the-slot gas fire. After considering it for several weeks, Paul decided it was worth it. One Friday at six he made for Madelon's stretch of sidewalk with a pound note in his pocket; he had left the rest of his week's money in his room; he couldn't trust himself not to give her everything he had if she asked for it. Madelon wasn't there. A curtained light showed in an upstairs window; she had a customer. Paul thought incoherently about what she was doing up there as he waited across the street.

The light went off; Madelon appeared in the doorway with a man: short, middle-aged, in a bowler hat and a raincoat; he kept pulling at Madelon's arm as she twisted to get away from him. He was saying something in a thin, pleading voice. Madelon's answer floated clearly across the street to Paul. "Bugger off, you bah-sturd." She wasn't French. The man came half-running toward him through the haze; as he passed, Paul saw the cave of his mouth below the neat mustache, the distorted cheeks. The man was sobbing.

It was a moment of realization for Paul. A romantic, he was always searching for what his imagination told him must be there; at the same time, he could be coolly self-protective. He looked over at the girl his fantasies had named Madelon; she was back on her beat, on the lookout for another customer.

Paul turned away and walked home.

He was eighteen that December. His aunt sent him two pounds as a birthday present. "Buy something you need," she wrote. He found a prostitute in Notting Hill. There is a drawing of her in one of his sketchbooks: a sullen, overweight woman in her thirties. She didn't want to have anything to do with him at first. "You're too young, dear." Finally, for a pound, she took him to her room: a cold basement kitchen furnished with a deck chair and a camp bed. She pulled off her woolen pants and gradgingly rolled up her girdle. Ten minutes later Paul was sitting in a movie house; silk, iced drinks, wisecracks, bare arms under bright lights; America fascinated him. He had no regrets about the squalor of his own introduction to sex; he had bought what he needed most at that age: experience.

He continued to spend hours in Soho, but his attitude toward Madelon and the others had changed; his romanticism was at a remove from them now; his feelings about them were like his feelings about the movies. One day that whole glowing world of the favored and fortunate would be his; he would earn it for himself; he would enter and live in it.

After a bad start, his work at the St. Martin's was gradually improving. He had always had a remarkable talent. When he was drawing, his right hand seemed to have a life of its own. Hour after hour, day after day, trying to translate Caesar's plaster head into line and shade, he learned that spontaneity wasn't enough. Like someone who has picked up the sounds of a language without understanding their meaning, he could jabber magnificently, but he couldn't say what he wanted to. He had to unlearn what his natural ear had taught him before he could speak with precision. He had to learn patiently, boringly, to control his hand.

He stayed in London alone that Christmas. The holy days were a nightmare; it was a city of dreadful loneliness, bleak and shut tight. For the rest of the short vacation he wandered around the Tate and the National Gallery, concentrating on the etchings, prints, drawings, trying to figure out how others had done it. By March he was deliberately experimenting in class: leaving out all detail in the

67

right side of Caesar's nose, letting the left side suggest it; overemphasizing, eliminating, above all simplifying.

"You seem to be progressing backwards, Tagliatti." His teachers used facetiousness like a rod; but on the whole they kept away from him; he made them uneasy; it wasn't natural for a boy to look like that.

That spring he made his first friend in London. There was a café in Greek Street, a place of bare lights and marble tables, where he liked to sit over a caffé espresso, pretending to read and listening to the gossip and grouching of the prostitutes who came to rest their feet there. One night a man sat down at the same table; Paul waited, ready to flare into savagery at any approach.

"What do you read, my lord? Words, words, words."

There was a companionable humor in the man's voice; they might have been two travelers who had met in the desert. Paul looked at him. He was in his late twenties; freckle-faced, snub-nosed; a belted fawn overcoat—Teddybears, they were called; a little green hat with a feather in it. He took it off with a mock bow; his smile accepted Paul as an equal.

Paul was reading *Journey to the End of the Night*. They talked about it. "Life is one vast attempt to catch you with your trousers down." The man echoed Cêline's black laughter.

His name was Denis Owen; he was an assistant cameraman in a film studio, frequently unemployed. His youth had been even bleaker than Paul's was now. Escaping the Welsh coal fields, he had come to London at fifteen; had worked as a darkroom boy at a pound a week; he had survived everything and remembered it with relish.

Without prearrangement, Paul and Denis began meeting in the café almost every night.

Joan Coster put me in touch with Denis Owen. We met several times in a pub in Fulham, and he talked about Paul Tagliatti for hours. A pale, flabby old man with wistful eyes, he was often rambling and repetitious, but Paul had left such an impression on him that Denis could recall whole conversations they had had over thirty-five years ago. "He was like a grubby little angel," he told me. "He dressed like a ragpicker, and did everything to make himself look as tough and dissolute as he could. But it was still hard to believe he was more than fifteen, until you

68

talked to him. Some of the people in Soho used to call him Satan."

It was through Denis that Paul first met the Costers. Still under forty, Howard Coster was one of the two or three best-known photographers in London. A varying group of writers, architects, men in advertising used to drop in at Coster's studio in Victoria Street at lunchtime. Joan Coster gave them tea and sandwiches, but they came to listen to Howard. He was an arresting personality in many ways—short, blunt, vital, with the face of a Blake prophet and the eyes of an Indian scout; his outstanding quality was a shameless honesty. He could express his deepest feelings without embarrassment; he would speak of honor, God, truth as though he had just discovered them. Most of the eminent Englishmen of the Thirties had sat for him; most of them he had little respect for; he had a special contempt for the Church. "That fat-bellied bishop, mincing in here in his leggings. 'Make—make me look dignified, Mr. Coster.' Four thousand a year that silly sod earns, and some poor bloke in a coal mine gets two pounds a week." A slight stammer increased the explosive energy of his judgments. The soft-handed advertising men would smile in agreement; they enjoyed Howard's indignation.

Paul took to Joan Coster at once. She treated him with the directness of an older sister. It was several weeks before he felt as easy with Howard. After his first visit to the studio with Denis Owen he began to go there during his lunch hour twice a week; he would have liked to go more often, but that self-protective element in his character restrained him; he needed to feel welcome there. Outside of his café meetings with Denis, those visits to Howard's studio were the only social life he had. One day he took a sketchbook with him, half filled with drawings he had made out of class: those joyless girls on the Underground; gray young men Sundaying in Hyde Park. As soon as he got to Howard's, Paul wanted to hide it.

"Let me see that. Come on. What did you bring it for?" It was a reasonable question. Howard turned the pages for some time in silence.

"By God, son, you've got—got it, all right."

Paul's father had resented the expense of his upkeep; his mother had doted on him intermittently; until he met

Howard he had never had his own hopes about himself confirmed.

The long summer vacation was an emptiness to be filled. With his knowledge of languages, he managed to find work with a travel agency. It gave him enough money to go to the movies every night, but the job itself was a disaster. He seemed to be going through a phase of involuntary absence. It was impossible for him to pay attention to what he was doing; even to be aware in any rational way that he was doing it. He was supposed to deal with inquiries from abroad; he would write fluent answering letters in French or Italian; but he was incapable of putting his replies into the right envelopes. The Paris office waiting for a Newhaven Return with Double Berth would receive a Dover Single with Accompanying Infant. When his mistakes were pointed out to him, he could only stare at the manager's face. All voices except those from a movie screen seemed to be directed at someone else from a great distance. He was fired a week before the beginning of the winter term at the St. Martin's. He walked straight out of the office into a double feature at the Plaza.

His second year at the art school was like a resurrection to Paul. It wasn't only that he was drawing from life, and found he could look at a naked woman for hours without any personal interest in her; the first-year course was planned to be as tedious as possible, to discourage the uncommitted. The second- and third-year students were all survivors; it gave them a sense of fraternity with one another. They met and talked after class; they organized puppet shows, visits to galleries, play-reading groups.

That second year Paul's looks became an asset to him; his beauty made him exciting to girls older than himself, who were beginning to experiment with their own emotions. Within a few weeks a student teacher took him to bed with her. She was an insecure, aggressive girl; it was not a happy experience for either of them, but it made him feel he was a member at last; he knew what intimacy was like; so far he had only imagined it from outside.

One day the spring of 1937 when Paul went to Howard Coster's for lunch, he found only one other guest there, a senior civil servant who had come for a sitting. He was an elegant man in his forties, with a way of gesturing with his cigarette when he talked, holding it precisely between the tips of his fingers. Paul had had a good morning in class; that term he had begun to work in conté; it suited him better than charcoal or pencil; he was talkative and lively. The elegant civil servant watched and listened; if he had been playful or condescending, Paul would have closed him out at once; he was almost deferential.

Two days later a note arrived for Paul at Coster's studio, inviting him to dinner.

Nigel West had a charming, walled house in Chelsea. The dinner was served by a butler. Several other guests had been invited too; their shirts were slightly starched, their jackets beautifully tailored, their ties significantly striped. Polite young men from the Foreign Office and the B.B.C., they pretended not to notice Paul's cheap suit. They were a languid group and seemed to feel it was bad taste to talk about anything that concerned them. They played the usual English game instead.

"Delightful wine, Nigel."

"Not too dry, you don't think?"

"Not a bit."

"You don't find it too dry, Peter?"

Ther was only one rule: keep the airy little ball moving.

"It was," Paul told Denis later, "a long, dull evening."

At nineteen Paul was anything but naïve about homosexuals. He knew without considering it that Nigel was infatuated with him. This time he did not react with his usual hostility. Nigel took him to the theater, to the ballet at Covent Garden. Paul accepted gifts from him; ties, shirts, a suit from Nigel's tailor.

"My dear boy, why not?"

There was an element of revenge in Paul's complicity. Nigel bored him; that was Paul's strength and his excuse. He gave Nigel nothing in return for his generosity. Nigel did not seem to expect anything; he never ventured even the most tentative physical advance; his sensuality was passive; it was enough for him to be with Paul, to be charmed by the boy's looks.

Paul had known Nigel for several weeks before he discovered that he was married. Nigel mentioned it for the first time one evening during the intermission of a dull play.

"My wife likes her," he said disparagingly of the leading actress. Paul had too little interest in any aspect of Nigel's life to be surprised. "I like her too," he said, continuing the conversation about the actress.

"My wife" occurred several times in Nigel's talk during their next few meetings. There was a slight mockery, but also a possessiveness in the way he spoke about her. Paul gathered she was in New York visiting friends; the frequency of Nigel's references to her increased; she was on her way home.

Paul met her for the first time one Sunday at lunch. Her eyes were puffy, as though she had just woken up after too many sleeping pills; she was petulant about the weather and the sherry; during the meal she paid no attention to Paul; he might have been one of the circumstances of her marriage, like the empty conversation, which she had learned to take for granted. For the first time Paul saw himself, his presence there, through someone else's eyes: he was one of Nigel's little foibles; it disturbed him. He made an effort to engage her attention and establish his independence. Nigel was bored by movies; Paul soon discovered that his wife wasn't. As they sat over coffee in the living room, he talked to her about an American film he had just seen. Nigel's wife criticized one of the women in it.

"She's got a magnificent body," Paul told her deliberately.

Nigel's wife did not have a magnificent body; but there was a looseness about her that attracted Paul. When she was in repose, listening, her mouth was always a little open; it didn't make her look stupid; it made her look wanton.

It wasn't long before Paul was taking Eugenia West to his room in the late afternoons and tumbling her on the unmade bed there.

11

"THE FIRST FRENCH ARMY, commanded by General de Lattre de Tassigny, forged in Africa and in Italy, enlarged by French Forces of the Interior, liberated Le Lavandou on August 17, 1944."

The plaque outside the town hall had the stale, deceived look of an old political poster. "All the Way with L.B.J." The Germans had not defended Le Lavandou. The General, landing farther down the coast, had bypassed it on his way to Marseille. But there was still some echo of truth in the triumphant inscription. Whatever the facts were—the young men in sweaty uniforms, forged by their resentment of the company sergeant; the slightly contemptuous French officers; the welcoming crowd, torn between pride that it was their own countrymen who had got here first and regret that it wasn't the more profligate Americans—there must have been an hour, perhaps a whole day, when the most exhiliarating of all history's illusions had caught at the people here: "At this moment, everything is possible."

The girl in the town hall, who listened to my inquiries about Mrs. West, did not share that illusion. "Impossible" was her favorite word. I was lucky I had been to French schools as a child; if I had shown the least hesitation with the language she would have found it impossible to understand a word I said to her. As it was, it was impossible to say where Madame West's villa might have been; it was impossible to find out if the house still existed; it was impossible to trace property from so long ago.

I don't go along with the popular idea that the French are a bunch of shits. They're difficult in their own way. They have none of the Italians' impulsive sympathy, that marvelous suspicion that you may be human too. But they are inquisitive. It's this quality that keeps breaking down their reserve, their tedious sense of superiority, and makes them so engaging. At least to me. After fifteen minutes of saying, "No, mademoiselle, absolutely not," the girl in the town hall was beginning to wonder if a rich American woman named Eugenina West *had* once owned a villa nearby. There might, she was beginning to suspect, be some file somewhere she hadn't peered into yet; she told me to come back in a few days; I thanked her to death and told her she was amiable; she said one would see.

The Petit Port had been rebuilt since the war, the tideless sea pushed back to make room for a new road, hotels, a pizzeria, a narrow crescent of sand. In May, Le Lavandou was an ugly little town. In July it would be a jungle of double-parked cars and angry people, each of them convinced that everyone else was an intruder, one of the new crowd who were ruining the place.

There was a square, part of the old town, back from the sea. I found the café I was looking for there; there were several drawings of it in Paul's sketchbooks; it had changed very little. Sitting at one of the tables outside, watching the men in blue trousers playing boules under the plane trees, I wondered if the "Café Owner" of Paul's painting, Madame Tranquais, was still alive. I turned to look for the waiter. . . .

He didn't move as I glanced at him. He had grown a mustache, and his English-style cap hid his receding hair; he didn't expect me to recognize him. I pretended not to; but I hadn't forgotten, could never forget those prim eyes, the way that slightly pursed mouth had asked, "Walter who?"

He was four tables away and slightly behind me. I sat there feeling his presence, like a touch, on the back of my neck. There was no reason to believe his being there was anything but a coincidence; it wasn't so strange to meet a man at the Museum of Modern Art and then see him again a few weeks later outside a café in the South of France.

I knew it wasn't a coincidence.

I suppose many people have fantasies about being followed. "Like one that on a lonesome road doth walk in fear and dread, because he knows a frightful fiend doth fast behind him tread." I used to walk down streets sometimes, pretending flight, stopping to glance in a store window for a reflected glimpse of the pursuer. It wasn't a fantasy now. Tartan Cummerbund did follow me back to my hotel. That English cap was unmistakable every time I turned my head. He didn't try to catch up with me; when I looked through the window of the lounge, he was sitting outside a café across the street. I watched him for a minute; the waiter brought him a cup of coffee.

Walter wasn't in his room. It was next to mine with a connecting door; I kept the key on my side; a room to myself with a door that locks has always seemed to me an essential luxury; I'd go mad in Russia. Walter had discovered Perrier water since we had been in France; there were several bottles of it cooling in his washbasin. It took one of them back to my own room with me.

I lay down on the bed, looking through the copies of Paul's sketchbooks Bone had sent me, all the drawings Paul had made in Le Lavandou: Eugenia West; Madame Tranquais in her café; Lilian Alan Fletcher on the beach; the villa; the garden. I couldn't concentrate on them; I kept thinking about Walter.

Walter who?

That was the trouble with him; he rarely seemed to know himself who he was. Most of the time he was that "we shall overcome" character; I could never accept him in that role; I don't believe we shall overcome—whoever "we" are. Most of the time, I don't think Walter did either; he just liked the idea of it.

I still enjoyed sleeping with him. He was so personal in bed. Sometimes with a man I imagine we're both someone else; the whole experience is a fantasy; I'm an eighteenth-century tart; he's a young thief condemned to the gallows next day; I'm trying to make him happy on his last night alive; it varies; a Roman girl and a gladiator; there is usually some element of consoling someone in his doom; not always.

I never did that with Walter. I was always myself in bed with him. He was always the same bony Walter, seeking solace from his own uncertainties in me; he used to say my name over and over when he was coming. It was his great charm: however unsure he might be of himself, Walter was always sure of others; they were fixed certainties to him.

I walked over to the window to see if Tartan Cummerbund was still outside the café across the street. It took me a moment to find his English cap; he had moved to another table; there was a Perrier bottle beside his coffee cup.

Walter was leaning forward in his earnest attitude. I could see he was being reassuring about something. As I watched him he finished his Perrier, touched his companion briefly on the shoulder and came toward the hotel.

He looked up. I moved away from the window before he could see me. Going back to the bed, I picked up Paul's sketchbook again. By the time Walter tapped on the door I had decided not to ask him who the man in the English cap was.

I didn't want him to say, "Who? Which man, Jane?"

I didn't want to listen to Walter while he lied to me about it.

12

"THERE, MADEMOISELLE."

The girl in the town hall had found the unexamined file. A Mrs. Eugenia West had once owned the Lou Nanon, a villa four kilometers out of Le Lavandou, on the coast road to St. Tropez. She knew the house; it had been bought by another foreigner in 1951; he had never come near the place since; a local notary managed it for him, renting it to summer people. A German family had stayed there last August, paying twenty thousand francs a month. "Imagine." Once started, she was a spring of information. She turned to the file for the name of the present American owner. I had already guessed that.

She didn't want my thanks; she only wanted to know why I was interested in the villa; I told her a famous painter had lived there before the war; she was disappointed; she had never heard of Tagliatti; her curiosity did not include painters.

Walter was waiting for me outside the town hall. We went to the notary and pretended we were interested in renting the Lou Nanon; it was vacant during the rest of May; he drove us there and showed us over the house the next morning. Walter unfastened a downstairs window while I was getting the notary to explain the hot water to me. We went back that afternoon and had the villa to ourselves.

A series of strangers had rented the house for the past twenty years, families eagerly displacing one another and settling in for a two-week holiday; breaking things and perfunctorily replacing them to fit the inventory; leaving beach towels and wine stains behind them when they went. The Lou Naon was little more than the walls of the house where Paul and Eugenia West had spent a summer together. The basket chair in which she had sat for her portrait was, not surprisingly, gone. I found a deck chair and

77

placed it so that the front of the villa, part of the window Paul had included in his painting showed behind it. There was no mimosa. Sitting in the chair, I tried to reassemble all the details of information I had. Madame Tranquais, the café owner, was still alive. She was a marvelous old gossip. She remembered Paul, the hours he had spent sketching and painting her, chatting with her in his effortless French. When I showed her the sketchbooks, she remembered two paintings he had made of her. "I didn't like the second one. It didn't look like me. I used to tease him because he was so proud of it; I pretended it wasn't me. I called it that woman in the bar." There were all those other drawings in his sketchbooks, the notes he had scribbled beside them about Eugenia and about himself.

Few tourists came to Le Lavandou in the Thirties. The single hotel on the main street was a stopping place for traveling salesmen, men who had business in the fish market. A scattering of English people owned villas in the neighborhood. Eugenia avoided them. Apart from Nigel's position as a senior civil servant, she was anxious to avoid talk, scandal, herself; she was almost twenty years older than Paul. The two of them spent most of their time confined here together. They saw no one except the local shop people, until later in the summer Paul met Lillian Alan Fletcher and her friends on the beach. . . .

Walter was inside, measuring areas, tapping walls, searching for hidden, papered-over closets. I had put the idea into his mind on the way out to the villa. We had to walk in single file, facing the oncoming traffic; Walter was in front, his bare heels bouncing up and down in his sandals. He had enjoyed deceiving the notary; his enthusiasm was lessening with every kilometer.

"We're wasting our time, Jane. If he'd left any painting out there, someone would have found them by now."

"Unless he hid them." I wanted Walter kept busy, out of my way, when we reached the villa.

"Why would he do that?"

"Put yourself in his place. He was going off to America. He knew it might be years before he'd be able to get back."

"I'd take them with me."

"The Germans were overrunning France, stopping people on the roads, searching them." I was gambling Walter didn't know the war hadn't started until a year later; he was interested only in the generalizations of history.

"I guess it's possible."

I could hear him tapping upstairs now. I closed my eyes, recalling the portrait of Eugenia West, as though projecting it on the back of my eyelids. She was a spoiled creature, accustomed to the license of her celibate marriage. She was also a woman who enjoyed humiliation; she liked being tumbled in a squalid furnished room. Later, when she was living with Paul, her demands became more perverse. She didn't actively enjoy pain, only the anticipation of it; she wanted him to join her in rituals.

"Now, threaten to whip me."

When he refused, she sulked. That evening she ordered a taxi and went off to the little fishing port of Le Lavandou alone. Paul found her in the café, resentful with drink.

"Order me another."

"Get me some cigarettes."

"Not *that* kind." Pushing his Gauloises away.

Finally, when he persuaded her to come home, she refused to settle the bill.

"*You* pay for a change."

Paul had no money; he was left to face the owner of the café, to explain that he would come in and pay in the morning.

It never occurred to her to doubt him; all foreigners were rich. "The next time," she agreed cordially. It was the beginning of his friendship with Madame Tranquais.

In the morning Eugenia was puffy-eyed and tremulous. "I'm sorry I was so awful." She promised, beseechingly, to be good. "I do love you, darling. I've never loved anyone so much." The words were a demand, a claim on him. That afternoon she told him he could spank her if he liked. "For being so dreadful to you last night."

The flaccid behind she exposed to him was an affront to his youth; all summer he had been longing for a girl with a body as young as his own. He gave Eugenia three hard slaps on the ass. It startled and angered her for a moment, but a different ritual had been established between them; she no longer needed Paul to threaten her; she could anticipate that sudden humiliating pain in being peevish, provoking him. He never slapped her again.

79

"Jane." Walter was shouting at me out the window. "Come up here. I've found something."

He met me on the landing, waving a paperback book. "Look at this." It was a Tauchnitz edition of *The Island of Penguins*. "Guess who left it here."

I took it into the bedroom and looked at the name written neatly in ink on the title page.

"He owns the villa," I told Walter.

"Bone?"

"The girl in the town hall showed me the papers. Didn't I tell you?" It would have served me right if Walter had slapped me. I gave him back the book; he sat down on the bed, crossing his legs, pulling up his feet into the lotus position; he said it relaxed him, helped him to think.

"Tagliatti left some paintings here, all right. The portrait of that West woman; *Quai, St. Tropez*; the Casino in Hyères. That *Café, Greek Street*—he probably painted that here too." He was beginning to put his conclusions into words. "They're all in the Wexford Bone collection now."

"Of course they are. That's why Bone bought the house: to get those paintings."

"I wonder what the law is on that." Walter wriggled his toes in his sandals. He was thinking again. "If Tagliatti had them—If Mrs. West didn't know they were here, she didn't have any right to sell them."

"She knew."

"I can't see Tagliatti giving them to her. He was an absolute squirrel about his paintings. The ones he liked. He wouldn't give Lilian that portrait of the Portuguese fisherman in Provincetown."

"You can be sure Bone did everything legally, Walter—put them on the inventory with the rest of the things in the house. One cane hamper with contents, four rolled canvases."

"Mrs. West would never have sold them if she'd known they were here."

"She didn't want them. They were nothing but an embarrassing memory to her by then. She had probably only held on to them in the first place out of spite, when Paul went off with Lilian Fletcher."

"Those paintings are worth around one million dollars."

"Oh, Walter, shut up." I couldn't stand him when he

talked like a Swiss banker. "Bone bought this house in 1951. No one had ever heard of Tagliatti then."

"No one ever heard of Van Gogh either until he was dead. But if I had a painting like *The Bridge at Arles* I'd have sense enough to hang on to it. I'd know how much it was worth just looking at it."

I wondered if he would. If any of us would. Except Bone, of course. Bone had seen Tagliatti's value long before anyone else. It was Bone who had made his paintings known: slowly, patiently, by a calculated process of revealing them to the right art critics, the right dealers at the right time; after Paul was dead, beyond envy, and his paintings had the assured scarcity value of Ming vases; no one could ever make any more of them.

"How do you mean, Mrs. West held on to them?" Walter's toes were busy again. He was wondering if she'd had any legal right to hold on to them.

"Paul felt he owed them to her." I could see the deck chair from the window. This had been her room; it was here she had played those perverse games with him. "He had no money at all. He had to ask Eugenia West for everything. Every drink, every pack of cigarettes. When they went to a restaurant or a café, she would hand him the money under the table to pay the bill. He hated it. But she didn't. It was her revenge for the humiliation that other side of her wanted."

I was still looking down into the garden; trying to recreate the incidents of that summer for myself; I had almost forgotten Walter was there.

"One night they went to the casino in Hyres. She gave him a thousand francs to play roulette with. He kept trying the numbers, a hundred francs at a time. A single win would have made him independent for a month. She smiled every time the croupier raked away Paul's chips. She was winning and gave Paul another thousand to play with. He lost it in a few minutes. She had a pile of chips beside her. She pushed them toward him, taunting him to try and win. He put them all on a single throw. He lost. Going home in the taxi, she kept laughing about it. 'What would you have done if you'd won, darling? Would you have left me, Paul?'

"He was wearing the tuxedo she had bought him in London. He told Eugenia he would give her his paintings, everything he had done that summer. The next morning he took them to her room—his portrait of her and the two others. She was contrite and pleading. 'I didn't mean it, darling. Please, darling, I didn't.' She accepted the paintings as a gesture to his self-respect. A few weeks later, he painted *Casino, Hyères*. He gave her that too. You can feel the anger and contempt in that picture."

I glanced at Walter. He hadn't been listening to me. He was looking at the paperback book he had found, turning the pages one by one as though he expected to find some coded message there.

I left him and went back into the garden. Sitting in the deck chair again, I tried to go on thinking about Eugenia and Paul. Bone, Walter's acquisitive zeal kept coming between me and the past. I wondered what had happened to that second portrait of Madame Tranquais, the one Paul had been so proud of, the one she had called "Woman in Bar." Had he taken it with him when he went off with Lilian?

Like his "Portuguese Fisherman" and the "Sixth Avenue El" painting Kevin had remembered, it was in none of the known collections of Paul Tagliatti's work.

13

I WROTE BONE A SECOND REPORT, listing all the paintings Paul had completed before October, 1938, when he sailed from Le Havre on the *Aquitania* with Lilian Alan Fletcher. I mentioned the missing "Woman in Bar" and finished by telling Bone I was coming back to New York.

Walter and I went straight to my apartment from the airport. There was a brief reply from Bone waiting for me in my mailbox. I took it upstairs with the reproachful inquiries from my mother and all the other bumf that had accumulated in four weeks. I read Bone's letter first. He was pleased with my progress. Did I think there might be other paintings of Tagliatti's which had never been found? He was "most interested" in this "possibility." He wanted me to continue with my research.

"It's great, Jane. All this space."

Walter opened his suitcase on my bed. I wouldn't let him unpack it. Once he had his jeans hanging in my closet, his shirts mingled with my underwear, he would feel entitled to a door key. He pretended to be offended when I told him he couldn't stay, and then became off-hand.

"Okay. I can go out to Southampton." It wasn't difficult to guess who was waiting for him there; the tartan cummerbund man had left Le Lavandou before us.

That was one of the reasons I wanted to get Walter away. We were beginning to compound our lies to each other. The strain of not mentioning things I wasn't supposed to know was beginning to make it painful to spend more than an hour or two at a time with him. In the end I let him stay the night. When we were silent and tactile together in the dark I still liked him as much as anyone I have ever known.

Lying to each other over breakfast the next morning

made me want to lock myself in the bathroom until he left.

"I better write to Bone and tell him I'm quitting." Walter could say things like that as though he meant them.

"If you think so. Sure." I couldn't look at him when I said them. I was too busy wondering if Bone knew Walter existed. Walter talked a lot about Bone, but I wasn't sure if he had ever actually met him.

"I can't go on taking his money when I'm not doing anything for him."

Please, Walter. Please, shut up.

"No," I agreed. "That wouldn't be fair."

"I'll write to him from Southampton."

"Good idea." Had Tartan Cummerbund paid for Walter's trip to Europe? Had Walter told him about the missing "Woman in Bar" yet? Was Tartan Cummerbund's mother—?

But the moment I began to ask myself questions about Tartan Cummerbund I came to a dead stop. I could see why he had been so suspicious when I accosted him outside the Museum of Modern Art, why he had been so persistent in demanding "Walter who?" What I couldn't understand was my own part in that meeting.

Waiting on Fifth Avenue that night, I told myself I was looking for a man alone, about forty years old, vain, not too sure of himself. Why did I pick those two, one after the other, first Cummerbund and then Bone? I had soon come to feel that Bone was manipulating me. It was far more disturbing now to consider that some part of my own mind, which I could not define and had never known existed, might have been manipulating me too. The possiblity reminded me, unbearably, of lemmings.

Walter was gathering together his razor and toothbrush, his manicure set—he was very neat about his nails—and putting them into his airline bag. I was suddenly sick of the game we were playing, the game I was playing with myself.

"Will you promise me something, Walter?"

"Sure." He was always impulsively co-operative. "What?"

"If I ask you a question, will you promise not to say, 'Who?' "

He thought that over for a second, resisting his impulsiveness.

84

"Sure."

"What's he got to do with Lilian Alan Fletcher?"

He thought that over too.

"Lilian was his aunt."

"What's his name?"

"Peter Alan Donner. People call him Pad."

"His mother—She's Lilian's sister, the one she wrote all those letters to?" I had always known there was a mother around somewhere.

"Sure." Walter kicked off his moccasins and sat down on the bed. He was getting ready to tuck his feet up. "Natalie Alan Donner. She's Lilian's younger sister."

"They're the ones who sent you a photograph of me?"

"Where did they get it?"

"I told you—it looked as if it had been taken in the street."

Then Berman hadn't been the only one trailing around after me that afternoon with Kevin; Pad Donner must have known who I was, where I lived by then; all he had had to do was follow Bone's limousine the night before.

"How did you get involved with them, Walter?"

"I've known them all my life." He was fitting himself into the lotus position. He hadn't been exactly truthful when he said it relaxed him. It made him feel protected; some people wear dark glasses. "They've got a big place in Southampton. I used to mow their lawns after school. They had one of those grass mowers you can sit on."

"Do you get a share if you find any of those paintings?"

"That's the deal." He fitted his left foot more snugly into its refuge. "I get expenses and a cut. Same as you with Bone."

There was no point in telling him he was wrong, that I hadn't even known there were any missing paintings when Bone hired me; Walter wouldn't have believed it. I was thinking about the Donners, the acquisitiveness of the rich.

Tagliatti was already famous, his paintings at a premium by the time Lilian Fletcher died. I could imagine Natalie Donner rereading her sister's letters then; the references to Paul's work, the missing "Portuguese Fisherman" must have incited her like a treasure map. Perhaps there were other canvases that had never been found.

"I suppose the Donners feel they're entitled to those paintings," I suggested.

"Why shouldn't they? Lilian helped Tagliatti for years,

85

years before he ever met Bone. All she ever got out of it was the five paintings she bought from him, and she left those to a museum. Natalie's Lilian's only relative. Why shouldn't she cash in on all her sister did for Tagliatti?"

I usually hated him when he talked like that. I understood him better now. There are poor Americans even in Southampton. The Donners with their lawns, their grass mower you could sit on must have fascinated Walter from the day he became aware of them. He had always wanted a share in all that.

"We know about three of them now," Walter was saying. "Those paintings exist somewhere. All we've got to do is to find them."

"All *you've* got to do is find them, Walter."

"You said we'd work together."

"We can't." We weren't going in the same direction.

"Don't be dumb, Jane." He sat quite still, looking gentle. It reminded me of that first night when he had taken his clothes off in my hotel room. He was very perceptive in his own devious way.

"We can help each other," he said. "I know a lot of things you don't. I know all about Tagliatti and Lilian. I know a lot about Angela Anson, too."

14

October, 1938–April, 1939.

THE SPLENDOR! The splendor! Paul walked for hours up
and down Fifth Avenue and into the East Fifties. He discovered a fresh vitality in himself. He enjoyed everything
too much to sleep. The women! The women! The sheerness
of the buildings. The streets and sidewalks, hosed down
each dawn. Everything gleamed in the clear October light.
It was all so diamond clean, dazzling, compared with London. It was all so definite. The city challenged him con-
stantly that first winter he spent in it. It never intimidated
him. From the day he landed he felt he belonged there.

Lilian had a duplex on Murray Hill. Although she was
thirty years old and had never been beautiful, Paul was
delighted with her after Eugenia. She was a cheerful
woman, full of healthy appetites. An excellent cook, fond
of casseroles, she did embroidery, read a great deal, played
the piano with enthusiasm but little precision, could
whistle like an alto flute and loved to sit up talking and
drinking all night. She had none of Eugenia's plaintive
complications; her only caprice was that she liked young
lovers. She enjoyed seeing herself as a Rubenesque nude,
reveling about with slender youths; her bed was mirrored
on both sides and above, so that she could see herself from
three angles. Paul's adolescent body enchanted her. From
the moment she had seen him on the beach in the South
of France she had been determined to get him back to
those mirrors on Murray Hill. She was rich and not mean.
Unlike Eugenia, she was not possessive. As soon as Paul
found a place of his own nearby, she was content to let
him go. She didn't try to keep him in dependence. She
gave him a thousand dollars.

The long depression was going into its ninth year. It had
created an elite club of its own. Money, any money, was

the badge of membership. It entitled the holder to the widest privileges. You could get a man to carry your bags for you, a plumber or an electrician at any time of the day or night. You could have liquor or sandwiches delivered at three o'clock in the morning. If you wanted to travel or go to the theater you could pick up a phone and your tickets would be brought around by messenger in an hour. You could get a waiter fired if he spilled your wine on you, or your maid arrested for stealing your towels. You could get a six-room apartment or a secluded house on the shore whenever you wanted one. You did not have to be rich to enjoy these privileges. Most of them cost very little. Money had such scarcity value that anyone with a job was one of the elite; anyone with a quarter could buy ten minutes' deference in a drugstore.

With his London-tailored suits and his thousand dollars in traveler's checks, Paul was a member in good standing. He found a studio near Gramercy Park, a single large room with a kitchenette and bath. The landlord threw in a paint job and a month's free rent; he was relieved to have someone living in the place. Lilian helped Paul furnish it.

The next six months were the happiest in his life. He worked, he made friends, he ate Lilian's casserole dishes; they sported together between the mirrors. He discovered New York; its contrasts fascinated him; a short walk through the insulated corridors of Rockefeller Center and he was in a town of old three-story brick houses, pawnshops, cut-rate bars and second-hand-clothes stores. Here all life ended every few minutes, obliterated by the uproar of the El. Paul made dozens of sketches of the Sixth Avenue El, its jungle of pillars growing out of the paving blocks of the street.

Paul was twenty-one that December. Lilian gave a party for him. One of the guests was a young actress who had a three-line part in a Jed Harris production. Her name was Angela Anson. She came late after the theater, a dark girl, good-looking rather than pretty, always just beyond the group Paul was talking to. She called him two days after the party and invited him to see the play she was in. He went alone; they met afterward, at her suggestion, in the Automat. He watched her while she ate cereal and fruit; she had beautiful eyes, but her jaw was too wide, the distance between her nose and mouth too long. He did not find her particularly interesting; she had little ambition as an actress; her part was no more than a temporary job to her; Jed Harris had hired her because he knew her family. She was Tyrone Fallon's stepdaughter. Paul walked her back to her room in the West Fifties. She didn't ask him in; he didn't try to kiss her. Again she called him. She had tickets to a Sunday-afternoon movie at the Museum of Modern Art. They ate after it at a delicatessen on Broadway. She asked him questions about himself, listening attentively to his answers. That Sunday she was wearing a beaver coat which she had bought for herself, saving for it, dollar by dollar. Fur had always seemed romantically erotic to Paul. They went back to Angela's room; she had a bottle of California Chablis, which she asked him to open for her as though it were a particularly difficult male trick. They lay on the bed, drinking the wine out of teacups.

She wouldn't let him make love to her.

He began to see her two or three times a week. Whenever he wanted to go to a movie or an art gallery and had no one else to go with he would call Angela Anson. Her phone was in the downstairs hall, and though the rooming house she lived in was full of suspense-ridden actors, she was always the first to answer it. She seemed to have no life apart from Paul and the few hours she spent at the theater every night. Paul began to tell her things about himself, about his parents, his wandering childhood, all the incongruous schools he had been sent to, which he had never told anyone before.

She would not go to bed with him.

They were often alone together at his studio until late in the night. Her refusal provoked him finally to physical anger. He shouted; he threw her beaver coat at the wall; he wrestled with her. She was surprisingly strong. He told her to get out; he was through with her.

He meant it. She called him. He hung up on her. The next night when he came home late from Lilian's he found Angela waiting outside his building.

"I came straight from the theater." For some reason she was whispering. She followed him upstairs and made them both some tea. They spoke very little while they were drinking it, watching each other with wary amusement. She went to the bathroom; when she came back she was wearing nothing but her slip. She refused to take it off until he had turned out the light. He wasn't vengeful or con-

89

temptuous with her. Just before he went to sleep she put her hand on his chest.

"You're really very nice." She sounded surprised.

"Turn your back while I get dressed," she told him in the morning.

When she got home she wrote him a ten-page letter; he found it in his mailbox that evening. "We must continue as friends—if at all" was the only phrase in it that made any immediate impression on him. The rest was a flow of free association about "you" and "us" and loneliness and night.

He called her at once before she left for the theater.

"We must continue as friends—if at all!" he shouted derisively over the phone. He was senseless with anger. "Go to hell, damn you, you bloody bitch."

She wrote him another letter the next day; she had two free passes to the Hayden Planetarium. "You often said you'd like to go there."

After that she slept with him whenever he suggested it. It was an act of greeting between them, little more. They didn't revel together as he did with Lilian; Angela would never let him see her naked; but he had come to depend on her in a way he had never depended on anyone before. If anything happened to him—a discovery, a small adventure, any sudden moment of excitement or failure—he couldn't wait to tell Angela about it.

One evening in January, Angela took Paul to meet her mother. Helen Fallon had just come back from Bermuda and moved into the Weylin, a residential hotel in the East Fifties. Her son, Kevin, who was a few months younger than Paul, was staying there with her until, as she put it with exasperated good humor, he settled down to something. Helen had been divorced from Tyrone Fallon for ten years, but her association with that giant, brooding figure still lent her mystery and distinction. She did her best to dispel the mystery. "Here I am," she seemed to be saying with an amused candor that had a quality of innocence. "You probably think of me as the wife of a great man, but you can't imagine how tiresome he was." The suite at the Weylin was a pleasant place, a bright refuge in the wintry times. Kevin and his mother seemed to Paul the personification of those favored and fortunate he had once hungered to join.

Angela sat withdrawn during the evening; she might have been watching the progress of an experiment she could no longer control. Paul could not understand why she had arranged the meeting. As he soon found out, Kevin had never liked his half sister; her mother was plainly irritated by her. From the moment Paul was welcomed into her family, Angela became the odd one out.

Kevin was supposed to be looking for a job. His father would do nothing to help him; the bitterness of his own youth, about which he had written so many airless New England sagas, had turned him against his son; but there were old friends of Tyrone Fallon's who were willing to do what they could. Kevin would leave the Weylin every morning promising his mother to look them up. He would come to Paul's studio instead and sit reading while Paul worked. He was the only person Paul had known who didn't distract him; there was a physical gentleness about Kevin that was reassuring to him. They had many interests and enthusiasms in common: Goya, Céline, W. C. Fields. They quarreled occasionally. Leaving the studio in the late afternoon, they would drift around the Village bars. Liquor made Paul wildly unpredictable at that time. Some chance identity would suddenly possess him. He would become unreachably convinced, for instance, that he was a newspaper reporter who had just come from identifying a murder victim in the city morgue. "Multiple lacerations around the vagina," he would report, drinking to dim the horrors of the dead body he had just viewed. It would amuse Kevin for a while, but as Paul's fantasies became more and more lurid, Kevin's natural reticence, the Puritan idealism that was the basis of his gentleness would revolt. He would tell Paul to shut up, for Christ's sake. They would part in a riot of exchanged indignation.

The next day Kevin would be amused. "You were something last night." Paul was never contrite. The craziness of those drunken fantasies seemed necessary to him. They restored his balance, lessened his constant nagging awareness of the gap between his aim and his achievement as a painter. Although he had worked hard for five months, only one of his paintings, *Sixth Avenue El*, seemed to him to approach what he had wanted it to be.

Paul never worked easily. His finished paintings achieve

an effect of having been painted in a rush of controlled energy. In fact, he often spent whole days wasting time, incapable of committing himself to a single stroke of the brush, alternately tense and exhausted, resisting a recurrent impulse to lie down, to scream, to masturbate, to give up and go out to a bar, until he reached the necessary pitch of frustration, and would suddenly find himself working.

By March, Paul's temporary security was coming to an end. He had lived comfortably for five months on the thousand dollars Lilian had given him. Their affair had settled into friendship; Lilian liked change, and acrobatic adolescents weren't hard to find. She was a candid woman; Paul knew he couldn't expect her to go on supporting him. He had no realistic hope of finding a job. A single want ad could produce a hundred applicants outside an employment office before it opened in the morning. When his last traveler's check was gone, he would no longer be a member of the club. He would lose all its privileges with dreadful suddenness.

Paul had a further problem. The year before, leaving England for the South of France with Eugenia, he had had to get himself a passport. He had no certificate of his birth in St. Louis and no idea how to obtain one in England. Both his parents had been British subjects; with the help of a friend of Eugenia's who was a Member of Parliament, he had managed to obtain a British passport which stated that his place of birth was London. He had used it to get a visitor's visa and been granted a six months stay when he landed in New York in October with Lilian. The six months were almost up.

By the middle of April Paul would not only be broke; he would be an illegal alien. He would have to either leave the country or risk being deported.

Paul wrote to Eugenia and told her he wanted to come back to London. He asked her to cable him the fare. Miraculously, she sent him two hundred dollars.

It was one of the deciding moments of Paul's life.

Germany had just occupied what was left of Czechoslovakia after Munich. Conscription had been introduced in England. Return to London would lead, rather sooner than later, to a suit of Khaki clothing for Paul, the gregarious boredom of an army camp.

Two hundred dollars was over a thousand pesos. Kevin had heard you could live on fifty pesos a week in Mexico. Lilian was fond of Paul; she was kind; she bought two of his paintings—*Man in Park* and *Street, Night*—for a hundred dollars.

Paul entered Mexico on April 12, 1939. He had bought himself another six months to get on with his work.

15

"I'LL BET SHE'S WEIRD."

Walter was back from Southampton, where he had gone to see the Donners and probably, I thought, try to get some money out of them. I was back from New Jersey, where I had gone to see Angela Anson.

"She's a sweet little old lady."

It wasn't true; Walter was right; Angela Anson was weird. Although she had no blood connection with the family, the curse of the Fallons had descended on her, that urge to narrow their lives to an inescapable, squalid end. She was living alone in a prefab near Point Pleasant. At first she thought I had come to hire her, as she put it; I gathered she did cleaning for the summer people; later she kept asking me if I knew she had once been an actress on Broadway.

"Do you think she's got any of his paintings?" That was Walter's only interest in Angela Anson.

"No."

"What makes you so sure?"

"She told me about Paul leaving suitcases and things with her. He always got them back." She was full of regret at her own lost opportunities; I was sure she wasn't hoarding any original Tagliattis in that prefab.

"Shall I tell you what I think?"

"Please don't go into the lotus position."

"Why does it bother you?"

"It always makes you so devious."

"Shall I tell you what I think?" He had brought a bottle of wine with him in his airline bag. He got up and uncorked it. I remembered that Pad Donner, as Walter called him, was always using expressions like that: "Shall I tell you what I think?" Things rubbed off on Walter. "I think he did eight paintings in his life which he really liked."

"Why eight?"

"It doesn't matter how many. I'm just using a figure. Let's say, *maybe* eight. Okay?" He was over by the sink at the other end of the room pouring the wine. He took a long time doing it. I imagined he was thinking.

"He really cared about those paintings. He thought they were the best he'd ever done. Right?" Walter handed me a glass of wine. I put it down on the table.

"There are three of them we know about now." Walter held up three fingers and flicked them down one after the other with the thumb of his other hand. "That woman in the bar. The Sixth Avenue El. And the young Portuguese fisherman." He dropped his hands. "And they're all three of them missing. Aren't you going to drink your wine?"

"No, thanks."

"It's good, Jane. It'll relax you. You're all uptight." He handed me the glass again. I took it and sat down in my comfortable chair. Walter had a point; if I was going to open the door to him, it was stupid to treat him as though he were selling magazine subscriptions. He was wrong about the wine; it wasn't good; I drank a little of it anyway.

"He loved those paintings. They were like his private collection. He wouldn't sell them or give them to anybody. Right?"

"Maybe you're right, Walter."

"Okay. Then what happened to them?"

"I suppose he took them to Mexico with him."

"The last time. Right? When he went back there at the end of the war. In 1945, or whenever it was we dropped the bomb on Japan."

"What's that got to do with it?"

"Nothing. Okay. The bomb's got nothing to do with it. But that's when he left the United States, and he lived in Mexico for the rest of his life. Right?"

"Please stop saying, 'Right,' Walter."

"He died there." His self-control was admirable sometimes. "He died in Mexico in 1952. Didn't he, Jane?"

"He did, Walter. In a place called Tetacata."

"Then that's where those paintings are now."

"In Tetacata?"

"No." Walter shook his head. "Somewhere else in Mexico."

I supposed they might be. I didn't know. Walter and I

95

went on talking about it, but I wasn't paying full attention to what either of us was saying. I kept thinking about Angela Anson, the embarrassed eagerness with which she had talked about Paul when I told her I was doing research for a man who was writing a biography of him. In spite of her regret, her resentment that he had never given her any of his paintings, she was proud of her association with Paul Tagliatti. She wanted to be in the book. She had been only two years old when her mother married Tyrone Fallon. It must have wounded her when she realized, waking from infancy, that he wasn't her father, that he didn't care about her, had no interest in her. Was that why she had introduced Paul to Kevin and her mother? Because her only importance, to herself, was that chance and an unrewarding relationship with Fallon? "Did you know I was once an actress on Broadway?" At least she had finally found something of her own to be proud of. But she had never been ambitious. Why had she let herself be bullied into living through other people's eyes? My thoughts were becoming brightly haphazard. I seemed to be on the verge of some encompassing question about her, about everyone, all of us. I couldn't quite state it.

"Was Bone in Mexico with Tagliatti when he died?" Walter was standing over me.

"Yes. At least, he told me he was."

"What else did Bone tell you?"

"He said Paul was shot by a drunken Mexican. That's sad, isn't it, Walter?" I felt it had a vast, ironic sadness.

"What did he tell you about those eight paintings?"

"Nothing. He never mentioned them to me."

"Bone knows where they are, doesn't he? He knows who's got them."

"Does he?" That surprised me in a distant way.

"Why did he have to hire you to get them for him?"

"He didn't. I'm sick of telling you—"

"My God. And you talk about being devious." Walter was walking away from me. "Okay. Let's wait a few minutes, Jane." He was receding across the room, growing smaller and vaguer.

I felt it then in my thighs, an uncomfortable lassitude, a slight irritation of the skin. I recognized it at once. I had been through it once before, because it was something I had wanted to experience for myself. It was too late to feel angry. I was past the capacity for detailed emotions; I saw everything instantly as part of a whole.

Every nation has its own morbidities. With the English it's ritual cruelty, floggings, hangings. Americans are obsessed, among other things, with compulsory veracity, lie-detector tests, truth serums. Perhaps it's part of that hunger for sincerity. If someone could only be forced to tell the whole truth, what marvelous revelations we would all enjoy. It was just the kind of illusion that would appeal to Pad Donner. I could imagine him suggesting it to Walter. "If you could make her tell you everything she knows . . ."

I had a moment's panic when I wondered if Walter had known how much acid to feed me. Thank God, I hadn't finished the glass of wine; I wouldn't drink any more of it. There was no stopping it once it started. Small quantities of Seconal were supposed to help; I didn't have any; you couldn't get it without a prescription. I wanted to think about that, about the whole concept of preventing people from harming themselves. John Stuart Mill didn't consider it a proper function of government. . . .

I could still direct my mind. It was like driving a sleigh across the ice; you couldn't turn the skittering runners; you had to give a sudden tug at the reins.

I was going to have to go through it to the end; seven or eight hours; the great thing was not to get anxious. Make the most of it. If you're going on a trip, pick your own country and take your own luggage. I knew where I was going. But not with Walter. I was going to choose my own traveling companion too.

The itchiness, that heated irritation of the skin, was passing. The doorknob, a pair of scissors on the table were bright with halos. I made an effort to look at Walter. For an instant I felt helpless again. Make him go away. Someone, please, make him go away. I was almost in tears. I gave a quick, hard tug at those reins. Walter was sitting in the lotus position on the bed; he was watching me as I leaned back in my comfortable chair. Escape was the apex of a right-angle triangle formed by Walter, myself and the door. I had it opened and closed and was running down the stairs before I was aware of Walter untangling his legs. Nothing happened, in my sight, until after it had happened. He was pulling on his shoes as I hurried out into the street.

The outdoors stopped me. Evening shadows were as positive as chasms. Cars passed. I wondered if they were following their headlights or pushing them in front of them. The question seemed related to the great problem of history. Do we follow our leaders or do they only sense the direction in which we are already moving? I would find my own answers to questions like that before the night ended. Walter had been standing in the doorway for some time. He was calling to me. I ran.

The creeps were clustered, watchful sentries, on the west side of Washington Square. They were my allies now; I ran, weaving between them; flight creates its own safety among the furtive; the pursued is a have-not. Walter, chasing behind me, calling my name, was their instant victim. He had something to lose. Me. His quarry. They closed around him with menacing questions; he would have to pay ransom for his urgency, his purpose. I looked back from the next corner. They were holding him upright, rifling his pockets.

When I walked through the lobby of the Milroy, the clerk was creating an intricate pattern of the switchboard, plaiting colored wires together as he thrust golden-tipped plugs into silver rings. He was too entranced to notice me. There was metal everywhere: metal doors outside, inside the elevator; all along the corridor to a metal number, 34. I didn't like metal; it was the only substance that didn't seem to share my existence.

I had another instant of fear as I knocked. By the time Kevin opened the door to me I was already wondering who it was who had been frightened. It didn't seem to be me. I tried to explain that at once, before I lost the sense of it.

"We say, I'm hungry, I'm cold, Kevin," I told him as he closed the door and I sat down on the bed. "And we say, I'm going to France, I want to paint that woman behind the bar. We use the same word, I, each time. But they're not the same I. They're completely different."

There was little light in the room, a single table lamp with a red shade. It was difficult to keep Kevin's face in still focus. Varying aspects of it kept overlaying one another like shifting slides projected onto a featureless head. All the slides were beautiful, even the ones that produced the fleshless skull. I was serenely happy; a fragile serenity; laughter was always on the edge of shattering it. Kevin sat

98

by the window in a peacock blue chair, the brilliant yellow brick surface of a building behind him. No one in the world could have been better disposed to accept me that night. At times we talked; at others I lay back, experiencing every cell of my body, from my growing toenails to the ends of my growing hair. That was one of the things I talked to Kevin about, the singleness of myself.

"Suppose it's raining, Kevin. You're hitchhiking along a highway. It's getting dark. You're not going to get another ride. You're going to have to spend the night by the road. Your body's going to get cold and wet. That's something you're going to have to share with it. You don't resist it. You just do it together. But if your mind is being subjected to some strain, boredom or accusation or something, your body rebels against it. It sweats and fidgets and tries to get away. That's wrong. Your mind isn't separate. It's just as much a part of you as your body."

The steam pipes resounded like deep, harmonious gongs. The patterned ceiling was a source of endless images. There was a solid stone ash tray on the table beside the bed. I could see the vein in the granite; I knew that stone and I were composed of exactly the same matter; we were part of each other, inseparable familiars. What had divided us, fractured us all? I thought I could understand a part of that too.

"Suppose you're looking for a drugstore, Kevin." I was filled with suppositions. "You're walking down a street, looking for a place to buy some aspirin or a toothbrush. So that's all you see. You don't see the houses or the roofs or the colors of the doors or even the people. All you see is whether there's a drugstore or not. You narrow your sight to your own objective. We do that all the time. When I worked on that damn fashion magazine, I used to look at what other women were wearing. All I saw was their clothes or their hairdos or their make-up. Children don't do that. When we're kids we see everything. It's only later when we have motives, a narrow purpose, that we begin to discriminate, to choose what to see. It makes us half blind. It fractures us. It separates us from our common unity with everything."

That amused me. I laughed a good deal from time to time. The laughter seemed to come from understanding. It was obvious to me that everything was essentially all right.

"We're all survivors, Kevin," I told him. "We can't help

surviving. A single fragment of skull is a part of the whole universe."

It was difficult to surrender the happiness, the security of knowing that. It must have been four o'clock in the morning by that time. I began to realize that re-entry was going to be difficult. The drabness, the small separate anxieties of daily living were going to be hard to accept. I had to tug at those reins, tell myself consciously that it wasn't so bad; life wasn't all that horrible; at least, not to me. Kevin came over and held my hand while I was falling back through the gravity of existence. I was lucky enough to be tired; I managed to sleep.

I awoke to a squalid hotel room looking over an area-way. There was a particularly ugly khaki brick building blocking out most of the daylight. The ceiling was patched with urine-colored stains. By the grimed window stood a sagging armchair covered with leaden blue cloth. A sudden clang from the steam pipes startled me off the bed. I was alone. There was a note from Kevin on the dresser.

"You were something last night. Sorry I had to leave you, but I guess you'll be fine when you wake up. I had to go out for my——" His ball-point pen had skittered across a grease spot on the paper; I couldn't make out whether the last word was shot or shit. I put the note in my pocket; I wanted to keep it.

When I looked back into the room from the doorway, the sight of it struck me with a quick sadness. This was what Kevin would be coming back to. Sitting there by the sightless window all day, *what did he think about?*

I stopped for coffee and a hot dog at Nathan's on the corner of Eighth Street. Kevin had been right: I did feel fine; but not quite fine enough to risk the west side of Washington Square even in the middle of the afternoon. I walked home along the avenue. It wasn't until I reached the door of my apartment that I realized I didn't have my key.

God knows I didn't want to see Walter at that moment: I wanted to close myself in alone and have a long hot bath; but I hoped he was still there to let me in. I knocked several times before I tried the handle. The door wasn't locked. I pushed it back against the wall more from habit than from caution.

The first thing I saw was the almost empty whiskey

100

bottle on the floor, some scraps of tin foil, the kind they wrap pills in.

Walter was lying face down on the bed. He was naked except for the top sheet covering one thigh and part of his hip. I closed the door behind me and fastened it with the chain.

I have had a fortunate life in many ways. Apart from being born white in a Western country, which is a piece of magical good fortune in itself, I have never been imprisoned, tortured, starved or seriously ill. I have never been in a war, never seen anyone fragmented. I have never watched a child die.

I had never even seen a dead body before.

I don't know how I knew so immediately that Walter was dead.

16

IT WASN'T IN THE LEAST like my idea of a police station. Its grimness was of a more intimate kind. I decided it had once been a school. The Sergeant, or whatever he was, in the downstairs hall was impersonally polite when I told him my name. I was wanted in Room 23 on the second floor. I might have been a temporary typist reporting for work, instead of a witness who had been summoned for questioning.

I walked up the stairs down which generations of children had struggled their way to the freedom of the streets. Room 23 was at the end of the passage. Two white men, one in a short-sleeved Hawaiian shirt; two middle-aged black women and a Puerto Rican boy of about twelve were sitting on a row of chairs just inside the door. At the far end of the large hall was a heavy wire cage with a door to it. There was no one in the cage. At unevenly spaced desks a dozen men, who looked as though they had been chosen only for their disparity, were conducting confidential interviews. They sat at right angles to their clients on the same side of the desk, leaning toward them for each whispered question and answer. None of the interviewers appeared to be waiting for me. I sat down next to the Puerto Rican boy. I was wearing a prim tan linen dress I had bought for temporary office jobs; the boy looked at me as though trying to see through it.

"What you do?" he wanted to know.

I told him I had found a dead body.

"In a automobile?" Transportation and death were evidently connected in his experience.

"In my apartment."

"Hey." That impressed him. "Your boy friend?"

"Not really."

"Who killed him?"

"He committed suicide."

"That's what you told the police, hey?" He didn't believe that story. I didn't know whether the police believed it or not. They had asked me strings of detailed, intimate questions after they had finally arrived, before they had finally taken Walter's body away with them. They had scarcely seemed to listen to my answers.

"You want another boy friend?" The kid's bright, almost black eyes were still trying to see through my skirt.

"Sure. Look me up in a couple of years."

"You'll be too old by then."

"Jane Claire." One of the interviewers was calling my name without looking around; he might have been speaking into a public-address system.

"No shit. I could fix you up," the Puerto Rican boy told me in parting.

"Sit down." My interviewer was young, olive skinned, with silky black hair that fell over his ears like an Apache's. The seat was still warm and faintly damp from the wide-hipped man who was walking away from it toward the door. The Apache asked my place and date of birth. He didn't turn to me when he spoke, pushing his head sideways at me, so that I could answer into the screen of hair over his right ear. It was like whispering into a confessional. He had a pleasant, tentative voice; it reminded me of a law-school student for whom I once typed an essay on sanitary codes.

"Occupation?"

I told him I was a temporary secretary. He was writing everything down on a ruled yellow pad.

"Walter Olvero." He looked at a typed report in front of him. Oliver, he had always called himself to me. Southampton, the grass mower you could sit on, his envious respect for the Donners fitted even more credibly into place for me.

"How long had you known Walter Olvero?"

"About a month."

"Where did you meet him?"

"In London. London, England."

"I know where London is." The Apache smiled, but he still didn't look at me. "You come back here from London together?"

"We went to France first."

"France?" That seemed to interest him. "How long were you there?"

103

"Two weeks."

"Had Walter Olvero ever been in France before?" Every time he spoke Walter's full name he made him sound less and less like anyone I had known, who had ever been alive. "Had he spent a lot of time there?"

"I don't know." I remembered Walter's excited discovery of Perrier water. "I don't think so."

He turned over a typed page. I was still leaning toward him; I saw the words "suppression of the central nervous system" and guessed he was reading the coroner's report on Walter Olvero's body. I had never seen a coroner's report before. His next question puzzled me.

"Did Walter Olvero often use suppositories?"

"No. I don't think so. I don't know."

"They use them a lot in France, don't they?"

"Yes." I wished he'd look at me; just once; he had no interest in me. It made me want to confide in him, to tell him about myself. "I used to go to school in France," I explained." Even when we just had a cold or a headache they made us—"

"Yeah." He turned another page. "Do you think Walter Olvero took his life by absorbing an overdose of barbiturate into his blood stream while under the influence of alcohol?" He might have been asking me to raise my right hand and repeat it after him.

"No." I didn't feel like repeating anything; I still wanted to confide in him. "No, I don't think he did."

"Why not?"

"Walter didn't drink."

"Never?"

"A glass of wine."

"He had a three point five per cent level of alcohol in his blood."

"He didn't take barbiturates, either."

"You said you didn't *know* if he took suppositories."

"I never saw him take anything."

"I guess someone else could have bought those things." There was a defeated weariness in his voice. "He wasn't the only guy who's ever been to France." He glanced at the stack of waiting papers beside him, then back at the coroner's report.

"There was no trace of excrement under his fingernails."

I suddenly wanted to be sick. When I told him I didn't

think Walter had killed himself I hadn't imagined the alternative. I was compelled to now. I saw a series of quick, too vivid pictures. Walter forced to drink himself helpless. Walter held down naked on my bed. The bullet-shaped suppositories being thrust one by one into his rectum. I didn't want to admit those pictures. I wanted to deny that was the way it had happened.

"He was *always* cleaning his nails!" I protested.

"Maybe." The Apache looked relieved. He put the report on Walter Olvero into a wire basket on his desk and reached toward the stack of other cases beside him.

"Maybe you're right." There was more hope than conviction in his voice. "He took the suppositories. Then he cleaned his nails." He pulled off the top set of papers.

"Emanuel Bido."

He had already called the next name before I stood up.

17

I MISSED WALTER.

In my memory some of his deviousness died with him;
his gentleness remained. When I was younger and refusing
to behave in some way my mother wanted me to, she used
to say, "You'll wish you'd done it for me one day." She
meant when she was dead. I never believed her. It seemed
senseless to me that I could ever feel guilty toward the
dead; it would be like wanting to repay them money you
owed them; what could the dead do with it? But for a long
time after Walter was murdered I wished I'd been nicer to
him.

I was sure he had been murdered. My apartment
seemed alight with reflections of silent violence. Perhaps if
I had forced myself to think about it, I might have
brought those reflections into focus; I might have understood then who had killed him. I couldn't. It made me
want to be sick. I would run down the stairs, go and see
friends, walk on lower Fifth Avenue.

Walking, I would sometimes try to puzzle out, in words,
who could have wanted Walter dead. I knew so little
about his relations with Pad Donner. The only thing I had
ever known for sure about Walter was that he wasn't telling me the truth. He had probably been lying to the Donners too; he might have been blackmailing them in some
way; I was too disordered with fear to think further than
that. Sometimes I was so frightened I decided to go back
to Room 23, confide everything to the Apache, all about
Bone and the Donners and Pad Donner being in France
and the missing Tagliatti paintings. I decided to go, but I
never went.

All purpose is subjective; there is no such thing as an
objective purpose. My own reasons for doing or not doing
something are often so frivolous they're inexplicable. I
think this is probably true of most people. Even Paul, who

at least had a single constant aim, his painting, often behaved in ways, made apparent decisions, that seem incoherent to me. I didn't go back to the Apache, because I felt he didn't want to be bothered with me. I know that's true, even if it is unbelievable.

I wrote another report to Bone, covering Paul's first winter in New York and telling him about the third missing painting, "Sixth Avenue El." In reply Bone sent me the usual perfunctory congratulations. "I am pleased with your progress." He also told me about a man named John Horne, a professor of Spanish at Westminster College in Fulton, Missouri, who had known Paul in Mexico in 1939. "Tagliatti told me he saw a good deal of Horne after he returned from Mexico at the beginning of the European war."

I was glad to leave New York, to get away from my apartment with its echoes and reflections of Walter. I flew to St. Louis and rented a car at the airport. Fulton was a hundred miles west along a two-lane blacktop. About halfway there I pulled off for gas. I wasn't thinking about what I was doing; for two or three minutes I sat fingering the steering wheel, staring at the pumps through the window—Super, Hi-Grade, Economy—before I realized the place was closed. It was hot. I got out of the car. The silence startled me. The still deadness in the air was like the spirit of vacancy. An unpainted wooden shack stood beyond the pumps. Every window was scarred in the same way: spider webs spreading out from neat milky-rimmed circles in the panes; dozens of other, less symmetrical scars patterned the gray wooden slats of the building. I had never seen bullet holes before. The stillness had a sudden positive quality in my ears; it was a silence of contrast, the dead end of violence. I had walked several feet away from the car. It was a relief to see it still standing there. The ignition key wouldn't turn. I had the car door open again and was going to run for it before I remembered to press in the key. That's the state I was in. I made a squealing turn and headed back toward St. Louis. Chicago was only four hours away. My mother would be having drinks on the lawn, her face flattered by the shade of a beach umbrella. There would be people on the tennis court and around the pool. She would be glad to see me. "Janey, Janey, darling, what a lovely surprise." She would mean it until she remembered the other arrangements she had made for the evening, and began to wonder how I was going to fit in with them. "How long can you stay, darling?" The corners of her lips going down.

I pulled into the first service station I came to and got the tank filled. I drove to Fulton.

No one in Fulton was glad to see me. The manager of the hotel looked at me as though I'd come to unionize his help. When I asked the waitress in the restaurant on the main street if I could have a glass of wine with my chopped steak she told me I wasn't in a saloon. I hadn't written to John Horne. I called him from a booth.

"Hullo? Yes?" He had a strident, high-pitched voice. I could hear gunfire in the background. After he had turned off the television set I still had trouble getting in touch with him.

"Paul Tagliatti's dead," he kept telling me. "It was in *Time* magazine. I saved it."

I said I knew he was dead. I told John Horne the same story I had told Angela Anson; I was doing research for a man who was writing a biography of Tagliatti. John Horne became less strident; like Angela Anson he wanted to be in a book, any book. He asked me if I had a car, where was it, which way was it facing? He gave me meticulous instructions how to drive out to his house.

I decided to walk. Away from the main street, Fulton was an attractive town of white frame houses with deep porches; tree-lined sidewalks that would be rustling and fragrant with leaves in the fall. John Horne lived in one of the smaller, shabbier of the houses. He opened the door before I touched the bell.

"Come in. Come in." He sounded as though he expected me to refuse. Grabbing my hand, he pulled me into the living room. He was one of the thinnest men I've ever seen. Long, narrow head with a stand of white hair; long, narrow feet; there was so little flesh on the bones in between he seemed to have no muscles to move them with; he gave the impression of being on strings like one of those dancing skeletons in shop windows on Halloween.

"Paul. The beloved vagabond. Paul." He had rehearsed the opening words of his reminiscence. "Pablo, we used to call him in Mehico. Pablo el Rubio. Paul the blond. The beloved—" His high-pitched voice was interrupted by a thunderous noise from upstairs. It sounded as though a barrel of wood chips were being rolled across the ceiling.

"It's only Celia," John Horne explained. "She's moving the bed again. We got married in college, my sophomore year."

While he was waiting for the noise to end, he darted to the desk by the window and snatched up the exhibits he had arranged there for me. He handed me the first of them: the copy of *Time* magazine he had saved; it was open at the Milestones column. "Killed. Paul Tagliatti, 34, American painter; in a shooting incident in Tetacata, Mexico. Tagliatti, whose 1945 exhibition of war paintings attracted presswide attention, had faded into obscurity in recent years."

The second was a snapshot: Paul and John Horne standing in front of a cantina. John Horne had been a rather dashing-looking young man with a Pancho Villa mustache and a tourist sombrero pushed back on his head. He had always been thin. Paul's face was slightly blurred; he was bareheaded and his eyes were half closed; he looked hung over.

The third exhibit was a post card. It had been mailed in Laredo, Texas, on September 12, 1939, and was addressed to John Horne, Westminster College, Fulton, Mo. "Dear John," it said in clear hand-printed letters. "I'm thinking of going to Canada to join the army or something. I'll stop off in Fulton on the way. Be good to see you."

It was unsigned except for a capital P.

18

PAUL HAD TWELVE PESOS, about two dollars, when the bus reached Nuevo Laredo.

The Mexican Immigration official who had posted a bond for him in April was relieved to see him. Paul surrendered his tourist card. Wearing his best suit and carrying his suitcase, he walked across the bridge to the American side.

"Where are you heading?" The U.S. Immigration officer's voice was friendly, welcoming, as he examined the visitor's visa Paul had obtained from the U.S. Consulate in Mexico City. "Planning to stay with us long?" The friendliness, the welcome were assumed. Visas were issued by the State Department. The Immigration Service was a branch of the Department of Labor. There was a long history of antagonism between the two bureaus.

"I'm going to Chicago." Paul had his story all ready. He had friends in Chicago; he would stay with them while he arranged things with the British Consulate there. He let that settle for a moment before adding modestly that he was going to Canada to enlist. "Now that we're at war, I'd like to get into the air force."

"How are you traveling?" The American wasn't at war. He hoped he never would be. In spite of Paul's best clothes, his large, respectable-looking suitcase, there was something that bothered him about this blond kid. It was a hot day. Why had he come dragging his ass across the bridge on foot? He could have got a taxi for a few pesos.

"How am I going to get to Chicago?"

"Yeah."

"By bus."

"Got your ticket?" The Department of Labor didn't want any aliens bumming around the United States; there were enough Americans on the bum already.

110

"I haven't got it yet. No."

"Have you got enough money for the fare to Chicago?" The Immigration official could have asked to see it; a cop would have; he had passed a federal civil service examination; he didn't think of himself as a cop.

"I guess so."

They looked at each other. Paul's eyes were as candid and untroubled as a statue's. He had a well-developed ability to absent himself from any threatening situation. He felt no anxiety.

"So you're going through to Canada, are you?"

"Yes, sir."

Perhaps it was the "sir" that did it. The American decided to believe him. He turned the page of Paul's passport to stamp it. He would let the kid in for ninety days.

"There'll be five dollars for the head tax," he said, inking the stamp.

The Mexican Immigration officer was not pleased to see Paul back. Although Paul had surrendered his tourist card, he was still technically in Mexico until he re-entered the United States. The Mexican, having posted a bond for Paul when he entered Mexico, was still responsible for seeing that he left the country. Paul understood this as soon as he saw the man's worried face. He explained what had happened. He said he needed five dollars to get into the United States. He didn't push it any further than that. Both of them knew he had paid the Mexican official twelve dollars and fifty-four cents for the bond back in April. If the man put up the five dollars, he would still be over seven dollars ahead on the deal.

It took the Mexican three hours to think it over. During that time Paul sat on a bench by the window in the border station reading a copy of *Jean-Christophe* which he had borrowed from the British Library in Mexico City. The Mexican did his best to ignore him, to forget him. It wasn't easy. Although Paul had lost some of that adolescent beauty that had made life difficult for him in London, he still looked barely eighteen. With the stark Mexican daylight behind him, making an aura of his unkempt blond hair, his face had the bland purity of an acolyte's in a stained-glass window. Just before four o'clock that afternoon, the Mexican official made up his mind. He gave Paul the five dollars.

111

The American official looked at the five-dollar bill Paul held out to him.

"Where did you get the money?" he wanted to know.

"I sold some cuff links." There didn't seem to be any point in going into a whole long explanation about the bond.

The American considered this. "Is that all you've got?" he asked looking at the bill Paul was still holding. "Five dollars?"

"No, I've got more than that."

"How much more?"

"About fifteen dollars altogether." The man hadn't asked to see it the last time.

The American shook his head. "I can't let you into the United States with fifteen dollars. What are you going to do when that's gone?" The unspoken words "public charge," "deportation at American expense" hung heavy on the hot desert air betweem them.

"I'm expecting some money in San Antonio."

"Yeah?"

"My father's cabling it to me at a hotel there. Two hundred dollars."

"Yeah?"

"To the Astoria Hotel in San Antonio, Texas."

"How do I know that?"

"I could phone the hotel and see if it's arrived yet."

"You'll have to pay for the call."

Paul had two dollars besides the five in his hand; it was only a hundred miles to San Antonio; he figured that would cover it. The American put the call through and asked for charges. Paul talked to the desk clerk at the Astoria. There was no cable for him, but there was a letter. Paul handed the phone to the American.

"Would you ask him to open the letter and see what's in it?"

The Immigration official identified himself to the desk clerk. The letter was read aloud to him over the phone.

Dear Mr. Tagliatti: The money you were expecting arrived by cable from England just after you left. Will you please let me know at once if you want me to forward it to you in San Antonio or to the address you gave me in Chicago.

It was signed, sincerely, with best wishes, by the manager of the Biltmore Hotel in Mexico City.

Paul looked relieved when he heard this news.

"You'd better have the money forwarded to you in San Antonio right away," the American advised him. Paul agreed. He paid his head tax. His passport was stamped. The operator called back with the charges. Paul paid them.

Paul entered the United States with a ninety-day permit and a dollar fifteen in change. In his suitcase, carefully rolled in oilcloth, were over a dozen paintings, including five he had completed in Mexico City. He also had the tuxedo Eugenia West had bought him. He pawned it for eight dollars in Laredo, Texas, and took a room in a cheap hotel.

That night he got drunk on rye with a Texan veteran of foreign wars he got talking to in a hamburger joint. He told the Texan he was an Austrian refugee, the son of a concert pianist in Vienna. In a mixture of German and Italian he described in detail what had happened to his father when the Germans entered Austria. It was a horrible story. The next morning he checked out of the hotel. He had nowhere particular to go. There was nothing for him in New York. Lilian might put him up for a few days but no more. The last time he had heard from Angela Anson she had just been fired from her job as a guide at the World's Fair.

At the back of his mind was a vague decision to go to St. Louis and get a record of his birth there so that he could establish his American citizenship. He remembered a young man he had met in Mexico City who was in college not far from St. Louis. He felt John Horne had been impressed by him; not because he was a painter, but because he was, apparently, English. As a national of a country at war, a young Britisher on his way to enlist in Canada, Paul thought he might be something of a trophy, a ten-day celebrity in a small college in the Middle West. He sent John Horne a post card from Laredo and started to hitchhike north.

He had to go through San Antonio on his way to Fulton, but he didn't stop to pick up his mail there. Paul's father had been dead for nine years. He had written the letter from the manager of the Hotel Biltmore himself before he left Mexico City.

113

19

"How long did he stay there?" I asked John Horne.

"About three months."

"What was he doing?"

"Teaching."

"Art?" I couldn't see Paul trying to teach anyone else to paint; the whole process was too private and personal to him.

"Languages," John Horne reassured me. "French and Spanish. He could speak Italian too. Even a little German. He was a whiz at languages."

"The college took him on as a teacher?"

"Not exactly. I mean, he wasn't on the faculty, of course." Horne had a haibt of weaving his thin fingers into basketwork patterns and holding them up to the light to examine the chinks between them. "He had a sort of an arrangement I fixed up for him."

It was the second evening I had spent in the shabby frame house. Our conversations were interrupted at strangely regular intervals by that barrel of wood chips rolling around upstairs. Whenever this happened Horne would say the same thing in the same reasonable voice.

"It's only Celia."

Sometimes he would add a scrap of biographical detail. "She never had any children," or, "She used to live in Webster Groves." We usually waited until the noise had ceased before returning to our questions and answers about Paul.

Paul had guessed right about his value as a trophy in Missouri. The president of the college was eager to keep him there. There was publicity to be got out of him, interviews in the St. Louis papers, debates with neighboring colleges. Everyone was anxious to hear what a live Britisher—particularly one of draft age—had to say about the war in Europe. It was understood that Paul would be

114

going on to Canada to enlist "as soon as he was needed." In the meantime he would stay on at Westminister College as a part-time student, giving private lessons in French and Spanish and, if anyone wanted them, Italian to pay for his board and room in the college dormitory. He was interviewed several times; he took part in a radio talk show; he was questioned by the students at the school of journalism at the University of Missouri, thirty miles away. He gave a lecture to the Deaf and Dumb Institute in Fulton, talking to the rows of soundless ears while an interpreter beside him translated his words into sign language.

He was a great success on all these occasions.

"What was his attitude toward the war?" I asked Horne.

"He wanted America to stay out of it."

I could understand that; Paul was privately trying to establish that he was an American himself. When Horne went home to St. Louis one week end he took Paul with him. The city hall was open on Saturdays until noon; the clerk was helpful; he looked up the date, December 8, 1917. A number of children had been born in the St. Louis area on that day. Paul's name wasn't among them. It was possible there had been some mistake about the date; the clerk had a cross reference by names; the only registered Paul Tagliatti had been born in 1926.

Paul knew he had been born in St. Louis. His father, who was still in the cotton business at the time, had been sent to America by the Allied Purchasing Commission in 1915. Paul's parents had lived in St. Louis for over three years, until after the end of the war. Paul could not have been born anywhere else. He was an American citizen by birth. In the meantime, his permit to stay in the United States would expire by the middle of December. He thought several times of going to the Immigration Service in St. Louis and trying to straighten things out. In the end he never did.

"He was weird." Horne was examining the chinks between his fingers, trying to define Paul's weirdness in a way I would understand. "He never made any effort to fit in anywhere."

"Did he do any work?"

"He didn't have to. He only took a few courses. History. Literature. Comparative religion. Being at school in

115

Europe and reading so much, he knew more than the other students already. He was smart as a whip anyway."

"I meant painting," I explained. "Did he work on any paintings while he was here?"

"He was always drawing. He did a painting of the college chapel. Old Bullet—he was the president then—Old Bullet had it framed."

"What happened to it?" I was getting as bad as Walter.

"It was hanging in the president's office for a long time. It isn't there now. I think somebody bought it."

"Who?"

He didn't hear me. We waited until the barrel stopped rolling overhead. "Do you know who bought Paul's painting of the college chapel?" I asked in the contrasting silence.

Horne didn't. He thought someone had come out from New York; someone who had heard the painting was there. Bone? It wasn't listed in the Bone collection. I asked Horne if he knew when the painting had been bought.

He wasn't sure. "It was after the war," he told me. "After Paul had that exhibition in New York, that big feature in *Life* magazine. I wrote him a three-page letter when he had that feature in *Life* magazine."

I tried to get him back to the college-chapel painting. He preferred to tell me about Paul's ingratitude.

"He never even answered." He wandered over to his desk. "I made a carbon of that letter I wrote him. It was at least three pages. I guess you'd like to see it for your book."

"I can't remember what I did with it." He was leafing ineffectually through some papers in a drawer. "Maybe it'll show up. Paul never answered it, anyway." He came back to his chair. "That's what I meant when I said he was weird. I was one of his oldest friends."

I didn't say anything; sometimes I could learn more about Paul by letting Horne go on in his own way.

"It was the same when he was here. He never had any sense of gratitude. He never tried to act like anyone else." He was plaiting his fingers again. "We used to double-date sometimes before I met Celia. Before I gave her my fraternity pin. Paul and I used to go out with other girls. I always had to pay for everything. The Cokes and the movies and everything. Then Paul would take my date home. He did that with some of the other fraternity men too. He made everybody sore because he never tried to fit in."

Horne went on about that for some time. Faced with the intricate tribal rituals of college courting in the Thirties, Paul had simply ignored them. "He never even sent his date a corsage!" I was aware of the weirdness of Horne's indignation; Walter would have interrupted to wonder how much that painting of the college chapel was worth now; but that wasn't the point either; Paul had had other values, other urges which Horne would never understand.

"Did he ever show you any of his paintings?" I broke in at last. "The ones he brought back from Mexico with him?"

Paul had; Horne was able to identify three of them from the Museum of Modern Art catalog. Others he wasn't sure about. There was one painting not in the catalog which he could recall in detail: a night scene in the Tenampa district. The painting had stayed in Horne's mind because he knew the Tenampa, a red-light area in Mexico City, rowdy with whores, thieves, drunks and street musicians. Paul had painted a section of one of the dance halls, a roofed-over square open to the street on all sides. Horne remembered the flaring gaslights, the vivid primary colors of the girls' dresses contrasting with the black and white of the Mexican workingmen's clothes.

"He'd got the atmosphere of the place, all right," he admitted. "You couldn't forget it."

I added "Tenampa, Night" to my list of missing paintings. It was number four in what Walter had called Paul's private collection.

"I don't see that he was really such a much as a painter, though." Horne was regretting his enthusiasm for the Tenampa picture. "Except for that one exhibition in New York and a few pages in *Life* magazine, he never had any success at all, did he?"

"Not while he was alive."

"I guess he put people off. You'd think when someone took the trouble—"

"Why did he leave here?" I didn't want to hear about that unanswered letter again.

"That's what I mean. No reason, really. He got twenty dollars for the painting of the college chapel and he just disappeared without bothering to say goodbye to anyone. He went off on the bum down to New Orleans."

Paul must have been bored at Westminster College, I decided; irritated by the hearty conventions, the ignorance and presumption. Sharing a room in the college dormitory, he couldn't find the privacy to work. There was nothing to hold him there. I wondered why he had chosen New Orleans. Perhaps he had heard the lonely flaunting whistle of trains at night. He had gone looking for Basin Street, the fine, wild romantic life his imagination told him must be there.

John Horne couldn't help me any further. I had to rely on the sketchbooks and on things Paul had told Kevin and Angela Anson to fill in the next few months of Paul's life.

I thanked John Horne for his patience and kindness; I promised to write to him with any news of the publication of the book I had told him I was researching. I never saw Celia.

20

December, 1939–May, 1940.

IT WASN'T LONG before Paul was broke. He spent his last
few dollars shipping his suitcase with the carefully rolled
canvases and his paints and brushes to Angela Anson in
New York.

For the next few weeks he worked the bars along Bourbon Street, offering tourists quick crayon portraits for fifty
cents. There was avid competition for the tourists' money;
the French Quarter was littered with men and women who
would do anything for a few cents; but Paul found it easy
enough to earn a living. The trouble was it was too easy;
too many of his sitters showed a personal interest in him;
they offered him drinks, a ride along the Gulf, a shared
hotel room. He always refused. Ever since his second year
of art school, he felt, he had been living, trading on the effect he had on people. It wasn't that he had any moral
guilt about Nigel, Eugenia, all the others who had been so
eager to help him. He was obsessed by the conviction that
what other people saw in him had become an impediment
to his own vision.

He left Bourbon Street; he hung around the docks,
huddled out of the wind in the pale sunlight, watching the
fruit boats unload, sketching the longshoremen at work.
There were occasionally ripe bananas to be had for the
asking; he slept at the city mission on Rampart Street. The
price of shelter and a bowl of oatmeal was an hour and a
half of hysterical accusation. Destitution was a proof of
sin; any man who pleaded guilty to this indictment, grov-
eling to Jesus for forgiveness, was rewarded with a bunk
for the night. Paul slept on the chapel floor. His clothes
were soon too soiled for any furtive laundering in a public
toilet to help. He was on the bum and he looked it.

Vagrants were like men in uniform; no longer individu-

119

als. Making the rounds of groceries, back doors in the suburbs—"Have you got any work I could do for something to eat?"—Paul found he had lost all identity except to himself. The shopkeepers and housewives, handing him odds and ends of food, saw nothing but his stained and shapeless clothes.

Paul had succeeded in disfiguring himself at last. He had become faceless.

He had never known such a sense of independence. Or of estrangement. He was fascinated by the experience; he spent hours in the public library reading any books he could find on Eastern philosophy. "If others can't see me," he scribbled in one of his sketchbooks, "what am I? Free? Or only misplaced?" His only regret was that he had no one to talk to about it. His fellow vagrants were no help to him. They had no interest in the mystic nature of their condition. Among themselves they had little solidarity, no group awareness, no life style. Their only concern was to "make it," to climb back into the class above them, the employed.

One night at the city mission Paul picked up with a former college student, Bob Steele, who had lost his athletic scholarship at Purdue when he broke his leg in freshman training. Like many physically big men, Bob had a quality of gentleness; it reminded Paul of Kevin. They took to wandering around the city together; Bob had never known anyone like Paul before; he liked listening to him talk.

By January Paul was getting tired of New Orleans; there was so much else of America he had never seen. Bob wanted to head for southern Florida. It was actually, not just comparatively, warm there, and there were golden rumors of jobs as dishwashers and bellhops in the resort hotels. They left the city together, riding freights along the Gulf.

The journey almost ended for Paul in Mobile. He and Bob were sitting around a hobo jungle near the yards when two Immigration officers appeared. On the lookout for Allied seamen who had jumped ship in American ports, they went from group to group along the railroad line questioning the vagrants, listening for foreign accents. They came to Paul. They asked him where he was from.

"Boston." Paul had been working on his American accent ever since Missouri. It was still far from native, but he knew who the governor of Massachusetts was, and their next question, the name of Boston's baseball team. The officers were still suspicious of him.

"How do you spell razor?" one of them asked.

"You mean the thing you shave with?" Paul hadn't seen the point of the question yet.

"Razor."

"R.a.z.o.r." Paul saw it as he answered; he said zee, not zed. The officers moved on.

I can't get this incident, its implications, out of my mind. Zee, not zed; an instant's slowness to see the trap; a single sound would have changed Paul's whole life. If those Immigration officers had arrested him, they would have found his British passport in his pocket; his visitor's permit had expired; he would have been deported then, returned to England in 1940. He would never have painted "Portuguese Fisherman" or *Chair* or many of his other later pictures.

He would never have met Bone.

Paul and Bob spent a few weeks at an unemployment relief camp near Jacksonville. There are several drawings of the camp in Paul's sketchbooks. One face recurs again and again: a Czech named Ardman, a man in his sixties, who had once owned several grocery stores in Chicago. The Depression had ruined him; out of all he had once owned he had only one possession left: a metal box about six inches long with a handle on it. According to Ardman it was a machine for sharpening razor blades. He never let anyone look at it; he was prepared to guard it, literally, with his life. In many of Pual's sketches of men lining up for food, huddled over bonfires in the woods, Ardman is holding this metal box. His hands seem to be trying to absorb it into themselves.

Bob was hoping for help from a classmate at Purdue; a money order finally arrived; Paul walked into Jacksonville with him. On their way they passed a stonemason's workshop. On one of the tombstones scattered about the yard was a Spanish inscription.

"Este Mundo Es Un Lago Profundo Donde Ninguno Sabe Nada." *

The phrase seemed to express for Paul some of his own ironic acceptance of his existence at that time. He copied it into his sketchbook.

In Jacksonville Bob bought himself some new clothes. The highways leading south from Jacksonville were rigidly patrolled, all obvious vagrants turned back. In a new pair of jeans, a clean shirt, Bob might pass as a construction worker or farm hand. Paul parted from him outside the public library. Bob started hopefully south. Paul went inside to the steam heat of the reading room. He had been wanting for some time to reread Swift.

He had hardly sat down with *Gulliver's Travels* when he saw Bob motioning to him from the door. He joined him on the steps.

"I've been thinking." Bob looked away down the street. "Why the hell don't you come with me?"

"I'd never make it." Paul meant that the first cop who saw him, his stained jacket, his broken shoes, would threaten him with a vag charge, head him back north. "You know I'd never make it."

"I've got enough dough left to get you a front too."

Bob probably had five or six dollars in his pocket; it was an extraordinarily generous offer. Paul thought of the warm sunshine, the beaches, the hotels. He shook his head.

"Why not?" Bob pressed him.

"I've had enough of that shit."

"What shit?" Bob was puzzled; he was getting annoyed. "What are you talking about?"

Paul thought that was obvious: Miami could be nothing but another Bourbon Street for him. Whether he hustled crayon portraits or got a job as a bellhop, it wouldn't be long before he met another Nigel or another Eugenia.

"People," he said. "Wanting to keep me. I've been through all that. It's more interesting being on the bum. At least it's new to me."

"You're crazy. I was only trying to help you, you goddamn fool. You're crazy."

Bob walked angrily away. Paul watched him out of sight. For two months they had shared every waking ex-

* This world is a deep lake where no one knows anything.

perience together, every thought and confidence that could help pass the time.

"Este Mundo Es Un Lago Profundo." The phrase repeated itself like a melody in Paul's head as he went back into the library.

Paul drifted slowly north as the winter receded. He was not heading anywhere in particular; movement had become an end in itself. He slept out whenever it was dry; he enjoyed the sense of his own isolation in the vast night land; when he asked the farmers' and millworkers' wives if they had any work he could do for something to eat he was rarely turned away. By the beginning of April he was in Norfolk, Virginia.

He heard an interesting story from one of the American seamen on the beach there.

Some weeks before, a Greek ship, the *Piraeus*, had put into dry dock in Norfolk after being holed by a German torpedo. The Greek crew had jumped ship to a man. The Neutrality Act barred American seamen from replacing them. The *Piraeus*, out of dry dock now, was bound for Liverpool with the next convoy. The Greek company's representative, a ship's chandler named Calevas, was reportedly willing to sign on any man, however inexperienced, who could prove he was not an American citizen.

Paul had been on the bum for four months. It had been an interesting experience, filled with new impressions: the loveliness of the outwardly tranquil land; the freshness of a dawn with the promise of warmth later; the forced meaningless religious hysteria of the missions; that exhilarating illusion of freedom created by his own facelessness. He had been deliberately floating, absorbing. Now he wanted to get back to work.

If he sailed on the *Piraeus* and was paid off in Liverpool, he would be allowed to register as a merchant seaman in England. That would keep him out of the army and he would have a few pounds, a few weeks before he had to ship out again. The only thing holding him in America was that suitcase he had sent to Angela Anson. He wanted *always* to be able to reclaim those paintings at will; they were the only proof of himself, of his life so far, that he had. As a seaman he would retain some physical freedom; he could surely manage to jump some ship in America later and get his paintings back.

Calevas was a dark, plump man in his thirties with a shrewd, pulpy face and those olive shadows around the eyes that are so distinctive of the Greeks. He saw at once from Paul's passport that he had overstayed his permit in America. He didn't mention it; it was a useful card to be played when he chose. He was willing to take Paul on, if it was okay with the captain of the *Piraeus*; the Captain was in Baltimore visiting relatives.

Paul was willing to wait around until the Captain got back, particularly if Calevas would help him out in the meantime.

Calevas could understand Paul needed a place to stay. He might be able to fix him up with a bed ticket at the seamen's mission.

Paul needed some clothes, too. He needed a shirt and a pair of dungarees and a sweater. He needed shoes and socks. It was important to make a good impression on the Captain.

Calevas agreed. He had a lockerful of good secondhand clothes that had been given him by one of the Help-the-Allies groups in Norfolk. He didn't mention that. He said he would try to find Paul what he needed; but Paul would understand that he wasn't a charitable organization.

Paul understood. He signed a note allotting Calevas five dollars out of his wages if the Captain agreed to take him on.

Calevas explained that he was still taking a chance. He was quite sure personally that Paul wouldn't run out on him. But it might be several days before the Captain returned and in the meantime he, Calevas, would have to be responsible for Paul's keep at the seamen's mission.

Paul agreed to leave his passport with Calevas as security.

The seamen's mission was luxury. Paul took a hot shower and scrubbed himself. He washed his hair; he shaved; he brushed his teeth with borrowed toothpaste. Clean socks, clean underpants, clean dungarees, clean shirt, clean sweater. He made a bundle of all his old clothes and dumped them in the trash can in the yard. It was extraordinary how erotic it felt to be clean. That night for the first time in four months he slept in a bed.

Hot oatmeal with sugar and milk in the morning, hot stew with meat and potatoes in it at night. It had been weeks since he had felt solid leather under his feet; it gave him a sense of confidence, almost of authority. Suddenly, too, he was no longer faceless. In clean workman's clothes he was an individual again. Paul had six days of it all before the Captain returned.

He was a thin, graying man in a dark suit and starched collar, meticulous as a small-town undertaker. His appearance was misleading. He had been a cabin boy under sail at fourteen. There was no folly, no treachery or baseness he hadn't seen and accepted in his rise to command of his own ship. His eyes barely glanced at Paul; the fastidious lines at the corners of his mouth deepened a little.

He shook his head.

Calevas began to argue with him in Greek. He produced Paul's passport; he stubbed his grubby finger at the birth date in it. The Captain didn't even bother to shrug. He looked past Calevas at the graded shackles hanging on the wall of the chandler's office. With quiet indifference he answered in Greek.

They went at it for ten minutes: Calevas gesturing and pawing at the Captain; the Captain examining the shackles as though they were the only things of interest to him.

Paul didn't have to know much Greek to understand what the argument was about. The movements of Calevas' soiled hands, his wheedling voice made that clear. This blond kid, he was saying, wasn't as young as he looked. He had been around. He had walked in here a few days ago on the bum. With a face like that a boy didn't get to be twenty-two without accepting nature. When the ship got to England the kid wouldn't make any trouble about a little sodomy on the voyage.

The Captain remained preoccupied with the shackles. This wasn't a street kid, he explained patiently. He had a passport; he had come to America as a passenger. The Captain knew the British authorities; he knew how prurient they could be when their class consciousness was aroused. He walked out of the office without changing his mind. He wouldn't have Paul on his ship, even if he had to sail without a galley boy.

"He'll change his mind. They won't let him sail without a galley boy. The cook'll jump ship if he has to clean his own pans." Calevas was reassuring Paul man to man. There was nothing to worry about.

It was Paul's turn to shake his head. He had changed his mind. It wasn't that he was concerned about being abused on the *Piraeus*; he had confidence in his own ferocity to resist assault. Although he hadn't known it until that moment, he had decided in the last few days to remain in America. The idea of returning to New York was exciting to him; he had been celibate for four months.

He asked for his passport back.

The time had come for Calevas to play the card Paul had handed him. First he mentioned the five dollars Paul owed him for clothes, then the sixty cents a day he had cost him at the seamen's mission. He was holding the passport in his hands as he added up these sums. Eight dollars and sixty cents. He pretended to discover Paul's ninety-day-permit stamp. It was beyond him to look shocked; he did his best to sound surprised as he pointed out that Paul was an illegal alien. Unless he wanted to be deported he should sign on the *Piraeus* or any other ship Calevas could find for him.

Paul could see there was no sense in trying to grab his passport. Calevas had all the authority of the Immigration Service to call on. He agreed to stay on at the seamen's mission and check in with Calevas every day.

Calevas locked Paul's passport away in his desk.

Paul didn't have the nickel for the ferry to Newport News the next morning. It took him all day to hitchhike around the peninsula and across the bridge.

The war in Europe was beginning to have its effect on industrial America. In Newport News the shipyards were working to capacity for the first time in ten years. The affluence of the payrolls was infusing the whole area. Paul got taken on as a bus boy in a cafeteria. By the time he got back to New York City in May he had a presentable secondhand jacket and a change of shirts. Winter was over.

Angela Anson had a job in a press agent's office. She knew the owner of a picture gallery who was looking for an assistant.

21

I HAD GOT OVER SOME OF MY FEAR by the time I returned to New York. My apartment was no longer so clamorous with echoes of Walter's death. I wrote to Bone about the fourth missing painting, "Tenampa, Night." I asked him if he knew who had bought Paul's painting of the chapel at Westminster College.

Kevin shuffled around the Village with me in a pair of soft moccasins I bought him. We sat together in Washington Square. I went out to see Angela Anson again. She told me about the job she had found for Paul when he came back to New York in May, 1940.

"All he had to do was answer the phone, show people around. It was a great chance for him." We were sitting in the yard of her prefab. If I craned to look past a scrap yard and over the twirling plastic propellers of a used-car lot I could see the shore. The tide was out and the smell of decay drifted in from the mud flats. I tried not to think of the desolation that winter would bring to this place.

"How was it a great chance for him?" I asked politely.

"Hans Picker would have helped him if he'd stayed at the gallery instead of running off to Mexico with Kevin. He'd have given Paul a show."

I doubted it; I had found out the names of some of the painters Hans Picker had been interested in. They were a forgettable and forgotten lot. I asked Angela where Paul was living when he worked at the gallery.

"He had a nice room on Perry Street. I found that for him too."

"Did he paint anything that summer?"

"How do I know? I hardly ever saw him." I gathered Paul had treated her badly after the first few weeks. "Even when I went to the gallery, he wouldn't pay any attention to me." He had taken up with a girl named Melanie Tyrrel. "I introduced him to Melanie. She had red hair.

127

She was always touching him." Angela's associations could be as disconnected as Kevin's. I wondered why the name Tyrrel was familiar to me. "Melanie thought Paul was in love with her. He wasn't." There was a sudden fierceness in Angela's eyes. "He was never in love with anyone except me."

I didn't say anything.

"You don't believe me, do you? I could show you if I wanted to."

"Show me?"

"It wasn't Melanie he turned to later when he needed someone." For the first time since I'd met her, Angela Anson was smiling. She got up and went into the house. When she came back she was carrying a packet of letters.

"Paul soon forgot about Melanie then."

The packet was tied crosswise with brown string. There must have been at least thirty letters in it. She held it out so that I could see the top envelope. "Miss Angela Anson, 149 West 4th Street." I recognized Paul's handwriting from his sketchbooks.

"Would you like to read them?" Angela sat down again, holding the letters in her lap. The way her hands clasped them reminded me of Paul's drawings of Ardman in Florida, clutching his metal box.

"Yes." I looked away from those hands. "I'd like to read them very much."

"Do you think he'd publish them?"

"Who?" I had forgotten for a moment that I was supposed to be researching a book.

"The writer you're working for."

The forlorn eagerness in her voice made me feel ashamed. It was a relief when she went on without waiting for me to answer.

"I might let you have copies of them. If it was worth it."

"Would you?" We were back in a comfortable area where shame had no meaning. She wanted money.

"How much?" I asked. It was an area in which delicacy had no meaning either.

"Five hundred dollars." She didn't hesitate for an instant. I wondered how long the sum had been decided in her mind. Would she have written and told me about the letters if I hadn't come back to see her? I looked past the junk yard, over the used-car lot; I wanted to help her and it was easy to be generous with Bone's money.

"It sounds fine to me," I said. "But I'll have to ask the man I'm working for."

"You can let me know."

I wrote to Bone that night, reminding him that Paul had stored paintings with Angela Anson for years. I told him I thought there might be valuable information in the letters. I asked him to let me know his answer as soon as possible.

I spent the next day with Kevin. It was hot even for July. We sat on the rim of the dry fountain in Washington Square. Kevin was wearing a flannel shirt with the sleeves rolled up; his forearms had the look of drawings in an anatomical textbook. He remembered when the fountain had worked; when kids had played in it on hot days.

I asked him about Melanie Tyrrel.

"She was an awful bitch."

"In what way?"

"She just was."

"Was Paul in love with her?"

"Christ, no. Old Melanie. She wanted to marry him."

Tyrrel. I remembered why the name seemed familiar to me. David Tyrrel was the name Paul had used when he was applying for a job at Abercrombie & Fitch in 1941. I asked Kevin about it.

"David was Melanie's kid brother. He used to make model ships. In bottles. Paul said it must have meant a lot of staying home nights."

I was getting used to Kevin's free association. It was only a question of letting him talk on, picking a phrase here and there and assembling the fragments until I could put the story together.

When Paul and Kevin decided to go off to Mexico together in December, 1940, Paul had no passport. "Some Greek stole it from him." I knew about Calevas, although he hadn't exactly stolen it. Paul needed something that would identify him as an American citizen to get across the border into Mexico. Melanie's brother, David, was eighteen that year. Melanie invited Paul and Kevin to his birthday party. "So Paul knew the date he was born. All we had to do was find out where. I guess I asked the kid that. I asked him if he was born in New London because of those whaling ships he made in those bottles." David Tyrrel had been born in Woodstock, New York. A few days later Paul wrote to the town clerk there asking for a copy of his birth certificate. He signed the letter with David Tyrrel's name. "I was living with my mother, so we used her address. It sounded better than the Village." The birth certificate arrived at once.

"It was useful as hell for Paul with the draft," Kevin remembered. "Being able to prove he was only eighteen."

They had entered Mexico through El Paso. "Paul said he was afraid they'd remember him in Laredo." They went on down to Acapulco. It was then, early in 1941, that they tried and failed to fill the war years ahead of them by walking along the beach to Panama. Kevin got the bus fare home from his father. "He sent me the exact amount to the dime. I was starving to death when I got to New York." Paul managed somehow to find the money for the train to El Paso, probably by making portrait sketches of the tourists. He showed the Tyrrel birth certificate at the border, and used the name for a few weeks to work in a department store in Dallas.

The money he earned there got him back to New York. He spent the summer in Provincetown with Lilian.

That brought me up to the end of 1941. Paul was working at Abercrombie & Fitch, living in a studio on Fourteenth Street, when the United States entered the war.

There were no fresh missing paintings to report to Bone. I was waiting for his reply to my letter about Angela Anson. It came a few days later.

Bone wasn't interested in buying photostats of Paul's letters. He wanted the originals, and was prepared to pay two thousand dollars for them. He enclosed a certified check made out to Angela Anson for that amount.

22

"WHAT DOES HE WANT the originals for?"

We were sitting in the kitchen. It was raining in the yard, a summer storm. Through the window I could see the drips skittering and gathering on the surface of an iron table. I watched them attentively, too entangled in my own lies to answer Angela Anson's question. I could only guess Bone was more interested in owning than in reading the letters; he apparently felt they were a collector's item worth rather more than two thousand dollars; he had always liked owning things.

"If you want to publish some of them in the book, why can't you use photostats?"

An irregular cascade was falling from one edge of the table to the cinder-littered ground. The surface was evidently slightly tilted.

"There's something funny about all this." She was getting angry; I couldn't blame her. "You come here and tell me you're working for a writer. You haven't even told me his name."

"I'm not sure why he wants the originals." What saddened me was that I knew she would sell me the letters; she kept looking at that check for two thousand dollars; but there was more to it than the money. She wanted to believe in the book about Tagliatti; she could already picture it, index and all. "Anson, Angela, 85–87, 104*ff.*, 138" ... a whole inch of page references. Our longing to survive, to leave some trace of ourselves is so strong that even a listing in a phone book is a reassurance. Angela was trapped by the hope of seeing her name safely linked with Paul's in the New York Public Library forever.

"Who is this writer?"

"Peter Alan Donner." It was a stupid trick to play on her; some sudden, unpremeditated cunning had made me hope for a reaction to that name.

"Donner?"

"His friends call him Pad." It meant nothing to her.

"I'm not going to give those letters up without keeping copies of them."

I couldn't see any objection to that. She thought it would cost eight cents a page to have the letters Xeroxed at the real estate office in Point Pleasant. I gave her twenty dollars and left Bone's check with her. She promised to mail me the originals before the end of the week.

The rain was still coming down as I walked back to the bus station. The hour with Angela had left me with an edgy sense of guilt. Although I was longing to read those letters, I was glad I didn't have them with me; it would have been like carrying evidence against myself: my betrayal of her hopes to preserve her name in print.

They must have been waiting in a car across the street from my apartment. They came up behind me as I climbed the stairs. I was too startled to run. Pad Donner caught my arm and gripped it hard enough to hurt. He had shaved off his mustache and was wearing a light straw hat with a scarf folded around it for a band. He pushed me against the door.

"We'll all go inside." His voice was as precise and disagreeable as I'd remembered it from the evening at the Museum of Modern Art. She came in after him. I had never seen her before, but I knew at once who she was. She had rather short white hair, carefully waved; there was nothing remarkable about her face: a prominent nose, a sharp chin. Her veined, ringed hands were the most memorable thing about her; the fingers never seemed to straighten completely; grasping and clutching were their natural functions.

"Where's Walter?"

Her question shocked me. I had been telling myself for days she knew all about his death. She was peering about the room as though she expected to find him there. Pad Donner had let go of my arm. I sat down in the armchair, sinking as low as I could into it. It was an instinctive reflex of submission. I was frightened of them both.

"This is my mother," Pad Donner said.

"I know." I tried to get a little farther down into the chair. Pad Donner was not an athletic man; his small pot made him look flat-chested; but he was heavier and stronger than I am. I knew he could twist my arms behind my back and hold me while his mother did anything she liked to me.

"Where's Walter?" She was looking at me as though she'd like to do something that would make me scream.

"He's dead."

She didn't react to that at all. "He was living here with you." She glanced at the bed.

"He stayed here sometimes."

"Where are his things?"

"He didn't have any." I felt I'd better explain that. "I wouldn't let him move in with me."

"He had an airline bag when he left Southampton. The taxi man told me."

"Where is it?" Pad Donner had moved behind my chair.

"I don't know."

He hit me across the side of the head with his clenched hand; I hadn't been hit since I was a child; it left a sullen pain down my face to the neck.

"I don't know." I tried to turn and look up at him. His hand caught me across the nape this time, knocking my nose against the chair. I jumped trying to retreat from them both. I have never been able to decide if there is any way of coping with violence; I would like to believe in passive resistance; I had been as passive as a plant ever since they arrived. I thought of fighting back instead, of grasping some weapon, but I knew I would never be able to stab anyone, anyone in the world, with a knife. There weren't any clubs or sticks in my apartment. If I picked up a bottle, Pad Donner would too. He was more likely to use it effectively than I was; the idea of jagged glass was horrible to me. It was humiliating to find I was crying; I hoped it was the bump on the nose that had caused my tears.

"We'll look." Mrs. Donner came straight to the point as usual.

As Pad Donner moved away from the chair, he put both his hands in his trouser pockets; the uneasiness in his eyes sickened me; it was because of his mother, not because of me, that he was trying to hide his erection.

"Sit down," Mrs. Donner told me.

I sat down and watched them search my apartment. They were thorough about it. They pulled out drawers and emptied them onto the floor, searching the spaces behind them with their fingers. Pad Donner took all the books out of my shelves, examining them three or four at a time and dropping them on the floor too. It wasn't anything as big as an airline bag they were looking for; they thought I had already gone through that and hidden whatever it was Walter had had in it. Mrs. Donner spent a lot of time peering around without touching anything; she was putting herself in my place. After a while I stopped watching them. I was thinking of Walter walking in that last night with his airline bag; the memory brought on a whole different set of fears; the Donners weren't pretending; whoever had killed Walter had taken that bag.

"This is his, Mother." Pad Donner was standing in the doorway to the bathroom, holding up a small black leather case. It was Walter's manicure set. I hadn't noticed it in my bathroom. I remembered what the Apache had said: "Maybe you're right. He cleaned his nails." Cowardice had made me remember that. Now that I could no longer blame the Donners for Walter's death, I wanted to believe he hadn't been killed at all.

"Where are the rest of the things in that bag?" Pad Donner was standing behind my chair again.

"Walter often kept that manicure set in his pocket." I didn't turn around; at least if Pad Donner hit me again I wouldn't bump my nose against anything.

He grasped my hair, curling it around his hand, and lifted me to my feet.

"Put your hands behind you." That quandary about violence again; he pulled my hair harder; I put my hands behind me.

He twisted my wrists up above my shoulder blades in exactly the way I had known he would. My head was forced forward toward his mother. I remembered the endless succession of dentists who had shadowed my childhood; I had always surrendered passively to the pain I knew they were going to cause me.

"Where did you hide it?"

Mrs. Donner slid the tips of her fingers across my cheeks, feeling the bones of my jaw. I couldn't understand what she was doing. Her bent fingers felt as cold and hard as metal. I tried to pull my head away from her.

I saw it happen in her face before I felt anything. Her mouth twisted down at both ends and her eyes opened with the effort as she forced her fingers into the soft place

134

she had been searching for just below my ears. I screamed.

There was nothing deliberate about it; I screamed with pain; but I knew at once I had done the right thing at last. Not that the sound of a girl screaming would make anyone on Macdougal Street do more than pause and listen before walking on; it was the effect the scream had on Pad Donner that counted. He let go of my hands and grabbed for my mouth. I kept on screaming. The pain of her fingers pressing into the nerves, or whatever there was there, just below my ears made it impossible to stop. Pad Donner got his hand over my mouth. I felt something between my teeth. I bit it as hard as I could.

When he wrenched his hand away he pulled my neck free of her fingers. The pain didn't stop at once. The dentist's drill which had been grinding straight into the nerve had only slipped a little to one side of it. I stumbled over the arm of the chair, but I managed to keep going until I was across the room and could turn and face them with clear space on all sides of me. Space to twist and struggle and run around in futile circles until they caught me again; but at least space, a distance from them.

The pain in my ears, in my eye sockets was beginning to subside a little. I could tell from the silence that I'd stopped screaming. Mrs. Donner was walking toward me.

"I don't know where it is," I shouted at her. "I don't even know what you're looking for. I don't know. I don't know." She stopped advancing. Pad Donner had his finger in his mouth. He was reaching in his breast pocket for his handkerchief with his other hand.

"We'd better go, Mother." His voice had a muffled, plaintive sound. He took his bleeding finger out of his mouth and wrapped his handkerchief around it.

Mrs. Donner peered about the disordered room, her head slightly tilted, as though listening for something. She frightened me more than he did. She had that determination which is like stupidity; she was beyond reach.

"All right, Pad. We'll go now."

It struck me at the time, it remains in my memory, that they didn't walk, they sidled out. They were both still watching me as they stepped into the hall. I slammed the door and chained it. The sudden vacant silence reminded me of that gas station in Missouri.

A girl I know whose apartment was burgled told me it was like being violated. I didn't feel that. Possessions have never meant anything to me; even my clothes have never seemed particularly my own. I felt quite detached picking up all the things and putting them back in their usual places. My ears still ached, but the worst of the pain was knowing it wasn't over. There was another appointment to be kept. Mrs. Donner still believed that what she was looking for was here, in my apartment, if she could just get her hands on it.

After I had put everything away, I made the bed again and lay down on it. One thing gave me a sense of satisfaction, of revenge. By leaving those letters with Angela Anson to be copied, I had cheated the Donners of them.

They arrived by registered mail on Monday morning. The black mailman climbed the stairs and knocked on my door. I had seen him only a few times before, in the hall, on the street. I had always liked him. He looked as though he had been a mailman all his life. It must be a wearying job; the mail is never delivered; like crime, there is always more of it, on and on, year after year into the future. I felt that this heavy-set middle-aged man had accepted that. He was one of the people who were helping to fend off chaos.

"Sign here." I had never expected him to like me.

There were thirty-two letters inside the Manila envelope. The dates on the postmarks ranged from March 3 to November 8, 1942. I opened the first one. Paul had written his address at the top of the page.

Room 211. Immigration Detention Center. Ellis Island, N.Y.

23

AT THE BEGINNING OF 1942 Paul was still living on Fourteenth Street. He had left Abercrombie & Fitch before Christmas, but he had saved enough to get ahead on his rent. Working two or three nights a week as a temporary dishwasher or bus boy, he had managed to complete four paintings, including the portrait of Priscila Franklin, by the end of February. When he got Lilian's letter telling him she was in New York and inviting him to lunch the next day at a French restaurant in the West Fifties, he thought at first of ignoring it. But he wanted to see her; he wanted to show her his new paintings.

Lilian, uncharacteristically punctual, was waiting for him at the table. Although she greeted him with her usual affection, she was inattentive and fidgety over lunch; she showed no interest in his new studio, his work. She treated everything he told her about himself as though it no longer mattered: it was all in the past now. Over coffee she told him why. An F.B.I. man was waiting outside the restaurant to arrest him.

She broke into a passion of self-justification. They had come to her in Provincetown, two young men in dark suits, "like tax men"; Lilian had a horror of tax men. They had been given her address by that gallery owner Paul had worked for last year; they knew all about Paul's spending the summer with her; they were disgusting about it, treating her like a moral delinquent. They were looking for Paul and they didn't want him alerted. What could she do?

"It's wartime, darling," Lilian kept saying that. How could she refuse to help the F.B.I. in wartime?

Paul could still distance himself from any threatening situation. He felt no immediate anxiety, no resentment against Lilian either. He thought impulsively of leaving the table, climbing out the washroom window if there was one, making a run for it. There didn't seem to be anywhere to run to. In the three months since Pearl Harbor, the United States had yielded eagerly to all the gratifications of war. A sentimental and self-righteous hysteria had replaced all motives except self-interest. He had been guardedly aware of this in his refuge on Fourteenth Street, and particularly in the restaurants he had worked in. It hadn't actively concerned him until this moment. It was impossible to escape it, he realized now; the war was everywhere, uniting the whole continent against anyone trying to evade it. Before he left the restaurant he gave Lilian the key to his studio. She promised to pack up his paintings and take care of them for him.

The F.B.I. man waiting on the sidewalk outside was a temporary wartime recruit to the Bureau. Glad to have escaped the draft, he was eager to believe in the vital nature of his job. Paul was a disappointment to him; he looked so harmless. Having asked Paul his name in a formal way, the F.B.I. man suggested that they go; he didn't say where. Paul kissed Lilian on the cheek. In the futureless limbo in which he abruptly found himself, her soft middle-aged body was a reassurance that he had at least had a past. She said she would try to find out where he was; she promised to write to him "there."

Paul was taken first to an office in Rockefeller Center. On the short walk, he felt nothing but an impersonal curiosity. It did not occur to him to ask if he was being arrested. He was twenty-four years old and had never registered for the draft. They had every right to arrest him. The question in his mind was what had brought him to their attention. He had left so few traces of his existence; he had never filled out a census or tax form, never applied for a driver's license, never been listed in a phone book; the only time he had ever had a job under his own name was the few months he had spent working for Hans Picker in his gallery.

There was no name, only a number on the office in the R.K.O. Building. Inside, a stout middle-aged man was sitting at one end of a long green-surfaced table. He did not look at Paul or the F.B.I. man as they entered. His air of patient indifference as he waited for the door to be closed reminded Paul of his math teacher at school, waiting for the class to settle down before he began the tiresome routine that had brought them all there. There was nothing on the table in front of him but a heavy glass ash tray. He put his pipe into it and announced with an English accent, and no conviction, that his name was MacDonald. He did not ask anyone to sit down.

The F.B.I. man was hovering behind Paul like an actor without a script. He retreated a few steps, found the door and leaned against it.

"Are you the holder of British passport five-two-eight-eight-one?" MacDonald asked Paul without looking at him.

Paul didn't know. He had never memorized the number of his passport.

"Are you the holder of a British passport under the name of Paul Francis Tagliatti?"

"Yes."

"Do you have it in your possession?"

That aloofness which had always protected Paul in precarious situations helped him again now. He was able to tell MacDonald about Norfolk, Virginia; the ship's chandler, Calevas, in a matter-of-fact tone that relieved his story of any suspicion of self-justification. He might have been giving an answer that could be verified in a textbook. MacDonald didn't interrupt him. Leaning back in his chair, his face slightly averted, he appeared to be concentrating on making as little contact with Paul as possible. He took no notes. Calevas' name, his appropriation of the passport aroused no visible interest in him.

When Paul had finished, MacDonald asked only three questions. They were all concerned with the issue of the passport. Where had Paul obtained it? London. When? Paul was able to give him only the approximate date. Who had signed the application for him? Paul remembered the name of Eugenia West's friend, the Member of Parliament. MacDonald took his pipe out of the ash tray and put it in his mouth. For the first time he glanced at the F.B.I. man.

"We know that," he said. "It's the same passport, all right."

The F.B.I. man didn't reply. Paul couldn't see whether he made any movement or not. He was struck by the bareness of the room; no filing cabinets, no pictures on the wall; a single steel bookcase was empty except for some rumpled *New Yorkers*. MacDonald stood up and walked over to the window. Paul noticed how short, how tight across the hips the jacket of his suit was. The F.B.I. man

139

was touching his arm; the interview was over; it had lasted less than five minutes.

Outside on Sixth Avenue, the F.B.I. man, still holding Paul's arm, began waving for a cab with his free hand. The war had made empty cabs hard to find. Any taxi letting off a fare was the immediate center of a tight, struggling crowd. In spite of this, Paul unthinkingly expected one to pull up at once for the Federal Bureau of Investigation. Surely they must have some secret signal of authority. They apparently didn't. The F.B.I. man, dragging Paul with him, managed several times to get his fingers on a door handle; each time, handicapped by his prisoner, he was jostled aside. The fourth time this happened, he let go of Paul's arm. "You stay here," he told him accusingly. Both hands free now, he strode out into the traffic. Paul was left standing alone on the sidewalk. He felt no fresh impulse to try to escape. A trancelike interest in his own situation, in his present reactions to it occupied his whole mind.

He had always liked Sixth Avenue. Although the El had been torn down since he had first discovered this area of New York, the cut-rate bars, the secondhand-clothes stores, reflecting the sheer symmetry of the facing buildings in their windows, were as familiar to his eyes as one of his own half-completed canvases.

They did not look familiar to him now. Even the York Bar across the street, where he had often talked away an afternoon with Kevin, seemed a part of an unknown foreign country. Every detail of its façade, the lettering curving across the window had an outlandish originality that fascinated him.

"Get in." The F.B.I. man had captured a taxi at last. He pushed Paul in and sat down crowding him against the door. Paul looked back through the rear window at the changing perspective of the street. The F.B.I. man gripped his arm again; he was eager to reassert his authority after his struggle for a taxi. He gave the driver an address on Ninth Avenue.

"It's the Immigration Service Building," he added, presumably for Paul's benefit.

He didn't speak again until they were clear of Times Square.

"Why should that Greek sell your passport?" he asked. "They're on our side, aren't they, the Greeks?"

140

"They were neutral then."

"They're not enemy aliens, anyway, I can tell you that."

Paul's trancelike preoccupation was passing. For the first time since Lilian had told him about the waiting F.B.I. man, he was beginning to take a practical interest in his own case.

"Who did he sell it to?" he asked.

"Who?"

"Who did that Greek Calevas, sell the passport to?"

The F.B.I. man hesitated. He was not handling Paul's case. He had only been detailed to pick him up, to take him to MacDonald and then deliver him to the Immigration Service. But he had seen Paul's file. His inability to get a cab outside Rockefeller Center still rankled; his bruised self-importance outweighed his caution.

"We picked up a German agent in Mexico," he told Paul. "He was using your passport."

Paul's claim that he was an American citizen, born in St. Louis, was not, after a few moments' discussion, recorded by the Immigration Inspector who questioned him in the office on Ninth Avenue. Paul realized that his best defense against the charge of not registering for the draft was that a draft board would have uncovered the fact that he was an illegal alien and had him deported.

He admitted under oath that he had entered the United States on a British passport in September, 1939, and that his visitor's permit had long since expired.

Thousands of enemy aliens, of hyphenated Americans, Nisei, Bundists and generally suspect persons had been rounded up since Pearl Harbor. The U.S. Government did not, understandably, feel there was any special urgency about the case of Paul Tagliatti. Paul was illegally in the United States. The Immigration Service, which had recently been placed under the Department of Justice, was not interested in establishing anything else about him that afternoon. It was enough, for the present, to hold him. Paul's birthplace was entered as "London, England." The sheaf of forms and carbons was rolled out of the typewriter. The Inspector turned thankfully to the next of the cases piled on his desk.

The F.B.I. man had disappeared. An elderly Irishman with an incongruous gun bulging under his tunic drove Paul downtown to the Battery. They caught the ferry to

Ellis Island. The second carbon copy of Paul's Immigration report was handed over in a Manila envelope to a younger guard with no gun in the reception room of the detention center.

"Good luck, kid." The Irishman ambled away to wait for the next ferry back to Manhattan.

Paul was given a clean towel and a small piece of yellow soap. A third guard escorted him down a long series of tiled corridors and opened a solid, white-painted door. Paul stepped inside.

There were double bunks against two of the walls, all four neatly made up with sheets, pillowcases and gray blankets. A large, thickly glassed window, screened with wire mesh, faced him as he entered. Beneath it were a flush toilet and a washbasin. There was a strip of coconut matting on the wooden floor.

The guard stepped back into the corridor. Paul was alone in the cell. The door was closed and locked on him from outside.

Alexander Solzhenitsyn says:
"Arrest! Need it be said that it is a breaking point in your life, a bolt of lightning which has scored a direct hit on you?"
And:
"Arrest is an instantaneous, shattering thrust, expulsion, somersault from one state into another."
And:
"That's what arrest is: it's a blinding flash and a blow which shifts the present instantly into the past and the impossible into omnipotent actuality."

Paul sat down on the lower right-hand bunk, holding the piece of soap and the clean towel on his knees. He had not, it was true, been officially arrested, only detained. But he had been brought here under armed guard and locked in a cell. He was not, he knew, going to be tortured or starved or beaten. He was not going to be sent to a forced-labor camp in Alaska.

All the same, if Paul had thought about it, he might reasonably have decided that the F.B.I. was sure to find out about his use of David Tyrrel's birth certificate. On that charge, coupled with draft evasion in wartime, he could expect to be sentenced to four or five years in prison. If the F.B.I. decided, on investigation, that he had also sold his passport to an enemy agent in Mexico, he might get life,

Paul didn't think about it. The moment the cell door closed on him he was aware of an extraordinary sense of euphoria.

It was irrational and inexplicable. Now, at last, he felt, he was going to be able to get on with things. His intelligence did not immediately define what "things" he was going to be able to get on with; he was simply conscious of being at the beginning of a whole new life. It was like the first day of summer holidays as a child; every possibility lay ahead of him now. More than that: it was as though he had just come from a doctor's office: there was no tumor, no need to operate.

Sitting in his cell, Paul began to make plans. As soon as he was permitted to write a letter he would ask Lilian to send him his paints and brushes, some canvases. It was after five o'clock now, but he could tell from the height and size of the window that for five or six hours every day the light in the cell would be fine. The glassed-in bulb in the ceiling was adequate for sketching even now. If he'd had the materials he would have started at once. He continued his exploration of the cell, considering its possibilities as a studio. He wouldn't need an easel: there was a wooden chair at the end of each pair of bunks. He pulled one of them out onto the strip of matting, adjusting it to the window. It was sturdy and didn't wobble; he could prop the canvas against its straight back; all he needed was some way of fastening it there. He remembered that in a paintbox he had left with Angela Anson was a roll of insulating tape. He wondered if Angela would be allowed to bring him that paintbox.

He had been sitting cross-leged on the floor. He jumped up. The thought of seeing Angela had had a startling effect on him. He had treated her very badly; he couldn't understand why; but all that was also in the past now—over. There would be a whole fresh beginning with Angela too. She was obviously part of his new future.

Paul had just made another unexpected discovery. Sometime during the past few hours he had fallen in love with Angela Anson.

I read Paul's letters to Angela from Ellis Island and the

later ones from West Street many times before sending them on to Bone. I made notes and copied out part of them.

They are full of details of his daily life, the men he met in detention, his thoughts. There is no self-pity in them, no apparent anxiety about his future. They are love letters, but of an unusual kind. Paul knew, of course, that his mail was censored; but I don't think that is the reason for their restraint, their lack of physical passion. The tone of them is the self-mockery of an intelligent older man writing to a very young girl, to whom he is cautiously trying to express his love without frightening her away.

For instance? "It's raining today. It makes no difference here, but I think of you just across the bay, out somewhere in the rain with your umbrella. I can see you closing it as you run into the Automat to escape a sudden heavy shower. You sit there at a table alone, or maybe some fortunate stranger shares it with you. The tea bag dangles from your finger. There is a Chinese boy here who says the Chinese discovered tea drinking. There is a Malayan who says the Malayans did. There is a Pole who says nothing."

As things turned out, Paul produced no paintings during the time he spent on Ellis Island. There is a certain irony in the reason for this. If the Immigration Service had been informed about his suspected contact with a German agent in Mexico, he would have been kept in a separate cell. But there was nothing in Paul's file except a note from the F.B.I. that he was "under investigation." As far as the Immigration authorities were concerned, he was a friendly alien, British, with no charge against him except that he had overstayed his visa. They saw no reason for subjecting him to the hardship of solitary confinement. The day after he arrived on the island, Paul was moved into what was regarded as easier, less restrictive detention in Room 211.

"Hit me."
"Stick."
"Dealer pays twenty."

There were always at least three open blackjack games running at the long tables down the center of the hall. The Greek, Polish and Norwegian seamen who formed the majority of the hundred-odd men in Room 211 were exultant

144

winners and noisy losers. Although the room was as big as a basketball court, the acoustics were bad. The high windows, protected with wire grilles, that ran down the right side of the hall were like amplifiers. Every sound bounced off them, acquiring a rattling, mechanical tone and inciting the gamblers to shout even louder. From eight-thirty in the morning, when the men were herded in after breakfast, until eight-thirty at night, when they were returned to their dormitories, life in Room 211 was a chaos of noise.

There was little to distinguish one hour from another. An elderly Italian selling candy and cigarettes wheeled in his trolley for an hour every morning; lunch was a half-hour interval in the dining hall at one; supper another twenty-minute break in the evening; mail was brought and distributed by a guard in the early afternoon. He stood at one end of the hall, yelling, "Kazinsky!" "Andersen!" "Florakis!" until the letters were claimed. For the rest of the twelve-hour days nothing interrupted the gambling and arguing and protesting of the Allied seamen who had been rounded up and brought there, to Ellis Island, in the weeks after Pearl Harbor.

Many of them had jumped ship in the early days of the war. They had settled in Brooklyn and the Bronx, found jobs and girls there among their own national groups. For two years the U.S. Government had tolerated their illegal presence. It was only when America entered the war that the authorities decided to try to get the men back to their ships.

They refused to go. To them, America was now their home. They were eager to volunteer for the American army—service in the armed forces carried automatic citizenship—but they wanted no part of their own national war efforts. No matter who won, they had no wish to end up after the war in Norway or Poland or Greece. Through the windows of the detention hall they could look across the bay to the splendid skyline of Manhattan. It symbolized the only desirable future to them. They would not voluntarily take one step farther away from it.

The U.S. authorities were caught in a tangle of legal impotence. They could not march the men down to the ships under guard and force them on board. At least, not immediately. A separate deportation order had to be filed against each man first. Each man had the right to appeal to Washington before the order could be enforced. With the wartime shortage of typists and file clerks, the whole process took about six months. And for every seaman the government could finally, legally force back on board a ship, there were at least ten more known deserters still to be rounded up.

While Singapore and Rangoon and Bataan fell, the blackjack games continued day after day. They would evidently continue into the foreseeable future.

Because they still had an unoccupied country of their own, British deserters had a tendency to go back to sea as soon as they were caught; there were usually only a dozen English-speaking men in Room 211. Like Paul, they were mainly "special cases." One was an elderly con man who had just been released from prison with a deportation order against him. There was no practical way of returning him to his birthplace in Scotland. It looked as if he would be spending the rest of the war in detention. He was not unhappy about it. After eight years in Joliet, Room 211 was a holiday. He ran one of the blackjack games. He was making a lot of money.

Another was a young man named Peter Willis. He had overstayed a student's visa in the United States and, his income from England cut off by the currency restrictions, had found a job as a hostess in a transvestite night club. It was his bad luck that the place was raided. He was frankly terrified of every aspect of the war. His physical cowardice was so explicit and unrepentant that there was an element of positive courage in it. Peter Willis was hard to talk to, because he kept plugs of cotton in his ears; he was eagerly friendly to Paul at first and then gradually withdrew. He kept more and more to himself, mincing up and down the hall and making derogatory remarks about the Greeks. After a few weeks he began to run a low fever and was sent to the hospital for observation. Paul never heard what eventually happened to him.

There were a number of Burmese, Javanese and Malayan seamen who spoke English. Patient, friendly men, they had no interest in the war; they had never owned any part of the world that was being fought over. Paul helped several of them fill out their long appeal forms to Washington. He was fascinated by the circumstances of their lives which their answers to the questionnaires revealed.

146

"List all addresses where you have lived for more than three (3) months over the past five (5) years."

"Do you remember where you were living in 1937?" Paul would ask.

The Burmese he was helping would patiently shake his head.

"Five years ago, when you were fourteen?" Paul would prompt him.

"When I was fourteen I worked on the docks in Rangoon."

"What was your address?"

"Address?"

"Where were you living?"

"On the docks in Rangoon."

There was a genial, English-speaking Dane who had been a pilot with TACA airlines in Guatemala. At first the authorities were willing to release him if he would volunteer for the U.S. Army Air Corps. He wouldn't. "I am not interested to become an American citizen," he told Paul many times. "I am interested to be sent back to Copenhagen." He was eventually reclassified as an enemy alien and disappeared from Room 211. The enemy aliens, most of them bound for internment camps, were more militantly organized than the Allied nationals. They had demanded and won the right to exercise outdoors. Paul could watch them from the window, marching briskly up and down. The Dane, if he caught sight of Paul, would smile and wave.

The Allied nationals were allowed to exercise only indoors. For four hours every afternoon another hall, like a vast empty greenhouse, adjoining 211 was opened for them. It was cold in February and later, as the summer came, oppressively hot, but Paul usually spent the full four hours there. Great wire-meshed windows ran the whole length of the east wall, framing Manhattan from midtown to the Battery. The pain of the sight was unavoidable; it never lessened. Paul couldn't help projecting himself among those buildings; he could feel himself standing on some familiar sidewalk, the corner of West Eighth Street, Gramercy Park; he could sense the whole animated texture of the city around him. Somewhere over there—it seemed within touching distance—was Angela Anson.

The seamen generally avoided the exercise hall. Paul

idled up and down, enjoying the quiet, with James Moy Yee.

Yee was a young Chinese from Singapore. Paul formed a close, random friendship with him as he had with Bob Steele in Florida. They confided incidents of their past lives to each other, shared every present whim and reflection to pass the time.

Yee had jumped ship in New York five years before. "It was all arranged," he explained. The Chinese, being barred by the Exclusion Act, had organized their own system of clandestine immigration. The job as a galley boy on a Portuguese freighter had been bought for Yee by his father. As soon as the ship docked, Yee went to an address he had been given on Mott Street.

"The old man who owned the restaurant there was expecting me, Tagliatti." James Moy Yee always addressed Paul by his surname, treating him with that ironic respect which the Chinese achieve with such grace. "I paid him the hundred dollars my father had given me and he showed me a piece of paper. It said Harry Sen Yung, Newark, New Jersey, June 4, 1920. He told me to remember that. If any American ever asked me who I was, that's what I had to say. I was Harry Sen Yung, born in Newark, New Jersey, on June the Fourth, 1920, Tagliatti."

In the office behind the restaurant the old Chinese produced a birth certificate in that name. The certificate was genuine. A Harry Sen Yung had been born in Newark on that date. When the child died, the parents had sold the document to the old tong chief on Mott Street. It was a common practice. As soon as James Moy Yee paid over another nine hundred dollars, the birth certificate would be given to him; he would become an American with a piece of paper to prove it. He could get a driver's license, perhaps even someday a passport.

So James Moy Yee became, for all his dealings with Americans, Harry Sen Yung. He got a Social Security card under that name and found a job in a hamburger place on Fourteenth Street. He shared a furnished room with two other Chinese. He was bright and adaptable; he soon lost his Singapore British accent. In spite of the faceless anonymity of being Chinese in America, he enjoyed New York. With the coming of war, he was increasingly anxious to establish himself as an American.

148

"Every week I sent another five or ten dollars to the old man on Mott Street, Tagliatti."

Paul and Yee paused, looking across the bay, their eyes evoking different images from the arrogance of those towers.

"Then one day a young Chinese came into the place I was working." They talked, they became friends. "His name was George Ling." After several meetings, George Ling began to trust Yee; he admitted he was from Hong Kong; he had jumped ship in New York three years before. The similarity of their experience, the common precariousness of their position brought them closer together. In 1940 one of the men sharing Yee's room moved out. George Ling was eager to take his place.

"He was scared of meeting the landlady. She was Italian, Tagliatti." Yee had a charming smile, shy and conspiratorial. "But she was nice. She never bothered us. I told George Ling not to worry. She didn't know one Chinese from another. But he was still afraid to give her his real name. He wanted to give her the name he used at work."

Yee and Paul were both smiling by this time. The name George Ling used in all his dealings with Americans was Harry Sen Yung.

"There must have been dozens of us, Tagliatti. All paying that old crook five or ten dollars a week toward that same birth certificate."

"How did they catch you?" Paul had stopped smiling. He felt a great affection and sympathy for the young Chinese.

"Someone reported me, Tagliatti." There was no resentment in Yee's voice. Acceptance of misfortune was part of his natural generosity. "It was probably that old man on Mott Street, I guess." He looked again at the towers across the bay. "I got picked up a few weeks after I stopped paying the money."

The guard was calling to them from the door. It was time to return to the chaos of 211.

The noisy weeks passed without distinction. Summer came. The gamblers stripped to their T-shirts at the blackjack tables. A dozen Greeks disappeared and were replaced by a dozen others. The Norwegians made a group deal to return to sea without being formally deported; they would be allowed shore leave the next time their ships docked in the United States; they could desert again. Their places at the gambling tables were immediately taken by thirty Yugoslavs who had been rounded up in Chicago. The Yugoslavs were noisier than the Norwegians but not as noisy as the Greeks.

Paul read; he wrote to Angela Anson; she visited him. They were allowed to sit facing each other across a table in another huge hall. The ardor of his feelings for her had made her a stranger to him. Angela was working at the Stage Door Canteen; she talked about the G.I.'s she met there, the sacrifices they were making to the war effort. "He was only nineteen and he had two Purple Hearts."

In a limited way, Paul believed in the war. He believed that the majority of people in the world would be better off if Germany were defeated. Angela's enthusiasm was less temperate.

"Did you know that the Russian soldiers go into battle with a song on their lips?" she asked him. She knew it for a fact; she had heard it on the radio.

At the end of her third visit Paul asked her not to come again. He could feel closer to her in his letters than he could face to face.

She had brought him his suitcase with the paintings and materials Lilian had collected from his studio on Fourteenth Street. He stored it in his locker in the dormitory. Sometimes in the evenings he took out his paintings and unrolled them on his bunk; his hunger to work was so great that he couldn't bear to look at them very often. When he tried once or twice to set up a canvas on a chair in Room 211, he became the immediate center of an inquisitive crowd.

Paul did fill two sketchbooks with drawings during the time he spent in detention. There are several portraits of James Moy Yee, a head of Peter Willis, many studies of the men at the blackjack tables. There is one self-portrait. Paul is lying on a bench, his head resting against the wall. The listlessness of the hands, the expression of the eyes and mouth are a study in indifference. Underneath the drawing is written: "There is safety in numbness." And the date, July 1942. Paul had been in Room 211 for five months by then. Since his original questioning on Ninth

Avenue he had seen no one in authority; he had been told nothing further about the case against him.

At the end of August a guard entered 211 one morning and called James Moy Yee's name. He was told to collect his belongings from the dormitory. He and Paul had only a minute to wish each other good luck. Yee shook hands with his ironic formality. "Goodbye, Tagliatti." Neither of them knew whether Yee was being released or escorted aboard a ship. The routine was the same in either case.

A few days later Paul received a letter from him. Yee was free in New York. "They're giving me a chance to become a Chinese-American," he wrote. "I've got twenty-one days to join the army.

"If I flunk my physical," the letter ended, "I'll see you back in Room 211 on September 19."

Paul never heard from him again.

Three weeks later, toward the end of September, Paul's name was called. He was not told to collect his things.

"Are those the best clothes you've got?" the guard asked him as they walked down the corridor. Paul had a clean shirt and jacket in his locker in the dormitory. He was allowed to change into them and to put on a tie before he was checked out in the reception hall of the detention center. A U.S. marshal was waiting for him there. He was an elderly man in a well-pressed uniform that looked as though it had been made for someone bigger.

"You aren't going to try anything, are you?" he asked Paul diffidently as they walked to the ferry. Paul shook his head.

"Hell, I don't want to use the cuffs on you," the marshal explained. Paul thanked him. He was pleased by the man's decency, his desire to spare his prisoner embarrassment.

They talked desultorily on the ferry; not about Paul; the marshal told him about himself. He was a retread, recalled out of retirement. He was bitter about it. "They wouldn't give me a new uniform. This damn old thing doesn't fit me any more. You can see that for yourself." Paul began to realize that the marshal had been thinking more of his own embarrassment than of his prisoner's in not using the handcuffs. He didn't want to draw attention to himself, to what seemed to him the shameful way he had shrunk.

There was nothing diffident about the young Assistant

U.S. Attorney who questioned Paul that afternoon. His name was painted on his office door in large, confident letters: Joseph G. Dovino. He was brisk and impatient; it was obvious Paul baffled him.

"You come from a decent family," he kept saying as he led Paul through the various inexplicable decisions that had brought him to Calevas' office in Norfolk, Virginia.

"Why didn't you stay in Fulton, Missouri?" he wanted to know. "You had the chance of a good education."

"I wasn't learning anything there."

"How old are you?"

"Twenty-four."

"When I was your age, I'd already graduated from law school."

Paul tried to explain he had never been interested in anything but painting, had never wanted to be anything but a painter.

"Did you ever try to get work from magazines?" Dovino asked.

Paul had to admit that he hadn't. His attempt to explain himself had enlivened him for a minute; he found himself drifting back into his usual detachment. From then on in the interview he knew he was there, the light from the window behind Dovino on his face, the elderly marshal sitting by the door, only because he could picture it to himself.

The Calevas episode was abruptly dropped. Dovino turned a page of Paul's file.

"Why didn't you register for the draft?"

"I was here illegally. I was afraid if I registered someone would check up on me."

Dovino made no comment on that. He turned another page. "Now, this is important," he said unexpectedly. "How did you get a copy of David Tyrrel's birth certificate?"

"I wrote to the town clerk in Woodstock for it."

"Who told you you could do that—just write to the town clerk?"

"No one."

"Did your friend Kevin Fallon put you up to it?"

"No." It crossed Paul's mind that it must have been Kevin who had told the F.B.I. about the David Tyrrel birth certificate. "No," he repeated. "No one put me up to it."

Dovino stretched his arms above his head. It was a threatening, not a relaxed, gesture. "I'm asking you to tell me the truth," he said softly.

"I am."

"It was Kevin Fallon's idea." Dovino evidently felt it would be a more rewarding case for him if he could bring Tyrone Fallon's son into it.

"No."

"Okay." Dovino lowered his arms. The interview was over.

The marshal walked Paul back to the ferry. That day was the first time in seven months Paul had been on a street. The buildings and store windows, the people around him, particularly the women, had the bright artificiality of a scene from a Technicolor movie. Paul noticed this with interest. He glanced at the marshal to see whether he too looked as vivid, as improbable as everything else.

"You should have told him the truth," the marshal warned him sympathetically. "You should have admitted your friend put you up to it."

Paul decided the marshal was essentially sepia.

"Dovino didn't like your lying like that. It'll go against you."

Paul's name was called again on October 14. This time he was told to collect his belongings. His paintings were already rolled in a cardboard tube with sheets of paper between them. He packed his materials and brushes, his sketchbooks, his few clothes into his suitcase. The same elderly marshal was waiting for him in the reception hall. His uniform seemed to fit him better; perhaps he was growing again now that he was back on the job.

He was less friendly this time. When Paul moved a few feet away from him on the ferry, he ordered him to stand still. An olive brown Dodge was parked outside the landing shed on the Manhattan side. The marshal drove Paul uptown through the trucking and vegetable district. Paul didn't ask where they were going. He felt that everything he saw—two men wrestling a crate into a loading platform, a woman with a baby carriage full of cabbages—had an isolated quality that gave it an unusual significance. He knew he would never forget the exact look of those two men, that woman. The street names became familiar: Morton, Barrow, Christopher. They were on the

153

west side of the Village. A few blocks away was the Old Colony Bar; its doors open; people, perhaps even people he knew, wandering in and out.

The car stopped outside the door of the Federal House of Detention on West Street. Paul was taken to the admission office, fingerprinted and booked in. That afternoon he was driven down to the Federal Court House in Foley Square and arraigned. .

The charge against him was "Misrepresentation." "In that he entered the United States under a false name, misrepresenting himself as an American citizen, and showing a birth certificate other than his own, and to which he was not entitled."

Paul pleaded guilty. He was taken back to West Street to await sentencing.

24

I COULDN'T STAY IN NEW YORK LONG.

Every time I went out for a few minutes, to buy a carton of milk or to meet Kevin in the Square, I was frightened sick by the thought of the shadowed flight of stairs waiting for me to return. I could feel the Donners moving in on me from behind at every tread on those stairs until I was safely locked back in my apartment.

I wanted to go to Mexico to try to fill in the last seven years of Paul's life after he had gone back there at the end of the war. I had to wait until I heard from Bone. When I sent him Paul's letters to Angela Anson, I asked him for addresses in Mexico, the names of people Paul had known there. There was no sense in leaving before I got his reply.

While I was waiting, I forced myself one morning to leave my apartment and walk over to the Federal House of Detention on West Street.

The black warden, or marshal, or whatever he was, who let me talk to him in his office there was friendly enough in a wary way. He obviously suspected me of being some liberal crazy, eager to believe all prisoners are innocent victims, but I suppose I was a break in his usual routine. He told me a good deal about the house of detention, the kinds of cases they handled there, the way the place was run. "It's the junkies who spoil things for everybody else." He wouldn't look up any records without authorization. I had a right as a citizen, he told me, to get the disposition of the case of *United States v. Paul Francis Tagliatti* from the Federal Court House in Foley Square.

"Anything else you want to know?"

As I was thanking him, he pulled a card out of a file and wrote down an address in Brooklyn for me. "Go and see old Mick Hogan," he suggested. "He was a guard here for forty years. He's retired now, but the war—he'd have been here in those days."

I thanked him again. There was no point in putting myself through the ordeal of the stairs to my apartment more often than I could help; I took the subway down to Foley Square; I exercised my rights as a citizen in the records office of the courthouse; I went on to Brooklyn.

Mick Hogan, retired, lived in the top half of a semidetached house in the Borough Park section. I caught him at home. I had the feeling I would have caught him at home any time of the day or night. He wouldn't open the door to me at first; he stood talking to me through a three-inch crack: a puckered mouth full of false teeth, a porous nose, part of an eye.

"I don't want to buy any books," the mouth told me. "I don't get time to read."

It wasn't until I mentioned the Federal House of Detention that Hogan unhooked the chain and let me see the rest of him.

"You been to West Street?" he asked. "They sent you here?"

I told him my usual story about the book I was researching. He had never heard of any American painter except the one who used to do things for *The Saturday Evening Post*, "I can't remember his name." He asked me to sit down.

It was cold in the small living room with its leather chairs, its stiff couch, its bare tidiness. The air conditioner groaned like the steam pipes at the Milroy.

"I've got it warm in the winter and cool in the summer," Hogan informed me when I started slightly at the first groan. He sat down in one of the leather chairs and put his feet up on a stool. He had been telling me the truth about his reading habits. There were no books, not even a newspaper in sight. How many people in cities sit alone in their cells doing absolutely nothing for hours at a time? Perhaps they watch television. I couldn't see one in Hogan's cell. I sat down on the end of the couch near him so we could hear each other above the air conditioner.

"What was he there for?" he asked when I mentioned Paul's name again.

"Misrepresentation."

"Nineteen forty-two?"

"Yes."

"That explains it. Misrepresentation. There were more cases of misrepresentation in those days than I've seen—"

156

He hesitated, showing me his false teeth for a moment in a painful smile. "Every two-bit kid, too young to get in the army, was walking around Broadway in a colonel's uniform. They weren't maybe doing anything except looking for free drinks, girls. But they had to be arrested. Misrepresentation. We got them all on West Street."

"It wasn't that kind of misrepresentation." I explained the charge against Paul. The Howard Coster photograph of him was in my handbag; I showed it to Hogan. He wasn't sure he could recall Paul's face. It wasn't surprising; Hogan had seen a lot of prisoners in forty years. Their faces were not what had remained in his memory.

"Ass holes," Hogan told me. "I seen more ass holes than any other man in the United States. Of course, that was my special job, being in charge of admissions. Every time a new man came in on my floor, or one of the prisoners was taken to court or somewhere. Every time he came back, that was my job. I didn't have to touch them. We weren't supposed to handle the prisoners anyway unless one of them was violent. I just used my flashlight."

I said I thought that was very interesting. I tried to get him back onto the more general subject of the house of detention, the war years.

"Louis Lepke. Brenner, the spy. Of course, Brenner wasn't as famous as Lepke. They didn't give spies much publicity in wartime. But he went to the chair too. And those four Nazi saboteurs. They did. All those fellows that were electrocuted. A lot of them are still famous today. I seen all their ass holes. Dozens of times."

I wasn't lying. It was interesting in a way, the thought of Hogan sitting there alone, hour after hour, remembering his unique relationship with the condemned.

To commit a federal crime in America requires a degree of specialization and intelligence. Murder, rape, most crimes of violence are state offenses. Paul's companions on the fifth floor of the Federal House of Detention were mainly educated men, forgers, embezzlers on a national scale. Many of them had been brought in from federal penitentiaries for questioning or to act as witnesses against former colleagues. It was a break for them being on West Street. They had enjoyed the novelty of the long train ride from Kansas or Georgia. They enjoyed the relief from monotony, the comparative physical freedom which

157

the change meant for them. In welcome contrast to the seamen in Room 211, they behaved with deliberate, studious calm.

They slept in groups of eight or ten in large cages built around the floor admission area which contained the guards' desks. During the day most of the cages, including the one to which Paul was assigned, were left unlocked. The prisoners were free to visit one another. They played bridge and chess, dominoes and cribbage at the long metal tables in the center of each cage. They wandered the corridors and exchanged news of friends in Atlanta and Leavenworth. They lay on their bunks and read books from the prison library.

The only prisoners deprived of this casual freedom were the spies and condemned murderers. Louis Lepke Buchalter, like the prize lion in the zoo, had a cage to himself, directly facing the guards' desks. He didn't spend much time there. Engaged in a long, finally unsuccessful effort to bargain for his life with the federal authorities, he was allowed to change into a conservative business suit every morning and was taken off by two guards for daylong meetings with his wife and lawyers. Paul could see him return every evening, a neat, gray-haired man with the tired, commonplace look of a neighborhood druggist. He would strip naked in his cage, hand his clothes to the young guard with bad teeth who was in charge of admissions and submit to being searched before dressing in his prison denims. It was difficult to believe he had once ordered men killed with that same patient indifference.

There were other prisoners for whom Paul felt more sympathy. One was a young Swiss, André Brenner. Brenner, a steward, had been arrested aboard the *Kungsholm* on one of its trips to New York. He admitted he had been carrying letters between people in the United States and their friends and relatives in Germany. He denied he had ever known what those letters contained. Like Buchalter, he was trying to bargain for his life. He was imprisoned alone at the end of one of the corridors leading off the admissions area. His meals were brought to him by a guard. Twice a week he was taken to the showers. The rest of the time he spent locked in his cage. There was no attempt beyond that to isolate him from the other prisoners. There was little need to. Brenner's English was tortuous and halting. When he found that Paul spoke French, he welcomed

158

his company. Paul would set up a board on a chair just outside Brenner's cage and they would play chess together, Brenner stretching his thin hand between the bars to move his pieces. It was another of Paul's random friendships. They were about the same age, but otherwise opposites in appearance and character. Brenner was dark with neatly combed hair, meticulous and unimaginative.

He rarely spoke about his case. Sometimes toward the end of a game, when he could see he was winning and his mind wandered from the chessboard: "It's ridiculous," he would say softly, incredulously in French. "It's absurd. I've done nothing."

Paul came to have great affection, a horrified sympathy for the young Swiss.

I believe that Paul's *Chair* was painted not in 1946, as the Museum of Modern Art Catalog says, but in the summer of 1943, when Paul was in London and the terrifying isolation of Brenner's situation was still sharp in his memory. Brenner was electrocuted in June of that year.

Paul spent a month in the Federal House of Detention. During that time he was questioned several times by a federal probation officer. He was lucky in the man, Robert Reeves, who was assigned to his case. Reeves wanted to be a writer; he found Paul less baffling than Dovino had. As part of his investigation he talked to Lilian Fletcher; she showed him some of Paul's paintings. Reeves thought they showed promise.

On November 12, 1942, Paul was sentenced in the U.S. Court House, Southern District of New York, to two years in a federal penitentiary.

The sentence was suspended on condition that Paul waive his right to appeal against deportation.

Paul was rearrested by the Immigration Service outside the courtroom. He was allowed to retrieve his belongings from West Street and was escorted aboard the British merchant ship S.S. *Oakwood*, of the Jacobs Line.

The Captain signed Paul on as an ordinary seaman. The *Oakwood* sailed the next day in convoy, bound for the Persian Gulf.

25

THE STAIRS WERE STILL WAITING FOR ME.

I had spent several hours in the public library after leaving Mick Hogan, trying to find out what conditions were like on British merchant ships during World War II. They were primitive. The crew usually slept three to an eight-by-seven-foot cabin. There were no showers, no running water except a cold faucet on deck. If the men wanted to wash themselves or their clothes they had to heat a bucket of water by running steam into it from the winches. By a system of extra watches known as field days, the crew worked a sixty-four-hour week at sea without overtime. The food from the galley was generally uneatable. The men lived mainly on bread and jam and tea.

I had a hamburger in a Chock Full o' Nuts and took a taxi home. There is usually a light in the hall, a sixty-watt bulb hanging above the mailboxes. It was out. I stood in the street doorway, listening. The hot night air was full of sounds. Two young men in jeans passed along the sidewalk.

"She might be in Minetta's," one of them said. I thought of going after them, asking them to walk up my stairs with me. It didn't seem like a sensible idea.

In the end I did what I usually do when I have to get something over with. I didn't think about what I was doing. I ran for the stairs and kept on running; my key was already in my hand; because I was acting automatically, it fitted into the keyhole at once. Some psychologists say you can drive a car better that way.

I snapped on the lights, slid home all the bolts, fastened the chain and leaned against the door.

Pad Donner was sitting in my comfortable chair.

I had two of the bolts pulled back and was reaching for the chain before he dragged me away from it. He was

160

wearing a seersucker suit; it was too tight in the arms; I could feel the damp heat of his flesh through the sleeves as he wrestled me across the room. I was trying to reach the window; I was going to scream down into the street. The window was closed. I screamed into the room. The seersucker arms were no longer holding me. He didn't try to put his hand over my mouth this time; he hit me with his fist below my left eye.

All the times I've seen men punching each other in films, even twice in life—once outside a pawnshop on Third Avenue and once in a bar in the Village—hadn't prepared me for the experience myself. It terrified me. I stopped screaming at once.

I was lying on the floor, saying, "Don't. Don't. Don't." I was probably whimpering. At least, I didn't say, "Please."

He got me to my feet by twisting his hand into my hair and pulling my face toward his. It startled me in a stupid way because I was wearing my hair up; I couldn't understand how he had managed to get hold of so much of it. His face was beaded with moisture like a chilled glass. He turned me around and pushed me across the bed.

It wasn't until I was crouching there with the familiar bedspread under one elbow that I realized what he was going to do to me.

To be truthful about it, I felt a sense of relief. I'm a physical coward. I've always been frightened helpless of anyone who wants to hurt me. A girl at school, who used to pinch my skin and then twist it until I cried, could make me do anything she told me.

After all, I'd been screwed before. Screwed, not made love to, by some man I'd gone to bed with, and then realized too late that his whole attitude toward my body was repulsive to me. It had been unpleasant and I'd felt sick afterward. Once in a hotel room in Spain where there was no washbasin I douched with Vichy water. But being screwed doesn't *hurt*.

Pad Donner was tugging at my skirt with both hands, trying to pull it up under my hip.

"I'll do it." I said that. I didn't want him to touch me any more than I could help. His hands were so damp and eager. I crumpled my dress up around my waist. I took my pants off myself, too, wriggled out of them.

Oh, God, don't let him make me take my bra off. Don't let him touch my breasts.

He didn't. He wasn't interested in me in that way; he had no urge to linger over me. I was no more than an aperture to him; something he had to get into at once. The worst part was the feel of his nervous hand searching between my thighs; I parted them as reflexively as I would have kicked my foot if he'd struck me below the kneecap.

My eyes were closed, screwed up tight, by that time. I made myself do what I had done in the hall: not think about it until it was over. It must have worked; there was no actual moment when I knew he had entered me, when it was suddenly done, the way ordinary things are, a lock of your hair cut with a click of the scissors, a light turned off.

It wasn't anything that went on and on, either. He was crawling off me. I kept my eyes closed; I didn't want to watch him pulling up his pants. The one thing I never wanted to have to remember was the look of his face at that moment.

I heard his steps cross the room; he hadn't taken his shoes off; I don't know why that struck me as so disgusting. The water was running in the bathroom. I wished it was pouring and washing over me. I could hear him retching above the sound of the water.

Oh, God, don't let him vomit. Don't let him leave that presence of himself behind.

The metallic sound of the bolts; the clink of the chain; the hesitant rasping of the hinges; the gasp and thud of the door closing.

I kept my eyes closed, listening to the silence for three or four minutes, until I finally believed he was gone.

I went straight into the bathroom. Even living alone I have never kept it hanging over the bath; it was folded away in a plastic case in the medicine cabinet. I turned on the hot water.

"Do *not* douche."

Why not?

"It will destroy evidence."

I didn't care. I knew I wasn't going to call the police. It wasn't only that I couldn't stand "detailed, intimate questioning." I didn't want to face any questions about Pad Donner; not even when I asked them myself.

How did you meet him? Go on, answer that for a start. I tried to pick him up outside the Museum of Modern Art. I was wearing a thin silk sari at the time; I slipped my

162

hand under his arm and practically rubbed myself against him.

I douched.

Thank God, I was on the pill. At least I didn't have that to worry about.

Why are you on the pill? Answer that. Because I never know when I'm going to meet someone I want to go to bed with. On the spur of the moment, as they say? Yes. Like Pad Donner? No. Like Walter, yes, but not like Pad Donner.

I took a shower. After the shower I had a hot bath. I lay down flat in the water and ducked my head. That still wasn't enough for me. I got some shampoo, turned on the shower again and rubbed lather right into my skull. Then I rinsed it all out again.

The clothes I had been wearing were lying on the floor. I picked up everything except my shoes and rammed them down into my trash can. I knew I would never wear them again.

What are you trying to obliterate? Memory. I knew that was a lie.

"Do not feel guilty. Being raped is not your fault."

I knew it wasn't my fault, but I didn't believe it. What did I wear such tight blue jeans *for*? For *comfort*? Why did I feel pleased when someone whistled after me in the street?

I had to talk to someone. I had to explain to someone why I had taken my own pants off. Because an inadvertent scream of pain, forced out of you, is the worst violation. I tried three girls I knew who would listen to me. None of them answered the phone.

"What do you do after you have been raped?"

The mimeographed leaflet was still pinned to the notice board beside my door. Perhaps there was a phone number on it, someone at the women's organization I could talk to. I walked over to the board and pulled out the map pin. There was something stuck to the board behind the leaflet. It fell to the floor. I picked it up.

It was a thin paperback book, a Tauchnitz edition of *The Island of Penguins*.

I was whistling as I made myself a cup of coffee. The discovery of that book had changed all my feelings about what had happened to me. My cowardly, passive behavior had become an act of defiance. I had put up with the

163

worst the Donners could do to me and I had beaten them; they had searched my whole apartment for that book; they hadn't found it. What did it matter that Pad Donner had "had" me? Having the Tauchnitz would have given him far more satisfaction than I had.

I sat down in my comfortable chair. I didn't feel guilty any longer; I felt vindicated as I started to examine the book for whatever Walter had found in it.

26

I FOUND IT toward the end of the book, on page 98.

The name Carlos Camara had been written in the margin, followed by San Miguel Allende, a town in central Mexico. Below it was a column of initials.

W.I.B.

S.A.E.

T.N.

P.F.

A.G.A.

C.

M.O.H.

M.W.G.

There was no mistaking the small, close handwriting; it was there again on the tile page of the Tauchnitz: his signature, Wexford Bone, and the date, 1951. I know nothing about ink, how it fades or congeals, but it looked to me as though Bone's signature and the name Carlos Camara and the initials had been written at about the same time. They had certainly been written with the same fountain pen, one with a hard fine nib that had indented the paper. The back of the book had been rubber-stamped, "The American Bookstore, Mexico, D.F."

Feeling melodramatic, I tore out page 98, rolled it into a thin spill and sewed it into the lining of my bra. I matched the new stitching so carefully to the old that only someone with a magnifying glass could have seen the difference. Once you yield to the spirit of conspiracy it takes possession of you; I tore the rest of the Tauchnitz into small pieces and flushed them down my john a handful at a time.

There was only one letter for me the next morning. It wasn't from Bone. John Horne had found his carbon of the letter he had written Paul, care of the Haggard Gallery, in 1945, to congratulate him on his show and his feature in *Life* magazine. "I thought you might want to quote from it in your book," he said in a covering note. I didn't feel like eating alone in my apartment; I read Horne's letter over breakfast in a coffee shop on Fourth Street. Most of it was about Horne himself; he was taking a postgraduate course at the University of Chicago; he described his progress with that insulting facetiousness—"Even you may have heard of García Lorca by now"—which students used to make friendship in those days; perhaps some still do; but the last paragraph fascinated me. Even though Paul had never answered Horne's letter, I couldn't believe he had ignored the information Horne sent him.

I found a phone booth that had a legible Manhattan directory in it. An Edna Haggard was listed on East Thirty-sixth Street. At the third try the dime stayed in the machine and I heard the phone ringing somewhere, maybe even in the right place. There was no answer.

I spent some time in the public library looking up the reviews of Paul's show at the Haggard Gallery. They were all unrestrainedly enthusiastic. I copied some of them into a notebook. Edna Haggard still didn't answer her phone. I didn't want to go back to my apartment. I looked up the feature in *Life* magazine and made notes on that.

The paintings Paul showed at the Haggard Gallery in 1945 are unlike any of his other work. But his style is recognizable in them, that effect of controlled vehemence which distinguishes everything he painted. They were exhibited soon after the Christmas of Bastogne, when the war in Japan looked as if it might continue from island to island for years. Their timeliness is probably what made them such a popular success. They are "war paintings." A line of disparate freighters in convoy, clumsily vulnerable against the Atlantic horizon; ships unloading in port, Bombay, Liverpool, Basra, a locomotive being hoisted ashore in Abadan. And always faces: the faces of Arabs, Indians, English dock workers; seamen, at work, eating, sleeping, in bars and brothels. There are sixty-three altogether, most of them water colors. They are inevitably journalism, reporting, rather than imaginative statements. None of them was included in Paul's retrospective show at the Museum of Modern Art. The forty-one of them owned by Wexford Bone are insured for a total of four hundred-thousand dollars.

I walked down Fifth Avenue to Thirty-sixth Street. Nobody answered Edna Haggard's doorbell. I still didn't want to go back to my apartment. At the corner of the block a young man who looked as though his face hurt asked me for a dollar. I gave it to him at once. He didn't thank me. I walked up Third Avenue and went into the first movie house I came to. The film was about a man renovating a church in Venice. He had large, interesting ears with exceptionally long lobes. He kept pulling at them.

When I rang Edna Haggard's bell after the movie, the answering buzzer sounded at once. She was waiting in a doorway on the second floor; but not for me; I could tell from her irritated expression she was expecting someone else.

"Yes?" She didn't move out of the doorway.

I started to tell her my usual story.

"So you're the girl," she interrupted me. She looked amused. "Come in."

I followed her into her living room. She bolted the door. It was one of those apartments you still find in parts of New York: light floor boards, scatter rugs, a grandfather clock. Except for the original Braque over the fireplace, it looked as though the interior of a Cape Cod cottage had been transported to the city. Edna Haggard fitted in it like a ship in a bottle. She must have been in her sixties, smaller than I am, with white frizzy hair, a long face and a prominent lower lip like a sheep. I couldn't be sure, but I thought she *was* the woman who had bumped into me in front of Paul's *Chair* at the Museum of Modern Art.

"Sit down, dear." She stood in front of the fireplace; there were real logs in it; I could imagine her roasting chestnuts over them in wintertime, popping corn.

"How long have you been working for Wexford Bone?"

There was no point in saying, "Who?" or "What?" There was nothing sheeplike about her eyes as she turned on the light beside me so that she could watch my face while I answered.

"About two months."

"What are you getting out of it?"

"It was just a job at first." That wasn't quite true. "And then— Now— I don't know. I'm interested in Tagliatti."

"In finding those paintings." It wasn't a question. For a
167

moment she reminded me of Walter; she was difficult to keep in focus.

"No." I could see she didn't believe me. "Not particularly, anyway." She still didn't. "I'd like to find them, of course. Anybody would."

"What would you do with them?"

I know it sounds absurd, but I'd never thought about that.

"Give them to Bone, I suppose."

"Why?"

"They're not mine."

"They're worth at least two million dollars."

She *was* like Walter.

"That's not going to do Paul any good now," I said. "The important thing is that they should be shown."

"Do you think that's going to do Paul any good? Now?"

I could see what she meant.

"You must believe in an afterlife." Her voice was serious, but her small blue eyes weren't. "You must believe Paul's up above somewhere, wanting you to find his pictures so they won't be lost to the world."

It was difficult to answer that. I had found out enough about Paul to know one thing about him. He wanted to survive. It might not make any difference to him now whether he did or not. But in painting those pictures he had tried to determine some part of the world we inherited from him: I didn't want to see that continuity broken by the accidental misplacement of his canvases.

"Have you fallen in love with him?"

"Who?" I couldn't help saying it this time; it was automatic.

"Paul."

I had never thought about that either. Can you love someone who's dead? Is love always a demand, an expectation of response? What response can the dead make? I didn't know.

"Why did you come to see me?" Edna Haggard asked. "What did you want to ask me?"

I didn't want to tell her about John Horne's letter. "That exhibition you gave Paul," I said. "It was such a success. Why didn't he follow it with another show?"

She offered me a cigarette. I don't smoke. I waited in silence while she took one for herself and fitted it into an amber holder.

"It was Wexford Bone who brought me those war paintings of Paul's. The Haggard Gallery was quite well known in those days and I had a reputation for giving young painters a break. I was interested, of course. Anybody would have been, particularly at that time. The war was still going on. Very little had come out of it yet in the way of art. Everyone was waiting for the post war generation of painters and writers. Paul Tagliatti looked like being the first of them. Bone had only brought me a dozen water colors. I told him I would have to see more. He said Paul was still working on the others. I told him to come back when they were finished and to bring Paul with him. It was difficult to take Bone seriously at first. He was still in his twenties, and there was something sissy about him. He looked like a college boy with a case of arrested development. Bone told me he was willing to put up all the money for the exhibition himself—pay for the printing, the publicity, the rent on the gallery." Edna Haggard turned her hands palm upward. "What could I say? I said yes." She sat down facing me. "Bone put up the money, all right, and he delivered the rest of the paintings on time. But he didn't bring Paul to see me. Paul didn't even come to the opening."

"He may have been afraid to," I suggested. "Afraid of the Immigration people. He'd been deported in 1942, and the only way he could have got back into the country was by jumping ship."

She was obviously disappointed that I knew. "You're right," she admitted. "An Immigration Inspector came to the gallery a few weeks after the opening and started asking me questions about Paul. I told the inspector the truth. I'd never met Tagliatti and I didn't know where he was. The only way I had of getting in touch with him was through Bone. I called Bone and warned him as soon as the inspector left. He didn't sound in the least disturbed. Or surprised, either. He told me Paul had already left the country. He was in Mexico City. The next day *Life* magazine called me. The Immigration people had been to see them too by then, and they were worried about it. They'd given a lot of space and publicity to a British deserter. They'd played him up as an American seaman, a kind of war hero. I talked to Bone. We decided the best thing to do was close the exhibition as quickly and quietly as possible. A lot of the pictures had already been sold. Bone offered to buy the rest. I was glad to let him have them at half their marked price."

She put out her cigarette. I waited for her to go on.

"Magazines come out every week. Exhibitions open and close. The war ended that summer. The atomic bomb. There was a flood of postwar novels and paintings. A year after his show, his feature in *Life* magazine, hardly anyone remembered Paul Tagliatti's name. But I did. There was something about the whole thing that worried me. I knew thousands of foreign seamen must have jumped ship here during the war. Thousands of them must have been caught and deported. I couldn't believe some immigration official had remembered Paul Tagliatti's name after three years and tied it in with those pictures in *Life*. That was another odd thing. Why had that inspector come to me first instead of going straight to the *Life* editors with his question? I had a friend in Washington, a lawyer, who had contacts in the Justice Department. I asked him if he could find out anything for me."

She started to walk up and down in front of me, excited, persuasive. I felt like a member of a jury.

"He found out that someone had informed on Paul. The Immigration Service had received an anonymous letter with details of his deportation from the country, the name of the ship he had deserted, everything. I can guess who wrote that letter, can't you?"

I could; I didn't say so. It would have spoiled her pleasure in her story, and I was beginning to like her.

"Wexford Bone."

The doorbell rang in the kitchen. She took my arm. "You'll have to go." Whoever it was she had been expecting was outside on the street.

"There's a back door at the bottom of the stairs," she told me. "Wait out in the yard until they've come up."

I didn't argue with her. I ran down the flight of stairs. That spirit of conspirarcy had possessed me again. I was grateful to it; it kept me from being frightened. I found the back door, opened it and stepped out, but I didn't close it completely; I stood watching through the two-inch opening. The answering buzzer sounded. They walked straight toward me for a few steps before they started up the stairs. I almost ran. Edna Haggard was right: it wouldn't have been a good idea for them to find me in her apartment.

I waited until I heard her greet them, heard the door of her apartment close, before I walked through the door and out onto the street. At least I didn't have to be afraid of my own stairs that evening. Pad Donner and his mother couldn't be waiting there for me. They were safe in her Cape Cod apartment with Edna Haggard.

I took a taxi home; I made myself some scrambled eggs and sat in my comfortable chair. Edna Haggard's guess was right; I was sure of that; it was Bone who had written that anonymous letter to the Immigration Service about Paul.

I was beginning to understand why.

"It was difficult to take Bone seriousy at first," Edna Haggard had told me. I hadn't taken him seriously myself that first evening at the Museum of Modern Art. But even in his twenties, disguised by a look of arrested development, he must have had a furious will. He had always had money; not the money of a city boy whose friends in those days would be driven to school by a chauffeur too. "He came from some place like Charleston, only smaller," Kevin had said. Wealth in a small Southern town would have assured him not only privilege but power. He could buy envy, dependents. Later, in the Village, he continued to buy them. "He didn't have any friends. All he had was money. He used it to make people hang around. Everybody was so goddamn broke except him." The war changed that. "Anyone— If you weren't in uniform, the G.I.'s figured you were queer. They used to beat you up—" Bone with his ulcer and his sissy look suddenly found himself frightened and alone. All his hangers-on had been scattered by the war; when they came to New York on leave they didn't need him; the bars were full of guiltily overage men eager to buy drinks for anyone in uniform. It must have been a bitter, humiliating time for him. There is something reproachful about a silent phone, a doorbell that never rings.

One evening in the late summer of 1944, Bone's doorbell did ring. Paul had just jumped ship in New York. He had to avoid most of his old friends. He must have known, with that reckless detachment of his, that there would be no intensive hunt for him, but if they checked his file, they would find Kevin's name in it, Lilian's, Angela Anson's. He had no desire to see Angela, anyway; he had come to despise his feelings for her as a romantic illu-

171

sion he had indulged in to give color to his aimless months in detention. Paul wasn't looking for illusions that night; he was looking for a place to hide, a place to work.

Bone was exactly the person to help him. Paul had counted on that. The interdependent nature of their relationship, tacitly understood that morning three years before when Paul had taken money from Bone's wallet, was openly recognized now. Paul had his carefully hoarded canvases with him, the dozens of notes and sketches he had made at sea. Bone had been one of the first to recognize Paul's extraordinary talent. It was confirmed for him by the paintings Paul showed him. Finding Paul a place to live on the upper West Side, safely away from his old Village associates; supporting him; hiring framers for his pictures; arranging and backing an exhibition for him; acting as his agent with Edna Haggard and *Life* gave Bone the reassurance and satisfaction he needed. He was no longer impotent; Paul owed more than success to him; so long as he was a British deserter, illegally in the country, he was helplessly in subjection to Bone.

And then that letter arrived from John Horne in Chicago. It was forwarded to Bone's address by the Haggard Gallery. Given Bone's possessiveness, his urge to retain control of the smallest details of Paul's existence, it was inevitable that he should open it.

I took it out of my handbag and read the last paragraph again.

Hey, boy, remember all that trouble you had about your birth certificate? Well, I did, and I happened to think of two things. (1) Your father was English. And what with being a wop (Sorry!) I guess he was proud of belonging to dear old England and all that, what? (2) Chicago is the nearest British Consulate to St. Louis. So I went there to see if I could find out anything about you. Well, old chap, you can forget your British accent now. Your birth was registered at the British Consulate here, all right. But that doesn't make you a limey. You were still born in St. Louis. So you're just an old Missouri boy like me."

It isn't surprising Paul never answered Horne's letter. Bone knew it would free Paul of his dependence on him. Paul could finally prove he was an American citizen; the

172

U.S. Government had never had any right to deport him; he could establish himself in New York at last with a more than promising career in front of him.

Bone never showed Paul the letter.

Instead, he warned Paul to get out of the country; the immigration authorities were after him; they had been asking about him at the gallery. Paul believed him at once. Bone gave him his own 4F classification and draft card to check out with. They were about the same height; both had "hazel eyes"; it was necessary only to alter the color of hair from sandy to blond. Paul had no trouble imitating Bone's signature on the draft card to get a Mexican residence permit; he had always had exceptional talent as a copyist.

A few days after Paul arrived in Mexico City the immigration authorities did start asking about him at the gallery. An announcement from Edna Haggard about the closing of the show, which Bone sent on to Paul in Mexico, confirmed that Bone's warning had been well founded. Good old Wexford had helped him get away just in time.

Bone had waited until Paul was safely in Mexico before writing that anonymous letter to Washington. He did not want to have Paul caught and deported. That was never part of Bone's plans for Paul's future.

I heard from Bone the next morning. He sent me several addresses at which Paul had lived in Mexico. He gave me the names of several people who had known him there in the last seven years of his life.

There was no mention of Carlos Camara in San Miguel Allende.

27

THE MEXICO CITY I FOUND was a very different place
from the one Paul had returned to in 1945. It wasn't only
that it had grown to three times its size. It had had an atmosphere of extraordinary clarity then: clean shadows,
sharp lines and colors. It was blurred with smog now.
There had always been a frantic quality about the city,
overcrowded, overstimulated, a perpetual rush hour. The
feverishness had become more self-conscious now; it was
like a communicable infection.

When I got off the bus from San Miguel Allende, I
asked a taxi driver, in my halting Spanish, to take me to
the railroad station. In most cities there is still an area
around the station that has withstood the present; the Hotel Grande del Estación in Mexico City had. In my
shabby, high-ceilinged room with its grimy French windows, I might have been back in the days of Díaz.

I bought a street map and for the next few weeks visited
all the addresses, tried to find all the people whose names
Bone had given me. Most of the buildings Paul had lived
in had been torn down; most of the people who had
known him were dead or untraceable. I did find a few—
among them an English painter, Lucia Collingham—who
could tell me some part of the circumstances of those last
seven years of his life in Mexico. Back in my hotel room I
spent hours lying on my bed with its leaden pillows, looking through Paul's Mexican sketchbooks, trying to fit those
parts together.

One morning when I went to Thos Cook for my mail
there was a note from Edna Haggard. Bone had given her
my address; she was in Mexico City, staying at the Capital
Hotel; she wanted to see me.

She answered from her room as though she had been
waiting for my call. I arranged to meet her in the bar that
evening.

174

I got there early. The Capital was an American hotel, not one of the most expensive ones, but trying hard to maintain that impersonal tastelessness, which Americans abroad find so reassuring. The cocktail bar was paneled with something that had been treated to look like wood. There were genuine handpainted pictures on the walls, two of which were identical.

Edna Haggard was punctual to the minute. I had forgotten how sturdy she was. She didn't waste any time asking me how I liked Mexico. With chilling seriousness she told me she was glad to see me again. She p-s-s-s-ted at the waitress. We both ordered tequila limonadas. They came with paper napkins with illustrated jokes on them. Mine had a drawing of a girl in a bikini carrying an airline bag. "Why do turistas fly to Mexico in the wintertime?" "Because it's too far to walk." Edna Haggard was fitting a cigarette into her holder; she was watching me.

"Bone tells me you've been in San Miguel Allende."

I had written to him from there because I hoped for some reaction from him; maybe I was getting it; I nodded.

"What made you go to San Miguel?"

"I was looking for someone."

"Did Paul ever live there?"

"Not as far as I know."

"Then who were you looking for?" Edna Haggard was smiling. "Why don't you tell me the truth, dear?"

Among the Cheyenne there were people called "contraries." They laughed when they were sad. They said yes when they meant no. They smiled when they were angry. Ever since that evening at the Museum of Modern Art, I had been meeting and living with people like that: Bone, Walter, the Donners, that girl at the St. Martin's School of Art in London. They were all contraries. Edna Haggard was still smiling at me.

"I had the name of someone in San Miguel who might be able to help me."

"Who gave you his name?"

I smiled back; I decided to be contrary too.

"John Horne."

"Who's John Horne?" I felt her curiosity was genuine; she had never heard of John Horne before.

"A man in Missouri who used to know Paul."

She lit her cigarette; she wasn't interested in friends of Paul's from the Middle West.

175

"Did you find the person you were looking for?" she asked.

"No." At least that was true. I had spent a week in San Miguel Allende. I went to the post office, the town hall, two priests, the shops, the cantinas, eventually all the pensions and hotels. No one there had ever heard of Carlos Camara. There was no Carlos Camara anywhere else in any Mexican phone book either.

"I'm going to tell you something about your friend Walter Oliver." Edna Haggard was no longer being contrary; she was getting to the point. "Walter told someone I know—"

"The Donners."

"Yes." She didn't even blink. "He told the Donners he had found a book in the South of France. A paperback edition of *The Island of Penguins*. On a page of that book was a list of eight paintings. *Woman in Bar, Sixth Avenue El, Portuguese Fisherman*. Walter wasn't sure what the other titles were. They were only listed by their initials. 'T.N.'—"

I could have told her the title of that one: *Tenampa Night*. I didn't interrupt.

"—'A.G.A.,' 'C.,' 'M.O.H.' and 'M.W.G.' Above the list Paul had written the name and address of the friend he had left those canvases with."

"Paul had?"

"Paul's name was on the flyleaf of the book."

So Walter had been contrary with the Donners too.

"What did Walter want?" I asked.

"What do you think he wanted?" She rubbed her thumb and first finger together. "Money."

"How much?" I couldn't help being curious.

"A hundred thousand dollars."

Modest Walter. "Why didn't the Donners give it to him?"

"They're not stupid. He wanted the cash in advance before he would even show them the book."

Practical Walter. So he had turned to Bone for the money. In writing to Bone he would have to tell him the truth: "I've got *your* book with *your* name in it." I remembered what Walter had said after feeding me that acid: "Bone knows where those paintings are, doesn't he? He knows who's got them." And then the insistent question he had asked: "Why did he have to hire you to get them for him?" Walter had been anxious to know the answer to that before he kept his appointment with Bone that night.

I had, really, known for some time that it was Bone— Bone with Berman's help, probably—who had killed Walter. I still didn't understand why. Perhaps it was simply that Bone wasn't the kind of man who was preapred to bargain with Walter for those paintings. It was a frightening thought. I realized I had been telling Edna Haggard the absolute truth when I said I'd given those missing canvases to Bone if I found them. I would give them to him, unconditionally, at once.

"Where's that book, Jane?"

"I don't know." I tried not to blink.

"Perhaps you don't know where it is now. But you saw it, didn't you?"

"No." It made my eyes smart. "I was with Walter when he found it at the villa, but he never showed me what was in it."

"All right. I suppose I'll have to believe you." She blew through her holder to clear it; it made her cheeks puff out; for a moment I saw her again as I had at our first meeting: a cozy little woman, roasting chestnuts, popping corn over a wood fire.

"What are your plans now, dear?"

I had been avoiding thinking about that for several days. Sooner or later I had to go to Tetacata, the small town to the south where Paul was killed. There was a question there I had to try to answer; I had looked up the bus schedule, but I didn't leave; perhaps I was already afraid of that answer.

"I'm not sure." I hedged. "I still have a few people here to see."

She opened her bag and took out an envelope. "I almost forgot. Bone asked me to give you another address." She lifted the paper closer to her eyes. "Señor— I can't read my own writing—It looks like Mendez."

"Who is he?"

"A picture framer."

"A picture framer?"

"Bone thinks he did some work for Paul."

"Thank you. I'll go and see him." I waited for her to give me the address.

"We can go together if you like."

177

"When?"

"Why not now?" She put the envelope back in her bag. "Do you have anything to do this evening?"

I didn't.

I know I was being stupid as I followed Edna Haggard through the lobby of the hotel and helped her into a taxi outside. But I didn't know it then. In any deception it's the detail that convinces. I would never have got into the taxi with her except for that single focused fact. A picture framer. It simply didn't occur to me that she had made *that* up.

28

WE STOPPED OUTSIDE an apartment house in the south-western district. From the shoddiness of the lobby it was a prewar building. The new buildings in that area are shoddy too, but in a less honest way.

The elevator took us, reluctantly, to the fifth floor. Edna Haggard rang the bell beside one of the unnumbered, badly fitting doors. A young man in a dark suit opened it at once. She asked for Señor Mendez.

"Yes," he said. "Come in. My father's expecting you."

I noticed the automatic way he spoke; I wondered *why* his father was expecting us; but I had no acknowledged impulse to withdraw until I had taken another step forward. The step brought a small hallway into sight, a table with a phone on it. Beside the phone was a light straw hat; it had a scarf folded around it for a band.

Beyond the elevator I had seen an archway leading to the stairs. Up or down? The question surfaced in my mind before I even moved. The young man reached for me with both hands. Edna Haggard was like a pillar behind me; as I turned I bumped into her, hard. She didn't give; I had to squeeze past her.

I was halfway to the stairs when the young man slipped in front of me; he smelled of Mexican cigarettes and lavender; he reached for me again. The sluggishness of the elevator was the thing that saved me; the door was still ponderously sliding closed.

Another inch to my bust and I couldn't have managed it. The door was slow, but it was heavy and determined. It did its best to crush my arm as I dragged it in after me. It heaved to a stop. It wasn't closed. The pointed toe of a man's shoe was wedged into the gap at floor level. Four fingers appeared at the level of my eyes. I kicked at the shoe and swung my shoulder bag at the fingers. I went on

179

doing it until they were both withdrawn. I pressed the button for the ground floor.

The slowness of the elevator was against me now. The young man and Pad Donner, even Edna Haggard could easily race it down the stairs to the entrance lobby. They were all going to be waiting for me there. Up or down? I pressed the *Alto* button and then 8; I went up to the top floor.

There was a narrow flight of iron steps leading up from there. The door at the top of them was unlocked. I stepped out onto the roof.

The roofs of the older apartment buidlings in Mexico City are like a second, more tranquil town built above the other: a town of open spaces, washing lines and simple houses once intended for maids but now usually converted into studios and penthouses. I was lucky with that particular roof; the whole block had been built as a single project. I ran to the low wall in front of me and climbed over it onto the next building.

Fear is inherent in the act of escape; it is contained in it like a dream in sleep. I was breathless; my skin was damp and chill by the time I had half-circled the block. I hurried to the parapet overlooking the street. I could feel Pad Donner behind me in the darkness, but I couldn't see him down there outside the building.

The door to the stairs was unlocked here too; the elevator was just as reluctant; I could hear it groaning somewhere below. I used the stairs. As I crossed the entrance lobby I felt stark naked, wading through space. I reached the heavy glass door to the street; I pressed my face against it and peered out. A young man in a dark suit was standing, waiting, on the sidewalk.

My mind was evidently working on two quite separate levels at that moment. The sight, the vision I have always associated with awareness recognized the young man instantly: Pad Donner's accomplice. Whatever was controlling my body made me push open the door and walk straight past him. He wasn't young; he wasn't even wearing a suit.

Five steps beyond him I started to run again. I had just sense enough to run in the right direction, away from that whole apartment block, toward a main intersection I could see several streets away. By the time I reached it I was almost rational. I could think about where I was running to, as well as what I was running from. I couldn't go back to my hotel; Edna Haggard knew where I was staying; she had winkled that out of me in the cab. She seemed to have made a decision for me too; I hadn't the least desire to stay on in Mexico City any longer; I might as well go straight to Tetacata.

I found a taxi a block away and asked the driver to take me to the bus station.

Safe in the moving taxi, I felt lightheaded and exultant. I wondered what they would have done to me if I hadn't recognized that hat. They would have held me there, probably, while they searched my room at the hotel. Then Pad Donner or his mother or both of them ... But I didn't want to think about that after all. They wouldn't have got anything out of me anyway; I was sure of that; it's easy to be staunch in theory.

I suddenly had to know if the bra I was wearing was the one I had sewn the page from the Tauchnitz into. I couldn't remember which one I had put on that morning; I buy my bras two or three at a time in Macy's; they all look alike. I unbuttoned my blouse and lifted the cup off my breast. I had made an ink dot inside the one with the page in it. It was there, all right. They might have found that page if they had stripped and searched me carefully enough. Carlos Camara San Miguel Allende. Those five words they were after with such rabid persistence; would they have told the Donners any more than they did me? There was no Carlos Camara in San Miguel Allende.

The taxi had stopped for a red light. I glanced at the street sign on the corner. We had crossed San Juan de Letrán and were skirting the old city.

I was always bad at algebra at school. I was better at geometry. Whatever deductive ability I have is visual. Given part of a pattern my eyes can sometimes complete it; my mind can't deal with abstract unknowns at all. I had thought about that address, Carlos Camara San Miguel Allende, so often since I'd come to Mexico that it had become as meaningless as a row of x's to me.

Whatever it was that happened in my mind at that moment—whether it was simply being there in the center of Mexico City—those five words suddenly ceased being an abstract equation.

I saw Bone pausing on a street corner, slipping that Tauchnitz from his pocket, taking out his expensive fountain pen, turning to page 98, writing that careful reminder to himself.

I leaned forward and told the driver I had changed my mind. I didn't want to go to the bus station after all.

I thought I knew where those eight missing paintings were.

29

THE TAXI LET ME OFF at the corner of the Avenida Pascal where the street began. I stood and looked up at the blue-and-white sign on the wall of the corner house. Calle de San Miguel Allende.

Bone had not, I hoped—I was almost sure—picked a page at random on which to write down the name of that street. Three blocks farther on, the numbers of the houses reached the even nineties. 92, 94, 96 ... So many of the addresses I had hunted up in the past few weeks had turned out to exist only in the past; the buildings Paul had known had been replaced by office blocks, hotels. But this house with its bulging wrought-iron bars over the lower windows looked as though it had been there a long time. The number 98 was bolted to the wall beside the door.

A light was showing upstairs. I rang the bell; I had to ring twice more before there was any sound from inside. The door opened a few inches.

"Who are you? What do you want?" a man's voice asked in Spanish.

"Señor Carlos Camara."

"What do you want?"

"Señor Camara?"

"Yes. What is it?"

With the hall light behind him it was hard to see his face; his hair was dark, combed forward across his forehead; he looked younger than I'd expected; about fifty, I thought. I asked him if I could talk to him for a moment.

"I'm just going to bed."

"Please." I was hampered by my Spanish; I couldn't remember if the word for important was the same as it was in English; I tried *urgente*.

"You're American."

"Yes."

"You've come to the wrong place." He spoke effortless English with a slight American accent. "I'm no longer—"

"Please let me come in." English made it easier for me to plead with him, to explain my urgency. "I've come all the way from New York."

"Oh, God. Oh, Mother of Heaven," he said in Spanish. But he opened the door. I stepped inside; he closed and bolted it. He hadn't been making excuses when he said he was just going to bed; he was wearing pajamas and a woolen dressing gown.

"Come in here." He turned on a light and led me into the living room. He was of medium height, thin, gray-skinned. Seeing him pass I would have taken him for a doctor or lawyer; he had that testy look I associate with those professions.

"I thought I was finished with you importuning Americans. I thought I'd heard the last of you." As he faced me under the light I noticed his hair had a mahogany shade at the sides; he had tinted the gray out of it. "All right. What is it?"

"I'm a friend of Wexford Bone's."

"Who?"

"Wexford Bone."

I repated the name as clearly as I could. The irritated expression in his eyes didn't change.

"Wexford Bone." I tried again; I couldn't think of anything else to say.

He shook his head. I was sure he wasn't pretending. The name meant nothing to him.

"It was a long time ago," I tried reminding him. "Nineteen fifty-one. Wexford Bone was an American. He was a tall man. He must have been in his thirties then. But he looked younger, I think. He was big and rather—rather fat."

"My dear young lady. In those days I met dozens, hundreds of Americans every week. Many of them looked younger than they were. Americans often do, for some reason, but never mind that now. And most of them were overweight." He took a packet of Delicados from his pocket and lit one of them in a resentful way as though he hadn't intended to smoke any more; I was forcing him to it.

"For over twenty-five years," he went on, waving out the match and dropping it into the fireplace. "Until my

184

mother died last winter and I was fortunate enough to be abe to retire, I was a clerk at the American Consulate here."

He didn't like me; I couldn't blame him; he had spent all those years listening to the complaints, the indignation of every American tourist who felt his nationality entitled him to make a nuisance of himself. I was another one of them, harassing him in his retirement, just as he was going to bed.

"Señor Camara," I said. "I'm really, honestly sorry to bother you at this time of night. I wouldn't if I could help it, but I have to fly back to New York in the morning." My contact with so many contrary people had weakened whatever integrity I'd ever had. "You see, the man whose name I told you. Wexford Bone. You see, he's ill, he's dying."

"Is he?" Carlos Camara didn't seem to regret it.

"When you—when he knew you down here in 1951, he was going off to France. He was living here, staying here, in Mexico City, when he knew you, but then he suddenly had to go off to France on business."

"Did he?" He walked over to the sideboard and poured himself a glass of sherry; he made me feel I was forcing him to do that too.

"He asked you to look after some things for him while he was away. He brought them here to your house."

"It was my mother's house then."

"He wrote down your name, this address, as the place where he left his things when he went to France."

"What things?"

I couldn't answer that precisely. I tried to imagine what kind of container Bone would have chosen to conceal those canvases. "A suitcase," I said. "A large suitcase. Almost like a trunk. It had his name on it." I was sure of that; Bone would always proclaim his possessions as he had written his name on the flyleaf of that Tauchnitz.

Carlos Camara didn't say anything for a minute; he sat, smoking his cigarette, sipping his sherry.

"You really are the most extraordinary people. I've always thought so. All those years at the Consulate. I've never been able to make up my mind exactly what it is about you. It's more than presumption. It's a kind of self-righteousness. This attitude that you're entitled to anything. Anything. You come here in the middle of the

185

night. You stop me going to bed. You tell me that twenty-three years ago a man left some things here. A suitcase, a trunk. You expect me to remember it. Of course I'll remember it. How could I forget a big, fat American? You expect me to find that suitcase for you. Now. At once. Search the whole house for it." He put the sherry glass down on the arm of his chair; he looked at me. "Don't you?"

I didn't do it on purpose. It might have been a belated reaction to my escape, to being frightened. I didn't howl; I hardly made any noise at all; but I could feel all the muscles of my face collapse, my mouth fall open in a gargoyle gape.

"Mother of God." My crying embarrassed him. He finished his sherry without looking at me. "Why is it so urgent?" he demanded. "Suddenly, now, after all these years."

"It just is." I didn't want to lie to him any more. He seemed to me the first straightforward person I had met for weeks; I liked his honest irritation with me.

"All right." He stood up. "I don' remember this man Bone. I don't remember agreeing to look after anything for anyone. But I may have . . ."

I followed him to the door, drying my face with Kleenex out of my bag.

"If I did, I probably put it down in the cellar." He opened a door at the end of the hall and turned on a light. "You can look if you want to. I'm going to bed. Call up to me before you leave so I can lock up after you."

I tried to thank him. He shrugged and left me. I could hear his slippers making a soft strapping sound as he climbed the stairs to his room.

The cellar was at the bottom of a twisting flight of steps, a large room that looked as though it might once have been a kitchen. It had obeyed the usual law of cellars: the more space there is for unwanted rubbish, the less of it gets thrown away. I started to tunnel through the accumulation of half a century, lifting down grimed cartons of letters, photographs, stacks of newspapers and magazines, bed ends, hatboxes, roller blinds, scrabbling to find Bone's suitcase underneath.

There was a trunk which I opened; it was full of women's clothes, a black fur as fragile as a puffball on top. There were only two suitcases, one tin and the other

186

cardboard, both too small to contain rolled canvases. I opened them anyway. One was packed with *National Geographics;* the other was empty except for a baby's shawl and a handful of cheap cutlery wrapped in newspaper.

I was getting desperate, heaving and sweating as I tried to lever aside some loose planks, searching for a cavity beneath them, the space that must contain Bone's suitcase. There was nothing beneath them except more planks. I went back to the trunk. Perhaps under those women's clothes . . .

I almost missed it. It was leaning against the wall, behind a broken piano, expensively made of stitched canvas and leather: a gun case.

I pulled it out. It was as heavy and rigid as I would have expected it to be with a gun inside it. A leather tag was fastened by a chain to the handle. I had to wipe the dirt off it before I could read it.

"Wexford Bone. Brill House. Columbia, S.C."

The gun case was closed with a zipper, and the zipper fastened with a small brass padlock. I found an iron stair rod, twisted like barley sugar, and after a lot of fumbling managed to screw it into the loop of the padlock and force it open.

Of course the zipper was stuck. I pulled the whole thing over to a clear space on the floor, braced my feet against it and heaved at the stair rod. The canvas-and-leather case gaped open.

There was no gun inside it. The weight and rigidity came from curtain rods, fastened together with adhesive tape and packed around with cloth. I slid them out. There was more wadded cloth behind them.

I was behaving like a fever case by this time as I started to tear it out.

I caught sight of a metal rim. Reaching through the cloth, I could make out the shape of a tube. I dragged out some more rags. The tube came free. It was about four feet long, as big around as my ankle, made of aluminum.

Running my fingers around inside the top of it, I could feel the stiff edges of several rolled canvases.

I did not think, Here I am holding two million dollars' worth of paintings. On Walter's dead heart, I swear I didn't.

I did want—more, I think, than I have ever wanted to do anything—to pull those canvases out of the tube, un-roll, reveal them. It was extraordinary how much like living things they seemed to me. They had been shut up in this cellar for twenty-three years. I wanted to set them free, put them up all around the walls, give them back their purpose, their life, look at them, show them.

I had been down there long enough already; Carlos Camara might start wondering what I was up to. I left the curtain rods on the floor and threaded the aluminum tube back into the gun case. The zipper stuck nine inches from the top. Pushing with the stair rod, I managed to force it almost closed. I cleaned off my hands and dress as well as I could with Kleenex. The light switch was at the top of the steps. I turned it off and closed the cellar door after me.

"You found it?"

Carlos Camara was stending in the hall. I had my arms wrapped around the gun case as though it were my only child. He walked toward me.

"That?"

I lifted the label so he could see Bone's name.

"You said it was a suitcase you were looking for."

"I didn't know exactly what it would look like."

"A gun."

"No." I bent the canvas to show him its softness. "There's no gun in it."

"What is there in it?"

He had been more than kind to me. I liked him.

"Some paintings. They're all rolled up inside a tube."

"Whose paintings?"

I lifted the label again. "They belong to Wexford Bone."

He looked at the case I was still hugging in my arms.

"A shotgun." He might have been tasting the words, trying to identify the memory of their flavor. "I remember him now. A big, soft man. Polite, ingratiating."

He seemed interested in trying to recall as much as he could; I felt I might as well make the most of his interest. "Did you see him often?" I asked.

"No." He pulled the pack of Delicados out of his pocket and then pushed it back again. "I only saw him two or three times. He invited me to lunch. I remember, he did tell me he was going away. He asked me if I could look after his shotgun for him. He didn't want to leave it at his hotel. He said it was a very expensive gun. It had been made by one of those people in England." He reached out and touched the case for himself. "There wasn't any gun?"

"No."

"Paintings?"

"Yes."

"Then tell me something." The pack of Delicados came out of his pocket again. "What happened?" This time he lit one. "Why didn't he ever come back for them? If those paintings are so important, why did he wait twenty-three years before sending someone for them?"

I kept my arms around the gun case. I tried to smile. There were things I couldn't tell him, things I couldn't tell anyone yet. They were too improbable; they rested on too many fragile suppositions. I still had to make that journey to Tetacata before I could answer his question myself.

"I don't know," I said. "At least, I'm not sure."

30

It was great being back in Mexico.

Paul had always loved the clarity, the hard sharpness of the country. From the sale of his war paintings, his fee from *Life* magazine, he had over four thousand dollars. He found a rooftop studio not far from the Reforma. In the first two and a half years after the war, he completed eighteen of the paintings shown at the Museum of Modern Art; he added another canvas, *Charlotte*, to his private collection, those hoarded paintings he considered his best work.

Charlotte Draper was a clerk at the American Library. At twenty-eight Paul's face had hardened out of any suggestion of prettiness; he was an exceptionally attractive and good-looking man. Watching him come in to change his books, Charlotte decided she was in love with him several weeks before he noticed her. She was an eager, practical girl, who enjoyed doing things for him, coming to his studio and cooking him meals, taking care of his laundry, sweeping out. Paul made love to her, gently and fervently, often at unexpected times. For a while Charlotte demanded no more from him. Paul felt he had what he had always wanted: affection; freedom from insecurity and intrusion; time to think, look, experiment, paint.

Perhaps no change is ever gradual, neither growth nor deterioration; it consists of a series of sudden developments alternating with inertia. Paul did not gradually tire of his life in Mexico. The change in his attitude was marked, and caused, by separate events.

There was the evening he had just finished his portrait of Charlotte. He took it down from the easel and stood it against the wall. Wanting to compare it with his other work, he pulled out several of his recent pictures and stood them around it. What he did next was not the result of any conscious decision. When Charlotte came by after the library closed she found Paul surrounded by his paintings. They covered every wall, the bed, the tables, the floor. She had seen most of them before, but never all displayed at once. She stopped in the doorway, overwhelmed by the blaze of energy and color.

"Having a show?"

Paul didn't answer at once. He gathered the pictures and stacked them back in their usual places, facing the wall.

"Where could I have a show?" he asked. "Who'd give me one? Edna Haggard?"

There were letters from Bone. He wrote every three or four weeks. It was an exciting time in New York, a lively interval between the war years and the McCarthy era. Bone enclosed enthusiastic reviews of the new plays, the new books and films, the new young painters. Paul replied with noncommittal post cards.

There were the three occasions when Paul managed to persuade a Mexican art dealer to come and look at his work. Each of them praised everything he was shown. Each explained that he was not, himself, in the least chauvinistic. But who in God's name wanted to buy American paintings in Mexico?

There was a letter from Edna Haggard. "There is still a strong feeling in America that the war was worth fighting ... out of the question at this time to arrange an exhibition for a young man who . . ."

There were increasingly querulous and resentful demands from Charlotte.

There was the morning Paul woke up after a prolonged drunk and realized he had less than a thousand dollars left.

"No man is thoroughly miserable unless he is condemned to live in Ireland." The 4F, Bone, who had spent the war years in the Village, knew that sooner or later Jonathan Swift's words would be true of any constraint, exile in any country.

He timed his first visit to Paul in Mexico very accurately. Paul had been drinking more and more, barely giving himself time to recover from one bat before starting the next. He had quarreled finally with Charlotte. He had for the moment lost any urge to paint. It was not one of his usual intervals of quiescence. He was not assimilating new impressions and ideas for a further burst of work. For the first time in his adult life he was bored.

Bone's chatter about the postwar "cultural explosion," his detailed description of films and exhibitions which Paul hadn't been able to see did little to lessen his boredom. Bone's praise of his new paintings meant nothing to him. All he wanted from Bone was practical help. He wanted him to arrange, to finance another show of his paintings in New York.

Bone was evasive. It was not the right moment. Paul's desertion in time of war was known to a section of the press, and probably by now, through Edna Haggard, to many people of the art world. If Paul showed his paintings in America there would be a spurt of righteous indignation in the newspapers; there would be no buyers. He warned Paul to wait.

Paul couldn't wait. Living in Mexico was still reasonably cheap because it was a poor country. But because it was a poor country it was practically impossible for him to earn any money there.

Bone stayed only ten days that first time. The morning before he flew back to the freedom and excitement of New York, he offered to buy three of Paul's new paintings. He paid him nine hundred dollars for them.

Soon after Bone left, Paul gave up his roof-top studio. He moved down to Taxco and rented a small furnished house there for twenty dollars a month. For a time the change, the reassurance of having sold some of his work, even though only to Bone, gave him a fresh stimulus. The first five months in Taxco he finished another nine paintings; he added another canvas, *Man on Horseback*, to his private collection.

Taxco was full of Americans. The letter from Edna Haggard followed by Bone's exaggerated warnings, had made Paul feel that the reason for the closing of his wartime show in New York was a matter of public knowledge. Although he felt no personal guilt about what he had done, he was defensive about what he assumed to be the attitude of Americans toward him. He avoided them.

The Americans in Taxco, in fact, knew nothing about him. They did not remember his paintings in *Life;* they had no idea he had ever been a seaman. But in a small

town dependent for entertainment on social gregarious-
ness, they did resent his unfriendliness. They made up stories to explain it: he had been forced to leave the United
States because of something unspeakable he had done to a
young boy, a black girl, a schoolteacher; Paul's victim
varied with the private fantasies of the narrator; he was
lucky he was allowed to stay in Mexico.

One of the few Americans who weren't influenced by
these stories was a man of about his own age, Jim Wager.
Jim had a small income from some property in Florida
and had never done anything since the age of sixteen but
drink, seduce girls and play chess. It was another of Paul's
incongruous friendships. He never discussed his work with
Jim, never showed him any of his paintings; but they saw
each other almost every evening; they drank and seduced
girls and played chess together.

One night when Paul had taken his queen Jim tipped
the board over.

"Let's get out of here," he suggested. "I'm sick of this
place."

"I'm not going to Paco's Bar again tonight."

Jim searched through some dirty shirts until he found a
letter. "I got this from a friend in Paris yesterday." He
waved it in Paul's face. "Read it. He's on the G.I. Bill
over there. He says if you've got a few dollars it's like
catching flies. Not these hangdog schoolteachers you get
around here, either. He's had dancers, trapeze artists. He's
been *shacking up* with a contortionist."

It wasn't the thought of the contortionists he was missing that hurt Paul. He had been to school in Paris; he and
Lilian had spent a week there on their way to New York.
He thought of the blue haze of the city at dusk, the smell
of Gauloises and wine, the yellow glow of the cafés in
St.-Germain. He had over thirty paintings stacked in his
house; he was sure he could get them shown in Paris.

"No," he told Jim. "I like it here."

Jim left the following month. Paul made other occasional friends; they came for a month or two, rented
houses, drank tequila limonadas, went back to America or
off to Europe.

Paul stayed.

Lucia Collingham told me that around that time—she
was vague about the date—Paul did try to get to Europe.

193

He thought he might be able to obtain a British passport. Lucia knew a man at the British Consulate in Mexico City. Paul asked her to talk to him. She put Paul's story to her friend as a hypothetical case: a British seaman who had jumped ship in New York and entered Mexico illegally using someone else's papers. Lucia's friend at the Consulate advised her not to involve hrself; he asked her not to tell him the seaman's name. He suggested that if the man wished to return to the U.K. he should give himself up to the Mexican authorities and ask to be deported. He might or might not be held in jail while all the formalities were being completed; that was up to the Mexicans; the British could not interfere. But if the man could prove he had been born in the U.K. the Consulate would ensure beforehand that the British officials at the port of entry admitted him.

The next winter Paul moved to Chapala. A dull, undefined town on the edge of a receding lake, it was cheaper than Taxco. He rented an adobe house in the grounds of a pension. There were few American residents in the area; the tourists who came to the pension tended to be retired people from the Middle West. A group of wealthy English homosexuals had built houses along the lake front; Paul found some distraction among them for a time, then quarreled with them when he rejected their advances.

Again Paul worked well for a few months. The boredom that began to distract him after that was as sensory as pain. It was as though his eyes themselves were bored with seeing. He could not bear to look at his room, the trees outside, the lake, the hills. His eyes avoided them as they would have flinched from a glaring light. He would wake with a sense of hopeless tedium; there was nothing to look forward to, not that day, not ever. He could argue himself out of this conviction at times, drive himself until his enthusiasm for painting revived. After an hour or two, staring at his own work, he would be overwhelmed by a sense of futility. He seemed to be living in a soundproof room. No matter how desperately he shouted for attention, no one heard him. It wasn't fame he wanted, only the barest acknowledgment that he existed; that he was there, trying to express a man's whole experience in those exhausting, agonized brush strokes.

Who would ever even see his paintings?

By the time Bone came back in 1949 on his second visit, Paul had left Chapala. He was living with a working-class family in Mexico City, drinking in the cantinas around the Tenampa, making few efforts to work at all.

Bone was staying at the Reforma Hotel; Paul refused to go there to see him; they met at a small restaurant on San Juan de Letrán where most of the customers were shabbily dressed. Paul was late. He had been drinking, but not disastrously; there was a stage in every evening when he had had only enough tequila to feel normal. He was cheerful and assured as he joined Bone at the table.

Bone was thirty-five at that time. Both his parents were dead, and as the only heir he had recently inherited another eight hundred thousand dollars from his grandfather's estate in South Carolina. He was no longer living in the Village; he had bought a house in Brooklyn Heights overlooking the river. In the past four years his natural selfishness had hardened into egotism. It was backed by determination; he was still prepared to be treated with occasional contempt; he was shrewd enough to recognize it as an inevitable reaction to his plump, boyish looks, his stilted celibacy; but he no longer forgave it.

He recognized Paul's exact condition as soon as he sat down. He saw that he was desperate; he understood that liquor had temporarily changed desperation into impractical hope. When Paul, after another two tequilas before dinner, began to tell him his plans for the future, he listened and nodded with apparent encouragement.

"I can get across the border somehow," Paul told him. "I've still got your draft card. I can bluff my way through with that. I'll go out to Los Angeles. There's a lot of interest in new painters out there at the moment. I won't have any trouble getting a show."

"Under your own name?"

"Any name."

Bone suggested that it seemed a pity to forfeit the reputation Paul had already established.

"That was four years ago. That damned show at the Haggard Gallery. Who the hell remembers it now?"

"I'm sure the critics do." Bone made it sound like a compliment.

They ordered dinner. The hot Mexican food had its usual sobering effect on Paul. He drank a bottle of beer and followed it with a brandy.

195

"You think any stupid critic's going to recognize my work after all these years?"

"Your work's unmistakable." Another compliment.

"There have been thousands of shows since then."

"Whatever name you use someone's bound to connect you sooner or later with Paul Tagliatti."

"I'll take a chance on that." The brandy was helping.

Bone said no more until they were parting; he would take a taxi to his hotel; Paul would drift off to the Tenampa. They paused on the corner of Madero.

"I don't think you should count on crossing the border with my draft card."

It was as close as Bone ever came to a threat. Paul wanted to smash his fat head against the wall behind it. He didn't; a lack of vitality restrained him; to hurt Bone, to frighten him, didn't seem worth the effort. More and more often lately he had felt the same exhausted indifference. Nothing seemed worth the effort.

Bone flew back to New York the following week. Before he left he bought another five of Paul's paintings. He paid him fifteen hundred dollars for them.

Paul moved decisively away from all his recent associations. He found a large, sparsely furnished room out near the university. He completed only one painting, but he worked several hours every day making sketches for others. What he needed, he began to feel, was a girl, the exploring freshness of an affair, to help him rediscover his interest, his curiosity. He met Iris Sherwood through an old friend from Taxco. She was studying Spanish literature at the university, more as an excuse for being a thousand miles from Kansas City than from any interest in the subject. Her ambition was to be a professional photographer, to do picture stories for magazines; she spent hours every day wandering around with a Rolleiflex. Like most girls Paul had been attracted to, Iris was practical, but she had more gaiety in her nature than either Charlotte or Angela. She was excited by Paul, admired and was envious of his talent; she responded to his interest in her with a laughing affection which was new and endearing to him. It was inevitable that within a week of their first meeting they should go to bed together.

Paul had been drinking very little that evening. They had dinner and returned early to his room. They kissed for a while and then rather formally undressed and got into bed like two people on their wedding night.

Paul was completely impotent. Iris was good-humored and encouraging. It happened to everyone at some time or another, she said. What disturbed Paul was that it had never happened to him before. They tried again a few nights later. This time he succeeded in partially entering her, but almost immediately became limp again. Iris pretended this was quite natural too. She ducked her head down under the sheet; she was loving and eager; Paul achieved another fragile erection; again he could not sustain it long enough to give either of them pleasure.

The next day, alone, Paul tried to masturbate. His penis felt tender to the touch and peculiarly cold; he found that although he could just make himself come, his sexual vitality was so low that even the orgasm caused him only a partial erection. A few days later he began to develop a dull aching in his thighs; his ankles and the soles of his feet felt inflamed. He realized, with relief, that he was physically ill.

The young doctor at the American hospital was more interested at first in Paul's ability to pay than in his symptoms. Reassured about this, he examined him with brisk contempt and told him he had probably picked up something. Blood and urine tests were negative; there was no discharge; but further tests revealed an unspecified infection of the semen. Paul was given several injections of penicillin. They did not seem to have any effect on him at all.

A doctor in Mexico City to whom I described Paul's case guessed he probably had a form of prostatitis: a virus had pocketed in his prostate and was causing an infection. There is no effective cure for this condition. The virus is immune to antibiotics, which at best can only lessen the symptoms. The illness is not critical in itself: it will normally disappear within two or three years. But Paul had no way of knowing this at the time; his infection was never diagnosed; and the active symptoms can be acutely unpleasant: a lessening of sexual vitality; pains and lassitude in the legs; periods of exhaustion alternating with extreme physical tension and irritability; general depression.

Iris wrote Paul a cheerful note full of exclamation

marks; she sure hoped he wasn't mad at her. He didn't reply to it. Any ordinary obligation—making a phone call, talking to another person—had become a desperate effort to him.

Paul had lost his gift for separating himself from threatening situations. He was ravaged by almost constant anxiety. He awoke to it every morning. The moment he became conscious of the circumstances of his life he felt a flush of panic. His renewed awareness of each detail of those circumstances was accompanied by a muscular spasm. He tried to analyze the causes of his fear. Many of them were rational enough. At thirty-two he was ill, with some venereal infection no one seemed able to explain or cure; he was impotent, unknown, trapped in a country in which he had no future, no hope of earning the barest living; he was almost destitute. But irrelevant, apparently harmless reflections could arouse the same panic. The most ordinary objects—a running faucet, a shoe—would fill him with loathing. The casual memory of two trees he had once tried to sketch caused him anguish.

The only thing that helped him at all was alcohol. He no longer drank wildly; he was admirably self-disciplined about it. Throughout the long wracked days, he put up with all the predictable afflictions of his condition, the fatigue, the recurrent impulse to flee, to hide himself in some close dark space, to run out into the street and scream. At five he allowed himself his first drink, an inch of light rum in a tumbler of water. After two of these, fear left him; his mind began to work normally; he could think calmly, even optimistically, about himself; he could hope that next day he could wake without panic; he would soon have the confidence to work again.

He would go out to a small cheap restaurant nearby, eating over a book as he had years ago as a student in London. For the rest of the evening until he went to bed, he would limit himself to three or four carefully spaced drinks, only just enough to preserve his tranquillity and make it possible for him to sleep.

Bone flew to Mexico for the third time in August, 1951. He soon realized the extent of Paul's helplessness. Some of it he gathered in the calm evening admissions Paul made to him about his illness, some of it during their rare daytime meetings. It was time, Bone saw, to make his last move.

"You wouldn't believe how much things have changed lately in America," he told Paul one evening over dinner in a restaurant.

"How?"

Bone took his time explaining that. There was a finer line these days between those who had wanted to see Germany defeated and those who had wanted to see Russia victorious. The phrase "premature antifascist" had become a dangerous accusation. A good war record was still important in politics, of course, but it was a doubtful advantage in the arts. Bone waffled on like this through his chicken *mole;* over his ice cream he hovered closer to the point. He thought there might be galleries, even galleries on Fifty-seventh Street, that would consider Paul's work on its own merit now, particularly if there was money behind it.

It was the thing above all Paul wanted to believe in: the hope of having his paintings seen. No promises were made, but he went to bed that night in a mood of fragile serenity. It was gone by morning, replaced by doubt and despair. Bone hadn't meant it; it was just talk; he would do nothing. At two o'clock, in a rigor of anxiety, he forced himself to go out into the street and call Bone from a café.

They met in Paul's room an hour later. This time Bone decided to be more specific. In his daytime condition Paul could not be reassured with promises.

"You need rest," Bone told him. "You need security to work."

"How? What the hell are you talking about? How can I ever have any security in Mexico?" Even in his worst periods of despair, Paul could control his voice; it was level and reasonable; but he could not control his imagination, the images of destitution that tormented him. "They'll turn the lights off in this place any day now. After that it'll be the rent. They'll lock me out. I've been through all this before in New York. At least I could work in a department store there. I've thought of carving crucifixes. Who'd buy them here? Every street's full of beggars hawking something."

Bone let him talk on. The greater Paul's insecurity the more likely he was to get what he wanted.

199

"How much would you need to live on down here?" he asked after a while.

"Not much. I could go somewhere in the country—"

"Two hundred dollars a month?"

"Why?" Paul wanted facts, not suppositions.

Bone had already worked out the figures. He pretended to be thinking aloud. Fifty thousand dollars at five per cent would bring in twenty-five hundred a year.

"I'll do everything I can to get the pictures shown," he promised. "I'll pay the rent on a gallery if I have to."

He did not press Paul then; he left the offer with him like a light to stare at. Paul considered it that evening after his measured drinks. In his sanguine state, when his mind seemed to have returned to its normal way of working, he did not feel he would be losing anything in accepting Bone's offer. He could always paint more pictures. At the same time, he did not see why he should sell them *all* to Bone. He would hang on to eight paintings. He would lend them to Bone for the show, of course; they were the best work he had ever done; but they would remain his own property. He felt Bone would agree to that.

The next morning, waking to those flushes of panic, he did not believe in Bone's offer at all; he remembered every inflection of it, but it seemed to have nothing to do with his own present identity.

They met again in Paul's room the following evening. Paul showed Bone the eight paintings he wanted to keep. Bone admired them; he could understand how much they meant to Paul; he did not commit himself any further than that. When Bone was thinking carefully about something, he had a way of taking his keys out of his pocket and sliding them one by one around the key ring, as though counting his possessions on an abacus: the key to his house, his car, his safe-deposit box. He asked Paul if there were any paintings he had left with friends or stored anywhere. He explained that he might have to acquire those too, to protect his investment, to keep from being undersold.

There was one picture Paul was anxious to retrieve himself: the painting of the chapel he had done for the president of Westminster College; he wanted it destroyed. Bone wrote that down. There were the four early canvases Paul had left in the South of France. Bone questioned him about them. *Woman in Bar* had been painted that same summer. Bone fiddled with his keys while he looked at it again. Paul told him about Eugenia West, the villa near Le Lavandou.

When Bone left that evening, the ownership of the eight paintings Paul wanted to keep remained undecided. In the following weeks, Bone was scrupulously businesslike. He had a contract drawn up by his attorney in New York. Paul was to receive an income of twenty-five hundred dollars a year for the rest of his life. In return Bone was to acquire absolute ownership of certain paintings. They were listed by title in approximately chronological order. *Woman in Bar* was among the first; the rest of the eight paintings were also named.

"I'm not selling those." Paul was calm and firm.

"I thought we'd agreed."

"No."

Bone put the contract away. He began to talk about various New York galleries, how well or how badly they had handled certain painters. While he talked, he lumbered about the room examining canvases, sorting and stacking them. Before he went back to his hotel that evening he arranged with Paul to have the ones he had set aside collected for shipment the next day. The eight disputed paintings were not mentioned again. The contract remained unsigned.

Paul went out when Bone arrived with two men from the packing company. He walked through the barren glare of the streets until he finally found a movie house that was open. Movies could still occasionally divert him as they had when he was a student in London; for a while he could forget his own despair in the simple wishful world they presented. It didn't work for him that afternoon. After an hour he left and hurried home. He ran up the stairs to his room.

The room looked startlingly bare, stripped and lifeless. For a moment he thought Bone had taken everything. But the eight paintings were still there, neatly stacked face downward on the table, the unstretched canvases separated by sheets of paper as he had left them.

He called Bone that evening. There was no answer from his room. He called again the next day. He left messages fixing the times for his calls. "Is no answer." The switchboard girl's voice was becoming hatefully familiar.

Paul's rent was six weeks overdue. Each time he came

201

home from calling Bone he expected to find the door of his room padlocked. The landlord would seize his few possessions. Rolling the eight canvases, he wrapped them in brown paper. He took them with him whenever he had to go out.

After three or four drinks in the evenings, anxiety turned to anger. Paul welcomed it. It was a relief to feel any positive emotion; his rage against Bone seemed like a sign of regained health. He rehearsed long silent harangues against him, rearranging the obscenities of which they were largely composed over and over in his mind.

Bone reappeared at ten-thirty one morning. Paul was lying in bed trying to cling to sleep, to the mercy of unconsciousness, when he heard Bone's voice at the door. He let him in with angry relief. Bone seemed surprised at his anger. He had taken the paintings to New York and stored them in his house in Brooklyn Heights.

"I couldn't risk sending them by freight."

"Why didn't you tell me you were going?"

"I thought you knew."

Paul was raw with fear. In that condition it was impossible for him to relate his thoughts to each other. They were beyond his control, like separate voices, whispers of irrelevant terrors merging into meaningless echoes in his mind. A single dominant question stood out at last.

"When are you going to give me the money?"

"You haven't signed the contract."

Paul was still trying to hold out. The weakness of his position lay not only in his immediate practical need, but in his recurrent indifference. He had hoarded and guarded his paintings for so long, carried them about the world with him, worried that they might be lost or damaged; it would be a relief to be rid of them all at last. Only the tired memory of his fury against Bone deterred him. He signed the contract just before noon. Bone gave him an extra five hundred dollars to get settled somewhere. Paul would start receiving his income in a few days, at the beginning of the month.

Bone put his copy of the contract away in a book he was carrying. He was flying to London that evening to see Eugenia West about her villa in the South of France. He might have to stay over there for a while, he said, but he would be back by December at the latest. They would discuss the details of Paul's exhibition then.

Bone picked up the eight rolled canvases. Although he was trying to hide it from Paul, he was in a hurry. He had an appointment for lunch with a clerk at the American Consulate. He wanted to stop by his hotel first and pick up the empty gun case, the aluminum tube, in which he intended to conceal the paintings he had arranged to store with Carlos Camara until he got back from Europe.

He must have felt pleased with himself as he left the building, walked down the sunlit street in search of a taxi. Except for the five pictures that Lilian Fletcher had and the war paintings Edna Haggard had sold through her gallery, he owned virtually everything Paul had ever painted.

31

THE GUN CASE was light enough without its curtain rods, but I couldn't carry it far through the city at night. It made me feel too conspicuous. I was sure the first policeman I met would stop and question me.

Another problem was that I had very little money: A hundred and fifty pesos, less than fifteen dollars. My book of traveler's checks was in my suitcase, and I couldn't risk going to the hotel for it; the Donners might be waiting for me there.

According to my street map, San Miguel Allende would end three blocks farther on in the cathedral square. They were long, silent blocks. The most insistent sound to me was the hue and cry of my own footsteps. I kept telling myself that only by the wildest coincidence could any of the cars that occasionally flared up behind me be driven by Pad Donner. I didn't believe it. Each one that passed without stopping was like a reprieve.

The cathedral square was as quiet as a museum after closing time. I walked three quarters of the way around it before I found a man sleeping in the front seat of a taxi. I tapped on the glass; he awoke slowly and irritably, like a tortoise, poking his head out the window. I asked him, inanely, if he was free.

"Where do you want to go?" He looked at me with my gun case propped up in my arms as though he had been awakening to the incongruous all his life.

I wanted to go to Tetacata, but I didn't have enough money to get there by taxi. I would have to take the bus, changing at Cuernavaca. There wasn't one until morning now, and I couldn't risk hanging around the bus station all night; it was one of the obvious places the Donners would look for me. I remembered a dot on the map on the road to Cuernavaca: a village, I thought, about ten miles away in the mountains. I didn't expect to find a café open there,

204

but there would be a square, a church; there might be a shed where I could wait until morning.

"Tres Roñas."

That didn't appear to surprise him either; we discussed the fare; he wanted a hundred pesos; we settled for ninety.

Tres Roñas surprised *me*. As we approached, the whole place—it wasn't exactly a town—looked as if it were on fire. The noise carried almost as far as the lights did. There was no square, no church, only a strip of highway a hundred yards long, packed on both sides with glaring, screaming cantinas. Tres Roñas was where people came to get drunk. It had no other purpose. I paid off the imperturbable taxi driver and edged into the nearest saloon. I didn't stay there long. I didn't stay anywhere long. I spent less than seven hours in Tres Roñas altogether, but by the time the bus picked me up in the morning I was a local celebrity. I was the girl who could run faster than a drunken Mexican. Any drunken Mexican. I proved that over and over again. Even hugging a gun case I was as elusive as a lizard. The lead-up to each chase was simple and monotonous. I would sit down at a table that appeared to be vacant. Sometimes it was as much as three minutes before all the other chairs around it were taken. First came the blurred, shouted questions, then the reaching hands, then the grab, and I was off. Usually I ran only one lap, down the highway, around the rear of the last cantina on the left, and back to the dark void where the road wound off into the mountains. I thought of hiding out there in the fields, but the open country was full of drunken Mexicans too; I felt less frightened on the built-up strip, where I could see them coming.

Things quieted down a little around daybreak; the jukeboxes still drummed and screamed, but there were fewer and fewer adult males left in Tres Roñas who could stand up.

I slept for an hour on the bus. Cuernavaca was warm in the morning sun. With four hours to wait for the connection to Tetacata, I sat in the square with my gun case across my lap. A man with an armadillo on a leash came and sat beside me. He wanted fifty pesos to photograph me with the torpid beast; I told him I didn't have fifty pesos; he didn't believe me. But there must have been a note of hysteria in my voice by then; after a few half-hearted insults he left me alone.

205

When I figured it was eleven o'clock Eastern Standard Time, I went to a tourist hotel on the square and persuaded the desk clerk to let me call New York collect. It took an hour to get through. By repeating Bone's name to a succession of switchboard girls, clerks and junior partners I finally found someone who agreed to accept the charges. I told him my name. He said, "Yes," as though he didn't want to either admit or deny that he knew who I was. I asked him to cable me three hundred dollars at the *lista de correos*, the post office in Tetacata. I spelled it out for him twice. He said, "Yes" again. He wasn't promising anything. I could only hope that he knew how to reach Bone at once.

I thanked the clerk at the hotel. He looked at my gun case with a smile of impersonal conjecture; I decided he was wondering what I would do if the money didn't arrive: sell the gun or shoot myself with it.

After paying for my bus ticket I had less than ten pesos left—about ninety cents—and two million dollars' worth of paintings.

I arrived in Tetacata just after four o'clock that afternoon.

32

PAUL SPENT SIX MONTHS IN Cuernavaca. They were
months of intended convalescence. He was trying with all
the force of his will to regain interest; an interest in
painting, in people, in looking, in the trivial pleasures of
daily life; an interest in anything. He spent hours studying
the Diego Rivera murals until he could close his eyes and
recall every detail of them. He read a great deal—Mon-
taigne, Proust, Dickens, a study of ants and their behavior,
biographies, thrillers—anything that could arouse his curiosity again, distract him for a while from his tortured indifference.

Now that he was receiving a sufficient income every
month, the focus of his anxiety had altered. Images of destitution no longer tormented him. His apprehension centered instead on the emptiness of his own future. He could
not believe he would ever recover the energy to work, to
want to work. All his life the sight of an attractive girl in
the street, the lines of a woman's body as she moved had
lighted his day for him with its memories and promise. He
felt nothing toward women now but a dull insensibility,
followed by a defensive withdrawal that came from the
knowledge of his own infectious condition. He would live
on in Mexico, impotent, aging, until he finally lost any
incentive to continue his existence.

He didn't indulge his despair. Day after day he forced
himself to get up, to eat, to sketch, to go out, to encourage
the affirmation of that terrified inner voice that kept saying, I don't want to die. I don't want to die.

It was not difficult to meet people in Cuernavaca. A
group of foreigners had built houses there. Many of them
were wealthy and idle, flaunting their perversions with a
malicious contempt for anyone who did not share them,
often using the power of their money gave them as an in-
strument of cruelty. Paul swam in their pools; he drank

their cocktails; he borrowed books from them; he smiled; he listened to them. Sometimes for as long as half an hour at a time he did not ask himself what he was doing there. Liquor remained a controlled remedy for despair. He never drank before evening and he never got drunk; his pride would not allow him to risk exposing his desperation in drunken candor; his common sense warned him that in his present condition the added insecurities of a hang-over might be literally unbearable; he could kill himslef. From time to time he met women who wanted to go to bed with him. He learnt to evade them early before their vanity was at stake. He was not popular in Cuernavaca; the other foreigners thought him prudish and arrogant; but they continued to invite him to their houses because for all his own boredom he was careful not to bore others. His very lack of interest in anything made him an excellent listener.

The single vital emotion he could still feel was anger. He cultivated it. Alone in the cool evenings he would sit for hours rehearsing and sharpening his hatred for Bone.

Bone spent several weeks near Le Lavandou, living in the villa he had bought from Mrs. West. He had always known how to enjoy his possessions. Except for the war years, when he had felt shut in by hostility, he had never minded being alone. There were interesting legal details to complete with the local notary and Eugenia West, the inventory to be gone over, meals to be eaten, those four additional paintings he had acquired with the villa to be examined and valued.

By December he was back in his house in Brooklyn Heights. He had matters to attend to there as well: investments and securities to be appraised, one or two friends to be entertained. He called Edna Haggard and invited her to dinner. She accepted out of curiosity; she had never liked Bone. He showed her Paul's paintings, setting them three at a time on easels arranged under a fluorescent light in his upstairs living room.

She was, in her own words to me in that taxi, shattered by them. "It was as though you had never heard of Modigliani, for instance—I'd even go as far to say Van Gogh—and you were suddenly taken into a room and shown forty of his paintings. It was difficult to adjust to the fact that they existed."

She asked Bone what he was going to do with them.

208

"I've been trying to insure them." He had always been literal-minded; the problem of insuring Paul's paintings was his immediate concern that evening.

"Why don't you let me show them in my gallery?" She tried to conceal her excitement.

"It's no use having the insurance company appraise them. They'd send some man over who'd say four thousand for the lot." Bone was fiddling with his bunch of keys. "That's less than I paid for them."

"How much did you pay for them?"

Bone found that difficult to answer precisely. He had paid twenty-four hundred dollars in cash for the pictures he had bought outright from Paul. Some part of the price of the Villa Nanon might reasonably be allotted to the four paintings he had acquired with it. There were various traveling expenses; the money he had given Paul when he jumped ship in New York. There was the two hundred which his bank in Columbia, South Carolina, was sending Paul every month.

"That depends," he admitted at last.

"Depends on what?"

Although Bone didn't say so, it depended in the end, of course, on how long Paul lived.

Bone drove to Fulton, Missouri, in April. The college authorities were delighted to give him the painting of the chapel, the work of some unremembered student, in appreciation of his donation of five hundred dollars to the library fund. Bone agreed with Paul that it was an inferior work, but he did not destroy it. It was not in his nature to destory anything he owned. He had the painting shipped back to his house in Brooklyn Heights. He drove on to Mexico.

When he had left for Europe six months before, he had stored his shotgun, wrapped in brown paper, at his hotel. He reclaimed it and put it in the back of his car. He did not pick up the gun case with the eight paintings in it from Carlos Camara's house on San Miguel Allende. It was safer, he thought, not to have it with him when he went to see Paul in Cuernavaca.

Paul had always been unpredictable, untrustworthy. He was quite capable of stealing his own paintings.

Although the money arrived promptly from the bank

every month, Paul had scarcely heard from Bone since he had signed the contract: a post card from London, a note from the South of France. Paul forced himself at last to write to him in New York, an angry letter, demanding to know what he was doing about exhibiting the paintings, insisting that he show them to the various gallery owners he listed. "Please let me know at once what their reaction is to my work," Paul ended. Bone didn't answer.

Paul's house was half a mile out of town, a white-washed two-room bungalow with a scrub of garden around it and a sagging tile-roofed porch at the front where Paul spent most of the day. He was lying there on a camp bed, reading, when Bone's car stopped outside the broken wooden gate. He watched Bone get out and walk up the dirt path; he put his book on the ground beside him; he did not stand up.

"I had a hard time finding you," Bone told him. "No one seemed to know where you lived."

"The mailman knows."

Bone pulled up a deck chair and sat down. "One of the clerks at the hotel thought he knew you, but he wasn't quite sure which direction—" Paul knew Bone would go on elaborating this subject until he was stopped.

"Why didn't you answer my letter?"

"I've only been back from Europe a few weeks. I had several important things to see to in New York—" He went on about that; he had always enjoyed talking about his business affairs to anyone who would listen.

"What have you done about galleries?"

"I showed your paintings to Edna Haggard."

"Fuck Edna Haggard."

"She was most encouraging."

"I can get a better gallery than that."

"Have you been working, Paul?"

"What did Edna Haggard say?"

"She isn't sure there are quite enough paintings for a show."

"Have you asked anyone else what they think?"

"I trust her judgment."

For mths Paul's fury against Bone had been aggravated by his own helplessness; he had no valid threats he could make against him; he could not force him to show the paintings. In the long evenings when his mind writhed with hatred and anger the idea of physical violence as an end in itself, vengeance, was most often in his thoughts. It was noon now. His legs ached with familiar lassitude. If he crossed them he could feel the bones weighing on each other like stones. His body would remain inert, seemingly immovable, for minutes at a time. Motionless, it seemed to him to be decaying.

I don't want to die, that frightened inner voice kept saying, I don't want to die.

"It's up to you, Paul." Bone broke the long silence. "You've got to get out of this rut. Start working again. Produce some more paintings."

Paul didn't answer.

"Perhaps you need a change," Bone suggested later that afternoon after lunch at a hotel.

Paul was back on the camp bed, motionless again. Although he had forced himself to eat some bread and soup while Bone chewed his way through the long courses, he had scarcely been aware of the interlude as a meal, only as a period of waiting. Time was a condition to be endured like cold. With his hands resting, inert, on his thighs he could see his watch without moving. Almost four o'clock. Every day the hour before five was the worst. The black time, he had named it to himself. It was then that his anxiety was most painfully acute. He was terrified, not of dying, but of being dead. The idea of not existing was appalling to him. But how much longer could he endure like this? His fear itself was slowly killing him. He knew it was irrational but at these blackest times the hope of having his paintings seen, recognized, his name spoken, of surviving death through his work, was the single active hope left to him.

He glanced at the solid, assured figure in the deck chair.

If Bone wanted to, he could burn all his paintings tomorrow.

"You need a change," Bone repeated. "We could take a trip."

"Where?"

"Anywhere. Just get in the car and drive. Stop at out-of-the-way places." Bone's voice ripened with enthusiasm at his own suggestion. "It would be a change for me too. I've always been interested in new places."

Perhaps if he moved, Paul thought. If he just moved off this bed. The fatigue of putting clothes into a suitcase, fastening the latches was almost more than he could face.

But he knew he could make himself do it. Even so wearing an activity as that would help him through part of the next hour. After that, all he would have to do would be to sit in the car. Time would pass while he did that too. He would take a bottle of rum already mixed with water. At five o'clock he would have his first drink. Vitality, optimism, designs for the future would gradually revive. His mind and his body would lose their exhausted immobility.

He got up and went into the bedroom and packed. Bone lifted Paul's scuffed suitcase into the back of the car with his own pigskin bags, the shotgun. They drove off soon after four.

It was late that evening when they reached Tetacata.

33

I DON'T THINK TETACATA has changed much since Paul and Bone drove there together twenty-two years ago.

Sometime in the nineteenth century it must have flourished as a market place. It put out streets like branches from its central square. Shops and homes sprouted on them. Then something, some wintry circumstance, kiled it. It ceased growing; it started to decay.

The bus let me off in the square. I walked up one of the side sreets until I found a hotel: half a dozen adobe huts scattered in weeds around a two-story house where the owner lived with his family and the guests ate their meals. Although I had no luggage except the gun case, the owner's wife showed me into one of the huts without asking for payment in advance. Dinner would start at eight, she told me.

As soon as she had gone I locked the door; then I opened the case and took out the long aluminum tube.

No experience in my life had prepared me for the excitement of that moment. What was so new, so exceptional to me about my feelings was their unity; there was no longer any separation between my mind and my body; the intensity of my emotion had fused them into one. For the first time in my memory I was complete as I slipped out those rolled canvases.

There was only one light in the room, hanging from the rafters. I dagged the bed beneath it and unrolled the paintings onto it one at a time, weighting down the corners.

The first was *Woman in Bar*.

For an instant I was sixteen—the irk of the school uniform, the grained reading-room table, the smell of its sour varnish; I felt exactly as I had then, the first time I'd seen a reproduction of one of Paul's paintings. Every stroke of paint was addressed to me, impaling me with its directness. As I brought myself back into the present, I regained that marvelous sense of unity; for a minute, ten minutes, some interlude in time, I opened myself to the forms and colors in front of me; I wasn't aware of looking and seeing; I simply absorbed them.

I went on to the next: *Sixth Avenue El*. I was held again.

They were all there, eight of them: the other four I already knew about—*Tenampa Night; Portuguese Fisherman; Charlotte* and *Man on Horseback*—and the two I knew only from their initials.

A.G.A. was the portrait of an Arab girl in Abadan. From Paul's wartime drawings I knew he had seen and sketched her when his ship unloaded in the Persian Gulf. She was sitting in front of a white wall, dressed in what were obviously her best clothes. Although there was nothing anecdotal, nothing even expository about the painting, it was a study in doomed pride. Like all his best work, it was a moment that contained eternity.

M.W.G., I guessed, stood for "Man with Gun." There were several notes about it in one of the later sketchbooks. Painted in Mexico City, just after Bone's second visit, it was the last painting Paul ever completed. A stout, sandy-haired man was standing by a window. It was more than a gun he was holding, reverently, in his freckled hands; it was the myth, image, the essence of all firearms, power, killing.

A little before eight I rolled the paintings up again with their sheets of paper between each one and the next and replaced them in the aluminum tube. I took it in to dinner with me, keeping it propped against the table beside me while I ate my way through a succession of snacks served as separate courses, a cup of soup, a dab of beans, three leaves of lettuce. Tired from all that running the night before, I left after a slice of indefinable meat. I slept with the aluminum tube in bed with me.

I took it to breakfast with me the next morning and then to the post office. There was nothing from Bone. The clerk there told me how to find the police station. It was on a steep, cobbled street near the square: an office that looked as though it had once been a shop and a cowshed with barred windows next to it. The Jefe—the Chief of Police—wasn't in yet. I sat outside a café across the street

214

and waited. For the next hour I was kept busy shaking my head as men, women, and children offered me bargains: a suitcase, a carved wooden crucifix, a tortoise. After buying a Mexico City paper I had just enough money left to pay for my coffee. The Chief of Police arrived at eleven o'clock. I followed him into his office.

He was a short, ugly man with a preoccupied manner. I hovered in front of his desk until he waved me to a bench along the wall. For ten minutes he ignored me as he opened a couple of envelopes, glanced through some fragile-looking carbon copies of something, searched the drawers of his desk until he found a pack of cigarettes. After he had straightened one of them and lit it, he beckoned me over. His hands were brown and delicate and his nails very clean. They reminded me of Walter.

"What have you lost?" He was still fiddling with those carbon copies; they looked as though they might fall apart in his hands.

"I haven't lost anything."

"Have you been robbed?"

"No."

"What is it, then?" He looked at my face for the first time. His eyes were set so wide apart they appeared to be independent of each other, like a camel's. I wondered if that was what gave him his preoccupied air: each eye looking busy with its own affairs.

"Can I sit down, please?"

"Yes."

There was a chair by the corner of the desk. He waited while I pulled it over and sat down.

"I'm interested in a man who was killed here. It was a long time ago." I had rehearsed the Spanish words while I was sitting in the café across the street.

"You can speak English if you like." His divided glance was wandering over me. "I understand English."

"Thank you." I tried smiling at him; his attitude toward me remained unchanged; I was a nuisance, but not necessarily a problem. I realized I'd better get on with it.

"The man who was killed was a foreigner. He was shot in a quarrel of some kind. His name was Paul Tagliatti."

"I wasn't here then."

"But you have heard about it, haven't you? Can you tell me—"

"Why are you interested?"

215

"He was a great painter. He's famous now."

"He's not famous here. You won't find anyone in Tetacata—"

"He's famous in America."

"In North America."

"I'm sorry." To call the United States "America" is a piece of arrogance that always irritates Mexicans. "I'm working for a North American who's writing a book about him. About Paul Tagliatti."

He sat back in his chair and put his feet on his desk. His eyes were still busy with their independent explorations of me. He seemed prepared to concede I might not even be much of a nuisance.

"The man who was police chief in those days is dead now," he told me. "But he was still alive when I first came here. What is it you want to know for your book?"

"Anything you can tell me."

"Two men were drunk. They were fighting over a shotgun. One of them got his head blown off. That's all. Even here in Tetacata it wasn't anything to talk about for more than a few days."

"It was over twenty years ago. In 1952." I tried smiling again. "But you still remember hearing about it."

"The old Chief of Police. He liked to talk about the incident because he kept the shotgun. It was a marvelous gun. Made in England. He liked to show it to people and tell them how he got it."

I thought I knew why he had been allowed to keep that gun. I wondered what else he had gained from the killing.

"What happened to the other man?" I asked. "The one who shot Tagliatti."

"Nothing."

"He wasn't arrested?"

"It was an accident."

"Was it?"

He found another cigarette and straightened it with his delicate fingers. "Suppose two Mexicans in San Antonio— Suppose they had an argument over a gun one night and one of them got killed— How much money do you think the State of Texas would spend trying to find out what really happened?"

"Two Mexicans?"

"Two Mexicans there. Two North Americans here. It's the same thing, isn't it? One of them shoots the other. Do

216

you expect the Mexican Government to go to all the expense of a long investigation, a trial, maybe having to feed some foreigner in jail for twenty years? Doesn't it make more sense to tell the man to get out, go home—" He shrugged. "And keep the shotgun in case he ever comes back."

I thanked him. He had told me what I had come to confirm. There had been no quarrel with a drunken Mexican. There had been only Bone and Paul. And Bone's gun.

The aluminum tube was leaning against the desk. I took it with me out into the harsh clarity of the street. The waiter at the café told me the way to the cemetery. It took me some time to find the grave; a man digging in another part of the cemetery finally remembered and showed me where the *extranjero*—the stranger—was buried. There was a single small stone with a rounded top; in twenty-two years it had come loose in the dry earth and fallen forward across the grave. I managed to lift it so that I could read the inscription.

PAUL FRANCIS TAGLIATTI 1917–1952

As I brushed the earth out of the shallow, chiseled letters I saw that something else had been inscribed beneath them. After a few minutes working away with a stick, I cleared the letters enough to read what it was.

"Este Mundo Es Un Lago Profundo Donde Ninguno Sabe Nada."

He was lucky with the Mexican police. It surprised him how easily he managed it. He surrendered himself and the weapon soon after the shooting. They locked him up for the night. The next morning, having produced his residence permit and established his identity, he let the police chief understand that he was willing to pay, as he put it, "all expenses." In the end it cost him less than two thousand dollars, and the shotgun, before his story of Paul, drunk, threatening him with the gun, was officially accepted. He left Tetacata immediately after the funeral.

He stopped for less than an hour in Cuernavaca to pack a suitcase full of sketchbooks. There was nothing else in the house worth taking. He drove straight to New York.

He did not stay in New York more than a few days. So long as there was the possibility of meeting anyone who had known Paul Tagliatti and had read or heard about his death he could not feel safe. The idea of San Francisco had always attracted him. He knew no one there; it seemed a perfect place to establish himself out of reach of any questions or curiosity about tha past.

He retained a firm of New York attorneys to handle all his business affairs for him and arranged for them to sell the house in Brooklyn Heights. He notified the bank in Columbia, South Carolina, to stop paying Paul the two hundred dollars a month. The collection of Tagliatti paintings was packed and shipped out to the Coast. bonce he had settled in San Francisco, he signed the necessary papers to transfer all his assets and investments to his new account at the Bank of America there.

Within a year he had bought a house on Telegraph Hill and collected a small group of friends among his wealthy neighbors. He was never bored.

His life had a single dominating purpose. He set about the long, calculated process of establishing Paul Tagliatti's fame. Money was an important asset to him, but he showed great patience ane shrewdness in the way he achieved this. He wrote gently flattering letters to art critics all over the country; he invited them to stay with him if they should ever happen to be in San Francisco; he entertained them; he showed them his collection. By buying other artists' work at their recommendation he made them gratefully indebted to him. The name of Paul Tagliatti began to occur occasionally in their columns and reviews.

He financed small exhibitions of selected Tagliatti paintings at galleries and colleges, at first in California and then later in Washington and Chicago. He arranged auctions at which he employed several agents to bid against one another so that Tagliattis changed hands, although only on paper, at increasing prices. When a Tagliatti was sold in 1961 to an unnamed collector for fifty thousand dollars, it was reported in the news sections of several newspapers. He genuinely sold one or two Tagliattis to people whose names would help publicize them. It took him ten years to get the movement started; after that it developed its own momentum. By the late Sixties Tagliatti's name was known in art circles all over the country. Galleries and museums were eager to acquire his work for permanent exhibition. When Lilian Fletcher died and left her collection of Tagliattis to the Museum of Fine Arts in Boston, reproductions of three of the paintings appeared in *Newsweek*. In 1971, a Tagliatti canvas, *Man Sleeping* (Mills Hotel), was sold a Sotheby's in London for a quarter of a million dollars.

Through all those years, only the thought of those eight missing paintings disturbed his contentment, his sense of gradual achievement.

The culmination of all his patient efforts was the night of the opening of the retrospective show of Tagliatti's work at the Museum of Modern Art. How could he resist the temptation to attend it himself? It was his single mistake. Edna Haggard did not recognize him there—any more than I recognized the stout, sandy-haired man with the gun as Bone in Paul's painting of him—but she asked one of the attendants who he was.

When I left the cemetery I stopped by the post office again. There was nothing for me. I hadn't expected there would be. Asking was no more than a gesture, like throwing salt over my left shoulder.

When I saw the news item in the Mexico City paper this morning I knew Bone wouldn't cable me any money.

He will come himself.

It was only a few lines on an inside page. I had no trouble translating it from the Spanish. An elderly North American tourist fell in front of a train at Zócalo Metro Station yesterday. It is thought that she had suffered from a sudden attack of dizziness. She was killed instantly. The tourist card in her handbag showed that her name was Edna Haggard.

I sat through the long, sparse dinner again with the tube of paintings beside me, then went back to my hut. I had nothing to read, I lay down on the bed and waited.

It's after midnight now. I can't sleep. My mind is too busy waiting, listening for every sound from outside, trying to decide what brought me to this. Was there always some lemming impulse in me? Because I don't think I've got much chance of survival now.

It isn't having no money that keeps me here waiting. I

could hitchhike to Cuernavaca; I could pawn my watch there; call my mother collect in Chicago. She'd cable me the money to fly back to New York or anywhere else. But then I'd be on the run forever. For as long as he lives. I'd have years, not hours, then, of being afraid. I can't bear the thought of that. That's why I called his attorneys and let him know where I was.

He might come tonight, have Berman drive him down from Mexico City. I'm sure at least I won't have to wait beyond tomorrow. I'll give him the paintings at once, of course. God knows they belong to him. After that I'll do my best to convince him that I have no reason, no intention of ever telling anyone what I know.

I wonder if Walter tried to do that. I wonder how much Walter did know. He may have understood what that note of Bone's in the Tauchnitz meant. He was certainly getting close to the truth with his realization that Bone knew where the missing paintings were. He probably wrote to Bone and tried to get money from him. How much did he tell him in that letter? Enough to frighten him, anyway. That's why Walter is dead.

Edna Haggard thought the Tauchnitz had belonged to Paul; she never saw it. She only saw my companion at the Museum of Modern Art and was curious about him. The Donners are lucky; their own suspicious, contrary natures saved them; Edna Haggard didn't trust them; she never told them the one thing she knew about my companion at the museum.

Did she too try to get money from him? Or was she interested only in the missing Tagliatti paintings? In either case she made the mistake of speaking to him at the Museum that night. After that he had to see her again. He probably tried to manipulate her, as he manipulated me. In the end, like Walter, she came too close to the truth.

What can I cay that will persuade him to trust me now? There was never any trust between us.

Is there any way, then, that I can convince him that I don't know the truth? If I try to do that, how can I explain how I found the eight paintings? How can I hide the fact that I must understand why he never collected those paintings from Carlos Camara himself?

Because, of course, he couldn't collect them. He didn't know where they were.

Only Wexford Bone knew that. And Wexford Bone is buried in that grave here in Tetacata.

The man I am waiting for is Paul Tagliatti.

Survivor.

Enemy.

My love.

THE BIG BESTSELLERS
ARE AVON BOOKS

☐ **Humboldt's Gift** Saul Bellow	29447	$1.95
☐ **The Auctioneer** Joan Samson	31088	$1.95
☐ **The Viking Process** Norman Hartley	31617	$1.95
☐ **The Surface of the Earth** Reynolds Price	29306	$1.95
☐ **The Monkey Wrench Gang** Edward Abbey	30114	$1.95
☐ **Beyond the Bedroom Wall** Larry Woiwode	29454	$1.95
☐ **Caro** Bernard Packer	31070	$1.95
☐ **The Formula Book** Norman Stark	31047	$1.75

☐ **The Relaxation Response**
    Herbert Benson, M.D.
    with Miriam Z. Klipper
	29439	$1.95

☐ **Between Heaven and Earth** Laura Huxley	29819	$1.95
☐ **Castles in the Air** Patricia Gallagher	27649	$1.95
☐ **Something More** Catherine Marshall	27631	$1.75
☐ **Getting Yours** Lotty Cottin Pogrebin	27789	$1.75
☐ **Fletch** Gregory Mcdonald	27136	$1.75
☐ **Confess, Fletch** Gregory Mcdonald	30882	$1.75
☐ **Shardik** Richard Adams	27359	$1.95
☐ **Anya** Susan Fromberg Schaeffer	25262	$1.95
☐ **The Bermuda Triangle** Charles Berlitz	25254	$1.95
☐ **Watership Down** Richard Adams	19810	$2.25

Available at better bookstores everywhere, or order direct from the publisher.

AVON BOOKS, Mail Order Dept., 250 West 55th St., New York, N.Y. 10019

Please send me the books checked above. I enclose $_____(please
include 25¢ per copy for mailing). Please use check or money order—sorry,
no cash or COD's. Allow three weeks for delivery.

Mr/Mrs/Miss_____

Address_____

City_____State/Zip_____

BB 2-77

Avon/31088/$1.95

THE AUCTIONEER

JOAN SAMSON

At first no one feared the smooth-talking outsider who ran the weekly auction. The slick, magnetic stranger was irresistible. The people of rural Harlowe, New Hampshire, willingly donated their antique junk for his auctions.

Then his quiet demands increased. Horrifying calamities befell those who refused him. What was behind his ever-growing power? After the heirlooms were gone, what would be next? The farm . . .? The children . . .?

**SELECTED BY THE BOOK-OF-THE-MONTH CLUB
SOON TO BE A MAJOR MOTION PICTURE**

EER 1-77